SIDELINED

USA TODAY & WALL STREET JOURNAL BESTSELLING AUTHOR
BECCA STEELE

Sidelined

Editing by One Love Editing

Proofreading by Rumi

Becca Steele

www.authorbeccasteele.com

AUTHOR'S NOTE

The author is British, and this story contains British English spellings and phrases. The football referred to in this story is known as soccer in some countries.

Enjoy!

For Sid the snail

Of all possessions a friend is the most precious.

HERODOTUS

ELLIOT

PROLOGUE

The golf club's interior had been decorated with strings of lights and swathes of billowing fabric in a shade of green matching our school colour. The setting reminded me of a wedding rather than my school's Year 13 Leavers' Prom.

Outside on the terrace, students milled around, making the most of the warm summer evening. Making my way to a quiet corner of the terrace, I leaned back against the stone balustrade and sipped my complimentary glass of Prosecco. It felt weird to drink at a school event, but I guessed that most of us were legally adults by now, other than the unlucky few who hadn't yet had their eighteenth birthday.

"E, my man." Marc, one of the guys from my business studies class, wandered over, tapping his glass against mine. "You drinking that fizzy shit? You need a pint."

I shrugged. "Yeah. It wasn't my first choice, but it was free."

"Fair enough. My date stole mine, but she bought me

this pint, so I ain't complaining. Who did you come with tonight? I guess you didn't have much choice, huh?" He gave me a sympathetic smile, and I sighed internally. Yes, I was gay, and yes, there were only a few other guys that I knew of in my school year that were gay or bisexual or pansexual or open to taking another guy to prom as their date, but even if the entire year had been gay, it wouldn't have made a difference. There was only one person I'd want to take me to something like this, and he was here with someone else.

"I came with a group. Not everyone's brought dates with them."

Marc's gaze shifted to the open doors that led into the golf club. "Yeah, good point, mate. Not Ander, though. Fucking hell, he is one lucky bastard getting to take Zoe."

I followed the direction of his gaze in time to see my best friend, his arm curved around his date, both of them smiling for the prom photographer as he directed them to pose. They looked so good together, two of the most popular people in our school, both poised and gorgeous.

I carefully suppressed the emotions that were trying to rise to the surface. It had been difficult enough to see them together earlier...

"One more photo!" My mum bustled around with the camera, arranging everyone to her liking. A group of us had gathered at my house before the prom, and a limo was going to pick us up to take us to the golf club. In her excitement, my mum had taken it upon herself to become our unofficial

photographer, and she'd bullied my dad into rounding everyone up and taking us outside where, according to her, it was "golden hour." My best friend, Ander, still hadn't arrived, but he'd sent me a text a few minutes earlier to say that his date was running late and they'd be with us in the next ten minutes.

There was a sudden shout of greeting from one of our friends, and my breath caught in my throat as Ander appeared from the side of the house. He must have let himself in like he'd done hundreds of times before.

"Oh, my! Ander, you look wonderful! And who is your lovely date? What a beautiful dress!" My mum was all bright-eyed enthusiasm, immediately rushing over and raising the camera to snap a photo. As for me, I stood in the back garden of my family home, struck dumb at the sight.

Now I got what my mum meant by the "golden hour."

The soft early evening sunlight danced across Ander, bathing him in its glow. He was clad in a navy-blue suit that fitted his athletic body like it was custom-made just for him. The sun made his chestnut hair shine with reds and burnished golds, and even from where I was standing, I could see the way his hazel eyes shone as his mouth curved into the smile I loved so much.

His arm was wrapped around his date, who had a long, shimmering silver dress on, her dark hair all curled and pinned up in a style that probably took ages to create. She looked beautiful, and I wished that I was a better person. I wished that I wasn't so overcome with completely irrational jealousy that I couldn't speak.

I wished.

But I knew that wishes were for fools.

Tearing my gaze away from Ander and Zoe, I redirected the conversation, and fast. "How do you think you did in your exams?"

Marc groaned. "Don't remind me of them. As long as I did well enough to get into Bournemouth Uni, I'm good. What about you? You're going to London, aren't you?"

"Yeah. London Southwark University, as long as I get the grades."

"Cool." His attention was diverted again, but this time, it was by his date, who greeted me with a smile.

"Hi, Elliot. You look nice."

"Thanks, Izzy. You too. Uh, nice dress. It suits you."

She beamed at me, so I guessed my compliment had hit the mark. Turning to Marc, she threaded her arm through his. "There's a photo booth inside. Come on."

A photo booth. I was suddenly hopeful. Maybe I could steal Ander for a few minutes so we could get some photos taken. One last memory of our school years before everyone moved away to different parts of the country, beginning their adult lives. One final reminder of our childhood together.

"Catch ya later." Marc gave me a nod, and then I was alone again. But I wasn't going to stand here moping on the night of my prom. Tonight was supposed to be about celebrating.

Finishing up the remainder of the Prosecco, I went inside on a search for something different to drink, preferably something with plenty of ice and plenty of alcohol. The only way I was going to get through this night was with the help of my friend, whiskey sour. I'd never actually had it before, but my dad liked it, and it sounded more exciting than the beer and cider that everyone else seemed to be drinking. Plus—ice.

"You sure you want that?" The bartender eyed me doubtfully after checking my ID to make sure I was eighteen. "Wouldn't you prefer a beer?"

I raised a brow. "Why would I prefer a beer?"

"He doesn't like beer." A warm weight was suddenly slung across my shoulders, and then Ander was pulling me into a sideways hug, a bright grin on his face. "But I agree about the drink. Come on, E, you don't wanna end up getting wasted, especially not this early. You're not used to drinking that kind of thing."

I glared at him, and he just squeezed my shoulder, smiling widely. For fuck's sake. I couldn't even be angry with him, not when he was this happy. With a sigh, I gave in to the inevitable. "What do you suggest, then, since you apparently know best?"

His brows pulled together as he scanned the various offerings behind the bar. "How about...gin?"

"Really? My *mum* drinks that."

"Yeah, but I think you'll like it. And if you don't, I'll buy you something else, yeah?" He turned to the bartender. "A gin with lemonade and plenty of ice, please. And I'll have a pint of Carlsberg. Oh, better add another Prosecco for Zoe too."

As if he'd summoned her, Zoe suddenly appeared by his

5

elbow, and he removed his arm from around me. "I got you a Prosecco. And here're the photos from the photo booth. I kept one, but you can have the rest."

She gave him a soft smile as she accepted the pictures from him. He smiled in return, and yeah, I was feeling like a third wheel.

"You having a good time?" Ander slipped his arm around Zoe's waist, but he was looking at me. "Wanna take advantage of the photo booth later? Try to break the camera with the faces we pull?"

"Yeah. I'd like that." I smiled back, and it was sincere because as much as my heart ached to see him with someone else, I did want him to be happy, and to want him for myself was a pipe dream. I got to have him in my life as a best friend, and that would be enough.

Zoe gave me a smile too, and my own smile fell away because hers was full of sympathy, and I knew why. Yes, I was here on my own, but so fucking what? There were plenty of people here without dates. Thankfully, the bartender was quick, and before I knew it, I had my drink in my hand, and with a murmured thanks to Ander, I made my escape. I held on to the thought of being in the photo booth later this evening, joking around and having fun with my best friend, creating a memory of tonight where it was just the two of us.

As the evening wore on, I found some of my friends, had a few more of those drinks, and I did my best to focus on having a good time. And it was good for the most part, dancing and talking and drinking, everyone caught up in the high of being finished with school. We were all about to begin a new chapter in our lives, to become adults, which was both exciting and scary. We'd never all be together again like this.

Eventually, though, people began drifting into their own smaller, more intimate groups, and I found myself on my own, my other friends having disappeared. I made my way back inside to the dance floor, sending the decorative green confetti stars scattering under my feet. Right after I entered, the DJ changed up the music. Calum Scott's cover of "Dancing on My Own" began playing...and believe me when I say that was the worst possible song that could be played at that moment in time.

Everything slowed right down. The atmosphere flipped, the lights dimming to a golden glimmer over the dance floor, and suddenly, all I saw were couples. I made my way to the corner of the room, suddenly sidelined. I didn't begrudge anyone their happiness—far from it. But for a single gay boy who had to stand there watching the boy he loved dancing with a beautiful girl, knowing that boy would never feel the same way about him...

It hit me hard.

And when Zoe's chin tipped up, her eyes meeting Ander's, and he smiled down at her and then dipped his head, his lips covering hers, the lump in my throat was so big I could barely swallow. My vision went blurry, and yes, I'd had too much to drink and was feeling sorry for myself seeing all these happy couples, but *Ander*.

I was so in love with him, and he would never be mine.

As I stood there, unable to look away, I noticed movement out of the corner of my eye. Turning my head, I saw the photo booth being dismantled. The booth that I'd wanted to use to create some memories with my best friend.

I felt my face crumple, and I couldn't stop the choked sound tearing from my throat. Fucking hell. This was supposed to be fun, a celebratory ending to our days as school students, and here I was, on my own and more miserable than I'd been in a long time. I'd never been more grateful for the volume of the music and the fact that I was more or less out of sight.

We never got to take any photos together.

Fuck. I had to get out of there. Stumbling through the doors into the night, I breathed in and out deeply, desperately trying to compose myself as I hid in the shadows.

I stayed outside for a long time, watching the happy couples through the windows, forgotten and alone.

ONE

ELLIOT

"Want a drink?

My best friend shot me his usual charming grin, and as usual, I pretended that it didn't affect me. It had become easier over the years to hide the way I felt, to keep Ander firmly in the friend zone even though my heart belonged to him and only him. It was a constant ache that I knew would never go away, but I'd made my peace with it. Mostly.

"Please. I'll get the next ones." I returned his smile, shifting in the booth. We'd come back to our hometown of Bournemouth for the weekend, the place we'd grown up together before Ander had persuaded me to apply with him to London Southwark University, aka LSU. We were well into the second year of our degrees, but it wasn't unusual for us to visit our families throughout the year—in this instance, we'd come back for my mum's birthday, which was tomorrow. In the meantime, we were in Cloud, my favourite bar, close to the seafront, relaxing after the long drive here.

I watched as Ander charmed both the bartender and the woman next to him, but I looked away when the woman at his side gave him a blatantly suggestive look and slid her phone in front of him. It wasn't like it was anything new, but it wasn't something I wanted to see.

When he returned from the bar, he slid a glass across the table to me. "G & T, and before you ask, yes, I got them to add extra ice. And one of those lemon slices—I still don't know why you like them." Taking a seat in the booth next to me, he ran a casual hand through his thick chestnut hair, the muscles of his arm flexing as he did so. I tried my best to ignore how good he looked. His hazel eyes sparkled at me as his lips curved into a smug, confident smile. "I did good, right?"

"Yeah. Thanks." I picked up my glass quickly, taking a gulp. It was the little things he did, things that proved how well he knew me, that made me wish for things I knew I could never have. Yeah, he was my best friend, and of course, that meant he knew me better than anyone else, but—

I cut off those thoughts, locking them deep inside me, where I wouldn't be tempted to access them anymore.

My phone lit up with an incoming message, and I pounced on it gratefully, laughing as I read the text.

"What is it?" Ander cocked his head, raising a brow.

"Noah. He wants to know if you know the best way to get tickets to Crystal Palace's FA Cup match so he can surprise Liam for his birthday—but he's said, and I quote, 'You and Ander are coming too. If I have to sit through eighty minutes of torture, then you can come with me, and

Ander can enjoy the match with Liam. P.S. you can pay for your own tickets.' Then he's included a load of emojis." I turned my phone to show him the screen.

Ander smirked. "Remind him that a football match is actually ninety minutes, not eighty, and that's not even including added time." He paused, then added, "You can tell him that I'll sort all the tickets if he wants, and he can just pay me back for his and Liam's."

I tapped out a reply and received a very unenthusiastic response to my reminder about the duration of the match, followed by a much more enthusiastic response to the part about Ander sorting out the tickets. Noah and Liam both lived in the student house next to Ander and me—and they'd been officially together for a week, although they'd been seeing each other—in the world's worst-kept secret— for a lot longer than that. Almost since the beginning of the semester, from what I gathered. Liam was a footballer, as was Ander, and while neither Noah nor I played, I quite liked watching it, whereas Noah wasn't exactly a fan. Not unless his boyfriend was running around the pitch in his football shorts, anyway.

"I still can't believe I lost my wingman," Ander lamented at the mention of Liam.

Another thing I should mention about my best friend— he was a bit of a player. His words, not mine. He loved girls, and girls loved him. I mean, how could they not? He was so gorgeous, tall, and broad-shouldered, with a body that looked like it had been carved by the Greek gods themselves and a face that literally took my breath away. In compari- son, I was...well, ordinary. Nothing to write home about.

11

My body was toned, thanks to my running and gym work-outs, but I was definitely on the lanky side. My hair was boring—light brown and kind of wavy, and my eyes were... the best way I could describe them was a pale, watery blue. In short, I was the kind of person that would always be in Ander's shadow, although he always took care to include me as much as possible.

"You don't need a wingman. You don't even have to do anything to get the girls to come to you," I said, keeping my tone light before fishing an ice cube out of my glass and crunching on it viciously, grinding it between my molars.

"That is so annoying, you know." Ander eyed me, amused, and I rolled my eyes.

"Really? I wouldn't have guessed. You've never told me that before."

"Fuck off, E." He nudged my arm playfully. "I guess I should be used to it by now since you've had the habit since we were six."

"Five," I countered.

"Nope. Six. It was right after your birthday, when my mum took us to that restaurant, remember? We could help ourselves to that drinks machine, and you filled up your cup with ice, then sat there for ages crunching all the cubes. Sooooo annoying." His grin widened.

It was easy to fall into banter with him. It was safe ground, where we were just two friends who'd grown up together. "I'm glad you have such fond memories of our childhood."

"I do. Remember that time you ripped your shorts on those railings, and you flashed—"

12

I clamped one hand over his mouth, the other going to his throat. "Do *not* finish that sentence unless you want me to choke you until you can't talk anymore."

"Kinky," he mumbled from underneath my palm, still grinning like a lunatic. I could feel his pulse under my other hand, and I was struck by a sudden desire to run my thumb over it, followed by my mouth. My dick stirred, liking the idea way too much.

I yanked my hands away, sliding across the booth and out of the side, and waved vaguely in the direction of the door that led to the toilets. "I'll be back."

Being in love with my best friend was the fucking *worst* sometimes.

TWO

ANDER

While I waited for Elliot to return, I glanced around Cloud's interior. We'd skipped our Friday lectures and driven straight to Bournemouth this morning, but now it was getting later in the day, and the bar was beginning to fill. Students mixed with the after-work crowd, interspersed with a few tourists here and there. I normally came here with Elliot when we came back for a visit—it was a bit of a magnet for Bournemouth's gay community, and if anyone needed help getting laid, it was Elliot. He was a good-looking guy, with his wavy light brown hair, clear blue eyes, angular jaw, and a lean, fit body, so he shouldn't have had trouble finding someone. But he hardly ever seemed to pick up guys, and those he did never lasted. It concerned me because he wasn't like me. He needed a proper relationship, someone to take care of him that he could care for in return. That was what my best friend deserved, and I hoped he'd find it one day soon.

My gaze was caught by Elliot making his way back

towards me. He was right next to the wall when he was stopped in his tracks by a guy placing his hand on his arm. I frowned, staring at them. I was sure I recognised that guy...

The guy leaned into him, saying something, and I watched as Elliot's expression changed from polite interest to horror, and then his eyes flared with panic as he sought me out.

I was already out of my seat, pushing through the crowds to him.

"What's going on here?" I folded my arms across my chest, giving the guy my best intimidating look. He was older than me, but I was taller and bigger, and I wasn't above using it to my advantage. Next to me, Elliot had gone silent, as stiff as a board.

"Oh, it's you, Ander." The guy flicked his beady gaze to me before returning it to Elliot, and the expression on his face made my skin crawl. I hadn't been able to see his face before, but now I took in the way he blatantly leered at Elliot, his hand going to adjust the bulge forming in his trousers.

Fucking gross.

"Sorry, do I know you?" My tone was icy as I stepped forwards, angling my body so that I brushed up against Elliot's shoulder.

"Gary. Marc's brother. Haven't seen you two around here for a while, but now I have, well...look at little Elliot. All grown up and pretty. I thought he might be interested in having a bit of fun with me tonight." His fat, slimy tongue came out to lick his lips, leaving a string of drool, and I nearly gagged. I remembered him now—the older brother of one of our school friends, he'd always come across as a creep. You know how some people just make your skin crawl when you look at them? He was one of those.

"I'm not interested," Elliot tried.

"Come on. Last I heard, you were single." His hand went to his crotch again, and I contemplated just kneeing him in the balls, but the bar owners were strict on any kind of violence, and I didn't want to get us barred from Elliot's favourite place.

My mouth and body swung straight into action before my brain had a chance to keep up. "He's not single," I bit out in the same icy tone as I slid my arm around Elliot's waist, pulling him into me. "He's with me."

Then I cupped the back of his neck with my free hand and slanted my mouth across his.

There was a shocked intake of breath, quickly followed by a sigh, and then I was suddenly making out with my best friend, backing him into the wall as our tongues slid against each other's, and his arms came up to wrap around my back.

Fucking *hell*, Elliot could kiss. Where had he been hiding this skill? I kissed him harder, my mind briefly reminding me of the fact that I was kissing my best friend in the entire world, who also happened to be male, but I ignored it in favour of enjoying the way his mouth moved against mine, his heart beating rapidly against my chest as I pressed him into the wall.

He arched into me, and, oh. He was *hard*. Was that from kissing me? A rumble of satisfaction came from my throat, surprising me, followed by my second surprise, which was that *I was also getting hard.*

17

Well, fuck me sideways. This was a very unexpected development.

I finally broke the kiss, not that I wanted to, but the Gary guy was saying something, an irritating buzz in my ear that made me want to punch him in the mouth. I resisted. Just.

"Will you just go the fuck away? Go and bother some other person. Elliot's not interested, and if you come on to him again, you won't like the consequences."

"You're really with him?" His eyes narrowed at Elliot as he did his best to ignore me shooting daggers with my eyes. After a long moment, during which I coughed discreetly, Elliot nodded.

"Did my tongue down his throat not give you enough of a clue?" I deliberately turned my back to Gary, facing Elliot. He stared back at me, his eyes wide and wild, his high cheekbones flushed, and his lips swollen and glistening from our kiss. He looked completely stunned.

Lowering my head to his, I rubbed my palm over his back in what I hoped was a soothing way. "Hey. E. Are you okay? Talk to me."

His mouth opened and closed a few times, but no sound came out.

"Did I break you? Was my kissing that good?"

Finally, he spoke, his voice a cracked whisper. "Did that really happen, or was it a hallucination?"

"Believe me, a hallucination couldn't kiss you as good as the real me," I stated, confident in my skills. I'd had plenty of opportunities to hone said skills, after all. But Elliot... "Speaking of, where the fuck did you learn to kiss like that?"

"I-I don't know," he stammered. "I don't know what's happening right now."

I raised my voice. "Gary thought you were single. You're not. He is, in fact, deluded, and he needs to take a fucking hint and leave us alone." The final part of my sentence came out as a growl, feeling Gary's slimy presence still right behind me.

"We should kiss again." Sheer panic came over Elliot's face as soon as he said the words, the colour draining from his skin, but there was something in his wide eyes...

I stared at him, my momentary surprise replaced by the reminder that I was helping my best friend out, keeping this creep away from him, and even though I wasn't gay or anything, it wasn't exactly a hardship to kiss him. "Yeah, maybe we should." Brushing my lips across his again, I lost myself in the sensations of his mouth, the kiss softer but deeper than before. His lean, strong body felt good against mine—not even weird because we'd hugged thousands of times over the years—and I had that same sense of gratification I'd had earlier when I felt his hardness pressing into me. This time, I experimented with tugging his lip between my teeth, earning me a barely audible whimper that made my dick pulse with satisfaction.

Fuck, I was good at this, wasn't I? Maybe I'd been missing out all these years. Why hadn't I ever tried anything with other guys? There was a whole world of opportunity out there that I'd been wasting. My hand slid down Elliot's back, making his whole body shiver as I pulled him even closer.

"No. Wait. Stop."

It took me a minute to recognise that he'd stopped kissing me. I drew back, blinking, and when the haze of lust cleared, the first thing I noticed was the wary look that had appeared on his face. The second thing I noticed was that Gary had finally taken the hint and disappeared. It was a fucking miracle.

"Ander, we can't do this...it's not a good idea." Elliot pushed away from me, and I dropped my grip on him.

"Hey, it's okay. It was just a kiss. Two kisses," I amended when he just stared at me. "We got rid of that creepy twat, and now we go back to normal. Don't overthink it. A kiss is just a kiss."

He mumbled something like, "Maybe to you," as he rubbed his hand across his face. When he lowered it and met my eyes again, he nodded once, decisively. "Just a kiss. And we'll never speak of it again, right?"

I shrugged. "'Course, if that's what you want. It's really not a big deal, E."

Something pained flashed in his gaze, but it was gone before I could make sense of it. "Yeah." He cleared his throat. "It's not a big deal."

THREE

ELLIOT

Ander kissed me. I kissed Ander.
It should never have happened.

He'd completely taken me by surprise the first time it had happened. The second his lips had touched mine, I knew I should push him away, but I didn't. I was helpless to resist, dying to know how he tasted, how his mouth would move against mine, to give myself a tiny glimpse of everything I wanted but could never have. Then I'd made it worse by blurting out the suggestion we should kiss again. What the fuck had I been thinking? When I'd finally gathered the strength to break away from him, he'd shrugged off the whole thing. What had been a life-changing moment for me had been nothing but a friend helping another friend out for him.

"You okay?" Ander glanced at me as he indicated to switch lanes. We were almost back at LSU, and I could see the sign for student parking up ahead. "You've been quiet this weekend."

Fuck. I thought I'd hidden it. I thought I'd been acting normally.

"I'm okay," I said eventually. "Tired, mostly."

He took his hand off the gearstick to give my leg a brief squeeze. Ander was a tactile person, always initiating contact without even thinking about it, having no clue that his touch lit me up inside. "Why don't we get a takeaway and watch Netflix in my bedroom? You can take it easy. I'll even use my magic hands on you if you want."

Getting a massage from Ander, just the two of us alone in his bedroom, wasn't a great idea with my current state of mind. "That sounds good, but I'm going to meet up with Noah." Neither of those statements was untrue. It did sound good—just completely inadvisable, and I'd texted Noah earlier, asking if he was free. Of all my friends, he was the one that I felt the most comfortable confiding in. I confided in my housemate JJ too, to an extent, but because he was good friends with both me and Ander, I found it difficult to bring up my Ander-related issues with him.

"Alright." He swung the car into a parking space and then turned off the engine. "But if you need anything, text me. Okay?" I nodded, and he smiled at me. "In that case, I'm gonna see if any of the football team want to get a drink tonight. But you're my priority, so if you need me, I'll be there. Bros before hoes and all that. Dicks before chicks."

"Dicks before chicks," I repeated, smirking. "That sounds like my kind of night."

He lightly punched me in the shoulder with a laugh. "Yeah, yeah. Have you ever thought about fucking a girl?"

"What?" I stared at him, caught off guard. "A girl? How

22

many years have we been friends? Has it escaped your notice that I'm gay?"

The corners of his lips kicked up in amusement. "I know. Just a question."

Shaking my head at him, I huffed out a breath. "I can tell you, hand on heart, that I've never once entertained thoughts of being with a girl." Just to get the point across, I gave a dramatic shudder, making him laugh again, which in turn made me smile. "Where did that question come from?"

He shrugged. "Just curious. Of all the things we've talked about over the years, I don't think I've ever asked you that."

"Well, it's never going to happen." I laughed, playfully nudging him with my elbow. "What about you, then? Have you ever thought about fucking a guy?"

There was a weighted pause, and then he said, "Yeah...I think I might want to try it."

I choked on nothing. That was *not* the response I'd expected. When I'd recovered from what might have been a close brush with a heart attack, I stared at him, open-mouthed, my heart racing. "*You what*? Where did that come from?"

Tapping his finger to his lip, he thought for a minute. "I liked kissing you at the bar. I guess it made me wonder if I'm missing out, restricting myself to girls only." His eyes widened, and he thrust his finger out, pressing it against my chest. "E! You can help me! You can be my gay guru. Show me the best places to find good-looking guys who want a piece of this."

My chest tightened, a lump appearing in my throat so

23

fast that I couldn't choke it back. I yanked my sunglasses down from the top of my head, covering my eyes.

Of all the things...

What the fuck did I do? I'd been in love with him for so long, and I'd trained myself not to react every time he was with a girl. But a boy? And Ander...he was so gorgeous with his perfect gym body and sculpted features that he would have zero problems getting male attention.

When I eventually managed to speak, I shook my head, staring resolutely out of the front windscreen. "I don't think I can do that."

He gripped my chin, turning my head to face him. I was so lucky that my sunglasses were dark. "Why not?" Hurt threaded through his tone. "You're my best friend, E. You're the one person I trust to advise me on this kind of shit."

I couldn't tell him the full truth, that the thought of helping him out was the worst and best torture I could ever think of, so I admitted something to him that I knew he was already aware of. "Remember that I'm nowhere near as experienced as you. Please don't ask me to do this." My cheeks heated, although I knew it was nothing to be embarrassed about. It wasn't like there was a rush to do anything, and I'd never been interested in casual sex. I needed an emotional connection. Kisses, yes, and even very occasional handjobs and blowjobs in a darkened corner or the club loos, but anything intimate...actually baring myself to someone...I'd never been able to contemplate that with anyone. Anyone except my best friend.

His brow furrowed as he pursed his lips. "Maybe we can both try this out together. Be each other's wingmen?"

24

"No." My tone was final. Abso-fucking-lutely not.

Sliding his thumb across my jaw, he gave me a soft look that was almost too much. "Sorry, E. I would never push you to do something you're uncomfortable with. I know that you're not into casual...like I am, I guess. I just want you to be happy."

I pulled back from his touch, unclipping my seat belt. There was only one thing I needed right now, and that was to get out of the car and away from my best friend so I could get my head around everything he'd just disclosed and regroup.

The second I was out and slamming the door behind me, I exhaled shakily. How had everything gone so wrong in the space of a few days?

Ander's door also slammed, and then a few seconds later, I was wrapped in his arms, my face buried in his shoulder. My sunglasses were digging into the side of my nose painfully, but I didn't attempt to move. Instead, I sighed, accepting the warmth of his hug. "I am happy," I mumbled. "I just can't be what you need me to be."

His arms briefly tightened around me. "Say no more. I'm sorry. I shouldn't have asked you." Releasing me, he studied me for a second with his brows pulled together before his expression cleared. He flashed me a quick grin. "Don't even worry about it. I'll talk to JJ instead."

Great.

"And now I don't know what to do." I sank back into the sofa with a groan.

"This is a mess." My friend and neighbour, Noah, gave me a sympathetic smile. "The whole thing with him wanting to experiment with guys—that's...surprising."

"Yeah." Rubbing my hand over my face, I sighed. "He made it clear that he wasn't interested in experimenting with me when he asked me to help him out. The kiss that meant everything to me opened up a whole new world for him, and now as well as girls, I'm gonna have to see him parading boys around in front of me. And I know I'll compare myself to them, as much as I'll try not to."

Noah sat in silence for a minute. "Okay. There are two ways you can play this. You can tell Ander how you feel about him." He held up his hand when I went to speak. "Or you can accept that this is going to happen, and you make a real effort to get over him. Because the way I see it, you're going to be seriously miserable if you just carry on as you are and he starts bringing boys home. I know you, and I know that it's going to tear you apart."

"I can't tell him how I feel. It's too much, and what he feels for me is completely platonic. I mean, look. The best fucking kiss of my life, and the only effect it had on him was to make him wonder if he should start kissing other guys!" My voice was rising, and I took a deep breath, making an effort to calm myself. "I need to get over him. That's it. I've been pining for him for way too long. What should I do? Download Grindr?"

"Noooo." Noah shook his head. "You need to ease yourself into it, and I don't think you'd...you don't want casual, do you? You need something else. I'm not an expert—look at what happened with Liam—but we can talk to Preston or JJ? See if they have any ideas?"

"Did someone say my name?" Noah's boyfriend, Liam, sauntered into the room and threw himself down on the sofa next to Noah. He eyed me with suspicion, to which I rolled my eyes. Even though it was clear to anyone with half a brain that Noah was completely in love with him, he still sometimes acted like I was competition or something. He was a little possessive of Noah, but Noah seemed to enjoy it for some reason.

"Yeah. Me." Noah smiled at him, and Liam immediately melted, leaning across to kiss his boyfriend. The way he looked at him—so soft, like he'd do anything for Noah...

I wanted that so badly. With one person, and one person only.

I had to get away. Rising to my feet, I cleared my throat.

"I'll work on what we discussed. Thanks, Noah."

Liam broke away from Noah, staring up at me. I could easily read the question in his eyes, but he remained quiet, which I appreciated. Still, it wouldn't hurt to tell him some of it. "I want something like you two have. I want to date, at least. Noah talked me out of Grindr."

An expression came over Liam's face, a combination of understanding and empathy. "Talk to JJ. He knows everyone," he suggested. "But tell him if he fucks anything up for you, he's got me to deal with."

"Thanks." I was oddly touched. "I'll do that."

As I let myself out of number 3 and made my way next

door to my house, number 1, I suddenly remembered that Ander had told me he was also going to talk to JJ.

JJ wasn't an option. It was time for me to take matters into my own hands and find a way to get over my best friend.

FOUR

ANDER

"JJ!" I lifted my hand in greeting from my position at a table inside the waterfront bar where we'd arranged to meet. My housemate and fellow student was dressed down in a canary-yellow LSU hoodie and tight jeans, with the chunky, black-framed glasses that he normally wore for studying perched on his nose. But even dressed down, there was something about him that drew attention.

"Ander." He gracefully lowered himself into the chair that was placed perpendicular to mine. "What's all this about? You were very cryptic in your text."

"I need some advice."

"It'll cost you." Flicking his gaze towards the bar, he frowned in thought. "Hmm. To start with, I'd like a rhubarb and sage spritz. Make sure they don't use the cheap gin."

"A what?" The worst thing about being friends with someone who worked in the VIP section of a club was that he had developed expensive and sometimes completely random tastes in alcohol. "Never mind. I'll go now." Muttering "rhubarb and sage spritz" under my breath, I made my way to the bar.

When I returned with what I hoped was the drink he wanted, plus a craft beer for me, I leaned my elbows on the table, meeting his gaze. "I kissed Elliot, and—"

I didn't get any further into my sentence because he spat half his drink across the table. My laughter was loud enough to draw attention to us, and once JJ had recovered from his sudden coughing fit, his laughter joined mine.

We eventually calmed down, and I continued where I'd left off. "As I was saying, I kissed Elliot. This slimy guy was coming on to him, so I kissed him to make the guy go away."

"Are you serious? *That* was the best idea you had?" JJ arched a brow at me.

"It was the first thing that came into my head, so I went for it."

"Okaaaay." His voice was unconvinced. "But you kissed *Elliot*? Your best friend? How's he doing after that happened?"

I shrugged. "Fine, I think. We both agreed it was just a kiss—y'know, just helping him out. He's my best mate. It's not weird."

"It is a *bit* weird, babe. For Elliot too, I'm guessing." Toying with the straw of his drink, he studied me from beneath his lashes. "So anyway, what does this all have to do with me?"

"I was getting to that. It made me think—why haven't I tried anything with any other guys before? I think I might want to fuck a man."

"You what?" His voice had gone extremely high-pitched, and he flung his hands around agitatedly. "No offence, Ander, but you're reeeeally not my type. Yeah, I know we flirt or whatever, but sex? That's a *fuck* no. Only if there was a zombie apocalypse, and even then, I'm not sure it would happen."

I ignored his zombie comment. "What, am I not attractive to gay men?"

He groaned loudly. "That's not what I meant. And FYI, not every gay man has the same taste. That's like saying every straight man has the same taste. There's no one on this planet that everyone would agree on. No. One."

"I realise that. But I mean...I'm everyone's type."

His eye roll was accompanied by a shake of his head. "Your ego never fails to astound me. You're not *my* type. I like my men a little less in-your-face. A little older. A little less..." He waved his hand at me, temporarily lost for words, and then settled for "...pretty boy."

Smirking at him, I grasped my pint and then lifted it to my lips. "You can talk, *pretty boy*."

He blew me a kiss, using his middle finger. "Yeah. I don't want to be with someone like me, thanks. Now, are you really here to proposition me, or did you want something else?"

"I actually didn't invite you here to proposition you for sex," I said, a little too loudly, going by the way the two women at the next table started giggling as they stared at us. Shooting them a wink, I turned my attention back to JJ. "I want you to be my guru. I'm...curious, I guess, and I want to try a few things, see if I like it. I now know I like kissing a man, and..." I leaned closer, lowering my voice. "I was starting to get a boner when I kissed Elliot."

"You get a boner at the drop of a hat," JJ said dismissively. "Seriously, you might actually have a medical problem."

Ignoring the evil gleam in his eye, I rolled my eyes, tapping my fingers on the table. "I get hard from kissing when I'm really into the girl and she's really into me. But this wasn't that kind of situation. For one, the slimy guy was standing right there, and then there was the fact that it was Elliot, who's my best friend. Not a sexy hook-up."

"Was it the same for Elliot?" Curiosity entered his gaze.

"Yep. He got hard. But that's the power of Ander Loverrrridge." I drew out the *R* in Loveridge while JJ pretended to gag at my words. "Girls get wet for me, boys get hard for me." *It meant nothing.*

JJ's brows climbed so high they were practically in his hairline. He stared at me for a minute before a slow smirk spread across his face. "Okay. Let's test it." He snapped his fingers. "Come with me. Bring your drink."

I followed him outside, past the tables placed at intervals along the riverfront and around the corner of the redbrick building. He stopped next to a large industrial bin. Glass crunched under my foot.

"Awww, JJ. You take me to all the best places."

"You know it, babe." He slipped straight into flirt mode, eyeing me over the top of his drink, his lashes fluttering dramatically behind his glasses. "Only the best for my man."

"You've ruined me for all other men." I gulped down

the last of my pint, then placed the glass on top of the bin. JJ followed suit and then turned back to me.

"You're going to kiss me now, just like the way you kissed Elliot. Let's see if your little hypothesis is true. If you make me hard and you also get hard, I'll give you a free lap dance at the club."

"Uh...thanks, but I don't want you to give me a lap dance," I told him.

"Not from me, obviously." He waved his hand impatiently. "But I can get you one from Honey Rose. She's always booked up, and she's expensive." *Too expensive for you* were his unspoken words.

"Deal," I said immediately. Honey Rose was the hottest female dancer at Sanctuary, the club JJ worked at part-time, and I was a poor student and so fucking here for it. "Get ready to pay up."

Moving closer, I cupped the back of his neck as I'd done with Elliot and moved in.

Okay, JJ was a really good kisser. Soft lips, smooth, confident movements, no hesitation at all. But fuck, it felt like kissing a brother. Not that I would kiss a brother like this. And I wasn't getting hard. Was he? I couldn't feel anything.

Without breaking the kiss, I snaked my hand between us to check.

JJ smacked my hand away, instantly pulling back from me. "Hands away from the crown jewels."

"Sorry, Your Highness. Wanted to see if you're hard."

He rolled his eyes. "Believe me, if I was hard, you'd

know about it. Although there's not much room for it to go anywhere in these jeans."

"I'm not hard either." I sighed. This experiment couldn't be a failure already, surely. "It felt like I was kissing a relative. No offence."

There was silence for a second, and then JJ huffed out an amused chuckle. "None taken. It felt that way to me too. Let's both agree to never repeat this experience."

With a short nod, I kicked at the ground, sending some pebbles and bits of glass skittering across the concrete, a cloud of dust disappearing on the wind just like my dreams of a lap dance from Honey Rose. My experiment was a failure. There was no spark there. Nothing that made my dick stir.

When I looked back at him, I was surprised by the sympathy in his eyes. "Just because it didn't work with me doesn't mean it won't work with someone else." He squeezed my arm lightly. "Wanna come out with me this weekend? I can introduce you to some people. You won't have any trouble pulling someone looking the way you do."

My mood lifted. Flashing him a grin, I leaned back against the wall next to him. "Yeah, okay."

"Okay. I'll introduce you to some people this weekend." His smile disappeared, and he placed his hand on my arm. "In the meantime, if you have any questions, I'm here, okay? All joking aside, if this is something you're genuinely interested in, I've got your back. But only if you're serious about it. I don't want to be responsible for you fucking with people's feelings. You need to be completely upfront with whoever I introduce you to, okay? Make sure they know exactly what the deal is."

Making sure to hold his gaze, I responded. "Yeah. I know I've been, y'know, joking around or whatever, but I *am* serious. I promise. Look—I couldn't stop thinking about it after I'd kissed Elliot, and I know that I want to at least explore my options. I don't wanna give anyone the wrong impression about what I want, and I'll make sure that they know where they stand with me before anything happens. I do that with the girls I'm with anyway—that's not going to change just because it's a man involved."

"Good. Because this is gonna involve real people, with real feelings." The seriousness faded from his expression, and he grinned at me. "I think you're going to enjoy this. Even if our kiss didn't work out the way you hoped, I guarantee there's someone out there who'll give you the kind of response you're looking for."

I returned his grin. "Thanks, bro. I hope you're right."

"No. You don't call me that. No bro nicknames."

"Sorry, dude."

He shot me a warning look. "You're buying me another drink."

I mentally prepared myself to take another hit to my bank account. "I guess I owe you one."

FIVE

ELLIOT

"**S**hit! Sorry!"

I straightened up, rubbing my head. A guy with tousled brown hair stood in front of me, first giving me a slightly apologetic smile, then wincing as he rubbed at his own head. We'd collided as I was entering the lecture hall and he was coming out.

"Elliot?"

My gaze swung to the guy's left, and my lips curved into a small smile. "Huxley, hi."

The corner of Huxley's mouth turned up, which was as good as a smile from him. "Might want to watch where you're going."

"Thanks for the helpful advice. I'll be sure to remember that in future." I adjusted my bag on my shoulder, shifting on my feet. "Uh. How's Cole doing?"

"He's your cousin. Why don't you ask him yourself?" Huxley smirked at me.

"He's your boyfriend." *And stepbrother.*

37

"Aren't you going to introduce me?" The brown-haired guy was looking between us with interest. His eyes lingered on me, and his lashes swept down as his gaze lowered to my mouth.

"Yeah, sorry. This is Elliot, Cole's cousin. Elliot, meet Curtis. He's in my band. Drummer." Huxley eyed his friend before turning back to me. "Cole's put us on the guest list at Revolve on Thursday." He paused, giving me a cautious look. "You wanna come?"

Huxley voluntarily inviting me to hang out with him—that had to be my cousin's influence. Leaning against the wall in what I hoped was a casual pose, I said, "Thursday? Isn't that a theme night?" I tried to ignore the way that Curtis was studying me with even more interest than before.

"Thirst Trap Thursday." Huxley rolled his eyes. "Not my choice, but it's two-for-one on drinks, and Cole wants me to entertain him while he's working."

Curtis took a step closer. "You should come," he said in a low, soft voice, and I suddenly remembered Noah's words. Maybe this was a good opportunity to dip my toe in the water. Open myself up to new possibilities. Cole would be there anyway, and I was pretty sure I could drag some of my other friends along.

I nodded. "Alright. I'll come. Get Cole to text me the details."

"Don't I get your number?" Curtis smiled at me.

"Not—"

I was cut off by the sudden arrival of Dr. Wilder, the principal lecturer for my international business management module. He was famously short-tempered and grumpy, and he didn't disappoint today, his face twisting into a scowl as he jabbed his finger in the direction of the lecture theatre. "Enough talking! Mr. Clarke, inside, now. You two, get out of here."

"Yes, sir," I mumbled, ducking inside and sliding into the first available seat, not wishing to incur any more of his wrath. All my other lecturers preferred to be referred to by their first names, but not him. The only acceptable form of address was "sir" or "Dr. Wilder."

Hiding my phone under my desk, I sent a text to Noah.

ME:

> I ran into my cousin's boyfriend and he was with a guy who I THINK was interested in me. I agreed to go with them to Revolve on Thursday night. Can you come? I might need moral support

Leaving my phone balanced on my knee, I returned my attention to the screen at the front of the lecture theatre, beginning to jot down some notes as Dr. Wilder went through the data relating to the on-screen chart. Around ten minutes later, I had a reply to my text.

NOAH:

> Yes! Want me to come on my own?

ME:

> No you can invite Liam. Preston too? The more of us, the better. Less potential for awkwardness

NOAH:

> Will do. Tell me about the guy

He followed up his message with a string of eyeball emojis, and I smiled.

> **ME:**
> His name is Curtis and he's a drummer in my cousin's boyfriend's band

> **NOAH:**
> I approve

> **ME:**
> You haven't even met him yet. I spoke to him for 2 minutes. Not enough time to form an impression

> **NOAH:**
> OK I'll reserve judgement until I meet him

> **ME:**
> Good. Speak later

I put my phone away and attempted to concentrate on the lecture. When it was over, I managed to get outside quickly, avoiding Dr. Wilder's eye, and I made my way to the student union café, where I was meeting Ander for lunch.

Ander was already at a table in the corner of the room, and I headed straight for him.

A bright smile lit up his face when he caught my eye, and as usual, I did my best to ignore the butterflies he gave me. "I got you the chilli—thought you might want something to warm you up. It's fucking freezing out there."

"Yeah, it is. Thanks for this. It's just what I needed." I sank into the chair across from his, unable to stop my smile as he unloaded the tray, placing steaming chilli with rice and a can of Coke Zero in front of me. Rubbing my hands together, I said, "I think my fingers have frostbite."

He laughed at that, and before I could register what was happening, he was reaching across the table and encompassing my hands in his. Slowly, methodically, he began to rub his hands over mine. "Better?"

I swallowed. "Much." My voice was way too hoarse.

"Good, because you don't wanna catch a cold. You can borrow my scarf for the walk home."

Thankfully, he let go of me, picking up his fork, and I was able to form sentences again. "You know that catching a cold from cold weather is a myth, right?"

"What about pneumonia?"

I shrugged. "I don't actually know how you catch that. What about bronchitis?"

Ander's attention was caught by someone behind me, and he lifted his hand in greeting. I twisted in my seat to see JJ bounding towards us, a red knitted hat pulled low on his head and a matching chunky scarf wrapped around his neck and the lower part of his face, just leaving his eyes showing, framed by his glasses.

"I don't know about bronchitis," Ander said as JJ reached us, and JJ raised a brow, unravelling his scarf and sinking into one of the two free seats.

"Am I interrupting something? Because if you need a medical opinion, I know nothing. My suggestion is go to the doctor."

His words triggered a memory...brown hair and a smile...the invitation to Revolve...Dr. Wilder snapping at us...

"Not Dr. Wilder."

I didn't realise I'd spoken aloud until Ander's lips kicked up at the corners.

"E, he's not a medical doctor. He's got a PhD in assholery."

"He's actually got a PhD in..." I thought for a minute. "Something businessy."

"Also, assholery." Leaning back in his chair, Ander folded his arms across his impressive chest. "That man is a fucking bellend."

"Well, yeah." I couldn't disagree.

"Who's this?" JJ's gaze flicked between us, sharp and interested, like a shark smelling blood in the water.

"No one. Just one of our lecturers. He's probably, what? Thirty? Thirty-two, maybe? Something like that. But he acts like he's some fucking all-knowing ancient being." Ander was dramatic as always, but again, I couldn't disagree.

"Oh, yeah. I've heard you both complaining about him before. But you're studying business. You should've picked drama or music if you wanted a lecturer who actually cared about more than ticking boxes." JJ reached out and grabbed my Coke Zero, taking a sip. "Let's change the subject to something less boring. What are we wearing to Thirst Trap Thursday?"

"You're coming?"

Placing my drink back down in front of me, he nodded. "Yeah, Preston invited me, and—" He cut himself off with a small shake of his head.

"It's okay. Elliot knows what's going on. I wouldn't keep

anything from him." Ander gave him a reassuring look and then turned to me. "I was there when Preston invited JJ, and I invited myself. So I'll be there."

His words fell heavily between us, a ton of lead dropping at my feet.

Ander was going to be at the club. *Ander.* Who wanted to experiment with other guys.

After the longest silence in the world, I cleared my throat. "Thirst Trap Thursday. Should be a good night."

"Yeah... Thirst Trap Thursday..." my best friend said slowly.

A reluctant smile crawled across JJ's face as he met Ander's eyes. He glanced at me and then back to Ander, who gave an emphatic nod. His shoulders relaxed, and he clasped Ander's arm briefly before releasing it. "You said you were interested in experimenting with boys, but are you ready to be thrown in the deep end?"

"I'm ready."

Those two words coming from my best friend's mouth... they fucking cut me. For so many years—*no*. I wouldn't torment myself. My only option was to move on, and I would do everything in my power to ensure it happened.

But the thought of seeing Ander with someone else, after everything that had happened between us over the past week...I knew that when I was faced with it, the cut would be even deeper.

SIX

ANDER

"Stop staring at Elliot, and come with me. I want you to meet some people."

Somehow, I managed to tear my gaze away from the sight of my best friend, looking so fucking... I didn't even have a word to describe him. Confident in a way I'd never seen him before. His body was writhing sinuously under the sweeping lights, the sheer sleeveless shirt he wore clinging to the lightly defined muscles of his torso. His legs looked long as fuck in a pair of tight black jeans that I'd never seen him in before. A huge smile was wreathed across his face.

Here, in this club, Elliot was so comfortable in his own skin, it...it made it hard to look away.

Turning to JJ, who was smirking, I raised a brow. "What? I've never seen Elliot like this before. It's...weird."

JJ stepped closer, curiosity entering his gaze. Despite the low lighting, his eyes looked even brighter and more

45

focused than normal, rimmed with some dark, sparkly shit. "Weird how?"

I shrugged. "Dunno, really. I thought I knew everything about him, but I haven't seen this side of him before."

He chewed on his lip for a moment, his expression thoughtful. "You've never been to a gay club with him before, have you? It's a different environment from the usual places you spend time together."

"I guess that makes sense." Shooting Elliot another final glance, I allowed JJ to steer me away from the bar towards a group of guys around the same age as us, dressed similarly in short-as-fuck shorts of varying colours and no tops.

"It's like I'm seeing seven of you," I murmured in JJ's ear as we drew closer. "Is there some kind of hot-boy clone factory out the back?"

"Babe, if you've got it, flaunt it." He shot me a grin. "Speaking of, it's Thirst Trap Thursday. Your T-shirt needs to be gone. Now."

"Okay." With another careless shrug, I lifted my tight white T-shirt, peeling it from my body, and tucked it into the waistband of my jeans. JJ was right. I had it, and I was fucking well going to flaunt it.

"JJ, who's this?" One of the guys, dressed in tiny electric-blue shorts, broke away from the group and sidled up to us. He was at least a head shorter than me, with the lean, defined body of a dancer and a mop of deep brown curls on the top of his head. Giving me a coy smile, he batted his lashes at me.

Before I knew what was happening, his blue-tipped fingernail was trailing down my abs.

JJ swatted his hand away. "Not for you. He's new to this. Very new. I don't want you scaring him off."

Both the guy and I laughed at the same time.

As if I could be scared away. I was fully committed to this.

"Hmmm..." The guy moved, circling behind me and then coming up to my other side. Gripping onto my bicep, he stood up on his toes, speaking into my ear. "Curious, are you? You know what they say about curiosity."

I shot him a smile, slipping easily into flirt mode. "What do they say?"

"Dance with me, and maybe I'll tell you."

"For fuck's sake," JJ muttered from my left. "Niccolò. Go and find someone else to play with. This is Ander's first time here."

"I don't mind." Holding eye contact with Niccolò, I replied to JJ. "What was it you said to me? Be upfront? I'm here to see if I can satisfy some of my curiosity. And I don't think I need to remind you that this was your idea to come here, anyway."

Out of the corner of my eye, I could see JJ shake his head in defeat. "Whatever. Just...play nice, Nic."

"I'm always nice," Niccolò purred. He began tugging me away from JJ and his friends, leading us in the direction of the dancing bodies. When we reached the dance floor, he plastered his body up against mine. "Ander. What brings you here tonight?"

A kiss.

A kiss I couldn't get out of my head.

My gaze flicked to the left of the dance floor where I'd

47

last seen Elliot. For a minute, I couldn't spot him, but then I caught sight of his familiar profile. He was no longer dancing but standing at the edge, his expression animated as he conversed with someone I couldn't see. As I watched, his head tipped back, a laugh brightening his entire face, and my chest did something weird. It felt like my heartbeat went irregular for a second.

I coughed. "Long story short. I kissed my male friend, and it made me curious. So I'm exploring new options."

"Oooh, fun. You kissed a boy, and you liked it. Let's dance." Niccolò grabbed my hands, and it made me smile, amused. I wasn't used to being bossed around, but it was clear to me that JJ's friend was just as direct as JJ himself.

He spun himself around so that his back was to my chest, threading his fingers through mine, and began to move to the music. I moved with him, dropping straight into the rhythm of the heady beat.

Niccolò dragged our hands up over his torso, angling his head to the side to glance up at me. "Feels good, doesn't it?"

Yeah, it did, in fact. I'd thought I loved the soft curves of a girl's tits, and okay, I definitely still did, there was no doubt about it, but this...this was new, and yeah, it was good. My dick didn't seem to be into it, not even slightly, but it was still early. Everything was still so fucking new, being in a gay club and dancing with a guy for the first time, it was probably getting a bit of performance anxiety. If nothing else happened, I'd just have to give it some extra special attention later to make up for it.

My mind flashed to an evening in Bournemouth...a male body pressed against mine, soft lips meeting—

I shook my head to clear it, meeting Niccolò's eyes. JJ's warning echoed in my head. Time to be upfront. "Good, yeah. Different, but I like it."

His smile morphed into a smug grin, and he dragged our hands down again, lower, then lower, until they were at his waistband. "There's a biiig difference down here." He sighed theatrically. "I promised I'd play nice, and there's a chance that JJ might shank me if I let you touch. But if you want to, there are plenty of dark corners that I'm intimately acquainted with."

"Uh..."

The grin faded, and he moved my hands to his hips. "We're just dancing, for now, curious boy. You can tell me later if you want anything more. No pressure."

I relaxed. It was all good. This was my new experience, and I was going to fucking well love it, even if I had to dance with a hundred different men before I found one that I wanted to take things further with.

I alternated dancing with Niccolò and JJ and his friends, who seemed to be either dancers or models, from what I could make out. None of them sparked an interest, but the night was still young. Now and then, I caught a glimpse of Elliot from across the floor, my gaze tracking his movements every time I saw him. I had to watch out for my best friend, after all. Noah, Liam, and Preston were all with him, but he seemed to be spending a lot of time speaking to and dancing with a guy I didn't recognise.

A couple of hours after we'd arrived, the music suddenly cut out. A loud siren noise sounded from the speakers, followed by an announcer's voice, almost drowned out by the shouts and cheers and whistles that filled the club.

"Revolve! It's time for the Thirst Trap Thursday lap dance challenge! All competitors, make your way to the left of the stage!"

The stage area suddenly lit up, illuminating a guy with a mic standing in front of a row of chairs. I didn't even get a chance to take it all in because JJ grabbed my arm, spinning me to face him. "Ready for that deep end I mentioned?"

"You signed me up for this, didn't you?"

"Uh-huh."

I grinned. "Bring it on, baby. Let me show the pro dancer that I've got moves too."

We made our way to the side of the stage, and I realised that out of all the dancers, I was the only one in jeans. Whatever, I was going to win this.

"Feeling confident?" JJ glanced at me as the guy with the mic strode towards us.

"Always."

When the mic guy reached us, he crouched down at the edge of the stage. "You have five minutes to find yourselves a partner. When you've chosen, come up onto the stage and seat your partner on one of the empty chairs. We'll begin when all the chairs are filled." He gave a saucy wink, which I swore was aimed at me, before straightening up. "Looking forward to the show."

"How pissed off would Liam be if I chose him?" JJ's eyes were bright with mischief.

I smirked, picturing Liam's face. "Mate, don't do it. Save yourself from the pain."

"I won't really, but I'm tempted to, just to see how he reacts. You gonna choose Nic?"

I shook my head. There was only one person I wanted. The person who was there for me through thick and thin that I could do this with and trust that it wouldn't get weird. "No. I'm choosing Elliot."

SEVEN

ELLIOT

W hat was happening? One minute, I'd been standing with Curtis, our conversation turning more and more flirty as the night went on, and the next minute, my best friend, who was currently shirtless, had wrapped his hand around my wrist and was pulling me towards the stage.

"Ander! You can't expect me to go up there!" I hissed, trying to yank my arm free from his grip. It was one thing to be up onstage, but to be up onstage with Ander grinding his hard, gorgeous body against mine...every single person would have a front-row view of the effect he had on me. There was nowhere to hide.

He turned the full force of his hypnotic gaze on me, his eyes going wide and pleading. "E, please. I know JJ thinks that I can't beat him or I'm gonna pull out of this, but I have to prove him wrong. You're my best friend, and I *need* you."

Bastard. He knew full well that I could never say no to

him when he looked at me like that. But then, he wasn't normally one to take advantage of my weakness.

Only in circumstances when he wanted something badly.

Like the time we were twelve and he'd heard that there was going to be a lunar eclipse, and he'd insisted that we should both set alarms for 3:00 a.m. and sneak out of our houses to take photos of the blood moon. We'd both ended up being grounded for two weeks for that.

Or when he told me he wanted to apply to LSU for his degree, and he'd begged me with his eyes to go with him. "I don't want to do it without you," he'd said, and then he'd wrapped me in his arms, and the only thought left in my head was that I'd follow him anywhere. Having said that, he had been fully prepared to give up his dream university had I decided not to go with him. The truth was, he was as incapable of saying no to me as I was to him.

I forced those memories away, raising my brows. "You do remember that JJ works as a dancer, right?"

"Only part-time," Ander shot back, and I shook my head with a resigned smile.

"Okay, fine. But you owe me for this, seriously."

"You're the best fucking friend in the world." He leaned in, and I felt the barest brush of his lips across my cheek before he withdrew, giving me a wide grin.

I stared at him. He was an affectionate guy, and he gave me hugs freely. But kisses? That was new.

Probably part of his experimentation. I hadn't missed how he'd been dancing with JJ's sexy friend earlier, although I'd attempted to reassure myself with the fact that nothing else had happened. Not that I'd been tracking his moves...fuck, okay, I had. Curtis had held a significant amount of my attention—more than I'd expected, in fact, but there was a part of me that was so attuned to Ander. I was expecting at any minute to see him with his tongue down another guy's throat, bracing myself for the sight because I knew that it would hurt. A lot.

By the time we were up on the stage and I was in the chair, I'd relaxed a little. Ander was playing around, flexing his muscles and showing off, as were the majority of the other guys up here with us.

I couldn't stop my grin as he spun around to meet my gaze. Cocking my brow, I eyed him with amusement. "I hope you know what you're doing."

"No idea."

It was such a typical Ander response that I couldn't help laughing. "I guess you never let that stop you before."

"Nope." Planting his hands on the back of the chair on either side of me, he leaned down, speaking into my ear. "E. You know that you're my best friend and you love me."

I shifted in my seat to hide the shiver that went through me as his breath skated across my overheated skin. "Yes..."

"You want me to win, right?"

"Yes..." Alarm bells suddenly blared, and I forgot all about the effect he was having on me. Angling my head away from him, I twisted so I could meet his gaze. I sighed. "Just say it."

Even though I'd angled my head back, we were so close that I could see the little flecks of gold in his hazel eyes, dotting the greens and browns. So beautiful. It was almost impossible to stop myself from getting lost in them.

Falling silent, he held my gaze, and I couldn't look away.

"Ander?" I whispered.

"Uh." He cleared his throat. "You...you're the only one up here with a top on. I think it'll look better if—"

"No. You can't— Have you seen how the others look?" Not that I was insecure, but I was realistic. Try being surrounded by thirteen other guys that looked like they spent the majority of their lives in the gym—it was enough to make any mere mortal feel more than a little inferior.

Ander's brows pulled together, and his mouth set in a flat line. "Elliot Clarke. Top. Off. Now. And check a fucking mirror because from where I'm standing, you have exactly zero reasons to worry."

"You can't make me," I hissed, irritation warring with the warmth that was spreading through my body at his words.

He seemed to deflate. "Yeah. I know. Sorry. Forget I said anything."

"Why do you do this to me, Loveridge?" My words came out as a sigh. "Fine. I'll do it. But you owe me so much for this. So, so much."

A gorgeous smile spread across his face. He straightened up and took a step back, letting go of the chair. "I'll buy you a hundred bags of ice."

"I can make my own ice for free in the freezer." My fingers curled around the hem of my top, and I took a deep breath. Better to get this over with as soon as possible.

Whipping my top off, I leaned forwards and shoved it under my seat, then straightened back up. My heart was pounding way too fast, and my palms were clammy.

I lifted my gaze to Ander's, but his eyes weren't on my face. His gaze was scanning my body as if he'd never seen it before, which was ridiculous because we'd seen each other shirtless a million times. His scrutiny made my cheeks heat, and I had to suppress the urge to curl myself into a ball and hide away from his gaze.

I was saved when the guy with the mic began to speak, informing us all how the challenge would be judged— loudest cheers at the end of the dance—and then the music started.

Then there was no time to worry about how I looked because I had a job to do, which was to look like I was enjoying being up here.

And despite everything, I *would* enjoy it because my hot-as-fuck, amazing best friend, who I loved, was going to be dancing for me.

The dance passed in a blur of colour and noise, sweat-slicked bodies sliding against each other, spurred on by the crowd.

I only had eyes for Ander.

Ander, whose body was so close to mine, winding and grinding and driving me completely and utterly in-fucking-sane. I drank him in, tracking his every movement with my gaze, not wanting to miss a second of what was probably a once-in-a-lifetime opportunity. My dick didn't even stand a chance, and there was no way that he could have missed it when he rolled his hips down into my lap. I white-knuckled the edges of my seat, my heart beating out of my chest, and tried to remember how to breathe.

His rhythm faltered, so briefly that I doubted anyone but me caught it, but then he was popping back up and spinning around, his hands going to the back of my chair as he rolled his body again. I focused on the beads of sweat running down the ridges of his abs, not daring to look at his face. My cheeks were flaming, and I could probably pass that off as being hot, but my erection...not so much.

A loud siren noise pierced through my panic, marking the end of the challenge, and I sucked in a relieved breath, collapsing back, my eyes falling closed.

"Time to decide our winner!" The mic guy's voice boomed through the space, and the noise of the crowd increased. "Revolve, make some noise for your favourite dancer!"

I opened my eyes again to watch him make his way down the row of chairs, pausing at each one. The cheers grew noticeably louder when he stopped in front of my chair. Ander stood facing out towards the crowd, the backs of his legs brushing against my knees. He flexed, blowing kisses and playing to the crowd, and the cheers increased.

"It's not over yet. Make some noise for our final dancer!" The announcer moved to the last chair in the row, which was JJ's. JJ had dragged one of his dancer friends up here to dance for, and he was waving his hands, encouraging them to cheer louder. JJ himself was wiggling around, showboating just as much as Ander had, if not more, and the noise from the crowd grew even louder.

The announcer leaned into JJ, covering the mic with his

hand, and JJ said something to him. When he turned back around, he waved his hand with a flourish.

"We have a winner! Give it up for dancer number seven, JJ!"

At his words, the music kicked in, and foam sprayed out across the club. Bubbles began pumping out from somewhere above us, iridescent globes that caught the rainbow of lights sweeping across them. JJ accepted the huge bottle of champagne that another guy brought over to him, then laughing, he shook it up, sending a shower of fizzing, sparkling liquid into the crowd, like he was a Formula 1 champion or something.

Ander swiped the bottle from JJ's hand, shaking it up and then dousing JJ with it. JJ grabbed it back, throwing his arm around Ander and tipping what was left over his head, both of them collapsing with laughter. Seeing Ander so happy made me happy, but it was bittersweet. He fit here so perfectly. Just not with me.

My realisation was hammered home when JJ shouted something to him about having his pick of the guys here tonight after that performance.

For the first time all night, I was filled with perfect clarity. I needed to do what was best for me.

I needed to let Ander go. Tonight.

EIGHT

ANDER

I disentangled myself from JJ, spinning back around to face my best friend. Except, he wasn't there. His shirt had disappeared too.

A weirdly disappointed feeling went through me, but I couldn't blame him for leaving. I'd coerced him into joining me onstage, after all.

He'd liked it, though.

I'd felt the hard press of his erection against my ass, and my dick had reacted, swelling in my jeans.

Although, if I were honest with myself, I'd been half-hard ever since...fuck, I couldn't recall exactly. But being up on stage had obviously done something for my dick. Did I have a previously unknown exhibition kink? Probably.

A thought stopped me in my tracks. *Had* Elliot liked it? Or was it a natural reaction? Because if I'd had a hot girl grinding all over my dick, there'd be no way I wouldn't get a hard-on.

Yeah. Fuck, what was I thinking? I'd dragged my poor

best friend up on stage under duress, and he'd had a natural reaction despite everything.

It suddenly hit me. I was a fucking *terrible* best mate. Why had I forced Elliot to go through all that when he clearly hadn't wanted to? He'd been hesitant from the start, and yet I'd steamrollered over his objections, only considering my own goals. I was so fucking selfish. I needed to find him so I could apologise, to promise I wouldn't coerce him into doing anything like that again.

Scrambling off the stage, I scanned the club, my vision obscured by the foam flying everywhere. *Where was he?*

Finally, after scouring the entire dance floor, my gaze caught on to the familiar sight of Liam and Noah and then slid to their right. I had to squint for a minute, but then I saw *them*.

My best friend, standing very, very close to the guy he'd been hanging out with for most of the night. As I watched, the guy leaned in and kissed Elliot.

My stomach churned. Fuck. I was going to be sick. The drinks I'd had must've been stronger than I thought.

I tore my gaze away. I couldn't watch them.

Liam caught my eye, and even from this distance, I could see his brows pull together. *You okay?* he mouthed, and I nodded, already on the move, heading in the direction of the toilets. If I was going to be sick, I wasn't going to make a fool of myself out here.

In the toilets, I bypassed the urinals and stalls, making my way to the line of sinks. I ran the tap of the farthest sink, splashing water on my face. In the mirror, my cheeks were flushed, and my eyes looked like I'd fucking done pills or some shit—wild, crazy, blown pupils. This night wasn't going to plan.

"Ander."

JJ's reflection appeared next to me, flanked by Niccolò, who squeezed in on my other side.

"What is this? Cosy chat time?" My words came out more sharply than I'd intended, but JJ just shook his head at me, placing his hand on my arm.

"Ander, listen to me. I saw you out there, and I've been thinking about all the things you told me. I...I'm going to ask you a question. Take your time thinking about the answer because you need to be honest with yourself. I don't even need to know the answer, but I want *you* to have it. Promise me you'll think about it, okay?"

I stared at him, our eyes meeting in the mirror. "Uh. Yeah. Okay. What's the question?"

His gaze flicked to Niccolò, and Niccolò gave a short nod. He stood up on his tiptoes, speaking into my ear. "My offer's still open if you ever want to take me up on it. But I think you might find your answers closer to home. Take care of yourself, *bello.*"

What was that supposed to mean? There was no time to ask him to clarify because he flashed me a quick smile and then disappeared out of the door.

JJ released my arm and turned, leaning back against the sink next to me. He bit down on his lip, clasping his hands together, and when his eyes met mine, I realised that whatever he was planning to ask me was going to be far more than a simple question.

"I think..." He paused, exhaling a long breath. "Have

63

you considered that your feelings for Elliot might be more than platonic?"

Nausea returned with a vengeance, and I rubbed my stomach.

"What?" I whispered, my mouth falling open. "*Elliot?*"

"Don't answer. Just think about it." Lifting his hand, he squeezed my arm again. "I might be reading things wrong, but I—" Cutting himself off with a shake of his head, he grimaced. "No. Never mind what I think. Just...*you* think about it. And if the answer is yes, you need to tread carefully. You owe it to yourselves to be honest, but you're both my friends, and I don't want to see either of you hurt."

Without giving me a chance to respond, he swept from the room, pausing only to spritz himself with the complimentary scents and shit that were in a basket close to the door, closely guarded by a bored-looking man. I collapsed forwards, my head falling against the mirror.

My best friend's name played on repeat in my head.

Elliot. Elliot. *Elliot.*

He was my best fucking friend. *Not* someone I was into. My feelings for him were 100 percent platonic. Always had been, always would be.

I closed my eyes against the flashes in my brain, but it didn't stop them from coming, one after the other, an incessant assault that I had no hope of escaping.

Flash. A kiss in a bar in Bournemouth.

Flash. A body moving under the club lights.

Flash. A long, lean torso bared to my gaze, up on a stage.

Flash. Light blue eyes meeting mine.

Flash. Soft fucking lips pressing against someone else's mouth.

Bile rose in my throat, and I dived for the nearest stall, slamming the door shut behind me. I staggered forwards and dropped to my knees, uncaring of the state of the floor. My vision blurred, and I blinked rapidly, curling my body over and leaning my head against the wall, waiting for my nausea to subside.

I remained there for a long, long time.

NINE

ANDER

"You're quiet." Liam's brow furrowed as he came to a stop beside me at the edge of the AstroTurf pitch. I handed him my bottle of water, giving a non-committal grunt that I hoped he wouldn't ask me to elaborate on. Sadly for me, he didn't take the hint. After downing the rest of my bottle, he crumpled it in his hand and then threw it on top of my hoodie, which was lying at the side of the pitch with our bags, before turning to face me fully. "What's up, mate? You can talk to me, y'know."

I stared down at the artificial grass as if it could provide an answer to the tangled mess in my brain. "It's nothing." I could feel my friend's eyes boring into the side of my head, but I kept my gaze fixed on the ground.

"Ander—"

The sound of the whistle blowing stopped his sentence in its tracks, and my head snapped up to see both our football coach, Bryan, and our team captain, Travis, shooting Liam and me impatient looks.

"Holmes. Loveridge. This isn't social hour, lads. Heads in the game." Bryan tapped his watch. "Back to it."

Liam and I jogged over to where the rest of the LSU football team players were queuing up in front of the lines of cones, ready to do drills. I took my place behind Levi, a first-year uni student and one of my housemates.

Levi twisted to face me with a sympathetic smile. "Having an off day? It happens to the best of us."

"You noticed?"

A heavy arm fell across my shoulders, and Travis was suddenly there, frowning at me. "We all noticed. You're normally the one keeping up the spirits of the rest of us."

"Guess I am having an off day," I mumbled as the line moved forwards. Travis' arm dropped from my shoulders, and I mindlessly dribbled the ball between the cones, my body working on autopilot while my brain was stuck on the same thing it had been stuck on ever since Thursday night.

It *couldn't* be Elliot that was making me feel this way, could it?

And if it was, how the fuck did I confront this? He was my best friend, the most important person in the world to me, and I never wanted to jeopardise that friendship.

When football training was finally over, after the longest two hours ever, I rushed out of the changing rooms with my gym bag slung across my shoulders, rubbing my fingers through my damp hair as if it would make it dry any quicker.

I was stopped in my tracks by Travis placing a hand on my arm. "Ander, wait up." Stepping closer, he lowered his voice. "Want to come to the pub with me, Liam, and Preston?"

"What, to your top-secret football-planning strategy session?"

He rolled his eyes. "It's not top secret."

"No?" I raised my brows, flicking my finger between us. "What's with the speaking in whispers and being in my personal space?"

"You're such a dick sometimes. I'm trying to do something nice because we're worried about you."

I deflated with a sigh. "Sorry, mate."

Clapping me on the back, he shot me a grin. "No need to apologise. So, you coming?"

I hesitated, eyeing him with suspicion. "I'll come...as long as you don't expect me to talk about my personal shit."

"Personal shit? Who said anything about that? We just want your input on some of the newer players. Levi, in particular. He's your housemate, after all." His words were innocent, but there was a gleam in his eye. I sighed, accepting my fate.

"I think you should utilise Levi more often." I sat back in my wooden chair, rocking slightly on the uneven stone floor. "I know he's only a first year, but he's good. Maybe the best we've had."

"Don't be afraid to piss off the third-year students on the team. Smith, especially. He's just pissed off because Levi plays in the same position, and he's a way better player.

All of them know their time is coming to an end." Liam smirked at Travis, who huffed.

"That's not it. I don't play favourites, and I make all my decisions for the good of the team. That's why the coach trusts me enough to do all this. Believe me, when I have my weekly meeting with him, he never goes against my decisions." He paused. "Mostly never."

Preston returned to the table, somehow managing to balance four pints of IPA in his arms. I relieved him of two of them, and he gave me a quick smile before taking a seat again. Glancing between Travis and me, he seemed to come to some kind of decision because he gave Liam a pointed look and then leaned into Travis and began speaking in a low voice, diverting his attention.

Liam cleared his throat. "So."

"So," I echoed, making a swirling pattern in the condensation on my glass.

"Uh. I'm not gonna ask you what's up again, but...you know you can talk to me, and it stays confidential, yeah?"

Swallowing a mouthful of chilled beer, I stalled for time. Liam and I...we were close friends, but a big part of our friendship had always been based on our mutual love of drinking and girls—right up until Liam had gone and got himself a boyfriend.

Wait. Liam had been straight, as far as I knew, and then he'd fallen for Noah. Maybe he *could* give me some useful advice. But then he might guess that I had feelings for—I mean, he'd get the wrong idea and think I was into someone specific.

Better not to say anything unless I wanted him to get suspicious.

"I appreciate it, mate. Just working out some shit in my head. How's Noah?"

"How's Noah?" His eyes narrowed. "Why the sudden interest? You only saw him the day before yesterday. Is it—" He cut himself off, his eyes going wide. Fuck. "*Oh.* Shit. That's why you were at the club?"

I nodded slowly. It was clear that he'd worked out some of what was going on with me, but if I didn't say anything else to incriminate myself, he could draw his own conclusions.

Liam shifted closer to me. "Got to be honest, I did wonder why you were there. You never showed an interest in going there before when Elliot or JJ went, and there have been shitloads of opportunities. So what...uh...did something specific prompt your interest?"

Fuck it. In for a penny, in for a pound, I guessed. "Yeah. I kissed someone, and it made me wonder if I'd been missing out all this time."

He stared at me, his eyes widening even further. "I can't say I was expecting that. Who was it?"

"No one important," I said, which couldn't be further from the truth. He threw me a sceptical look but refrained from commenting. Instead, he nudged me with his shoulder.

"I know a bit about that. Except, I guess, in my case, I really fucking wanted to kiss Noah...I just hadn't realised it at the time."

"That's not how it was for me." I gulped down more of my pint. "I was doing him a favour, trying to get some creep off his back. It was a spur-of-the-moment thing—never entered my head until that moment in time. It shocked me as well as him."

Liam's sharp intake of breath sent my stomach rolling. "Was it Elliot?" His voice was barely above a whisper, but it felt like he'd shouted it.

"H—how did you guess?"

He glanced over at Preston and Travis, making sure they weren't paying attention before turning back to me. "I can count on one hand the number of men you'd kiss to get someone off their back. Actually, two fingers. Elliot and maybe JJ. JJ...I can't imagine him needing you to come to his rescue. As for Elliot...he's your best friend. You're always looking out for him."

"Well, yeah. When you put it like that. But it wasn't like you're thinking. I helped him out, and then it made me wonder if I'd been missing out."

"Dicks are pretty good." Liam smirked. "Noah's, anyway."

"Please stop talking. I don't wanna know about Noah's dick. For fuck's sake, mate." I pretended to gag, and he laughed. Fuck this wanker. Time to give him a taste of his own medicine. Cupping my package, I leered at him. "I know dicks are good because mine is amazing. Uh-ma-zing. Porn-star-worthy, some have said. Wanna see?"

Liam looked unimpressed. "I've already seen it in the changing rooms."

"Already seen what?" Travis' voice interrupted our conversation.

"Ander's dick," Liam was quick to say, and I elbowed him in the side, grinning.

"I don't even want to know what you're talking about," he replied. Shaking his head, he picked up his pint. "Let's do a cheers to Liam for putting a smile back on Ander's face, even if he used questionable methods."

Preston raised his glass. "I'll drink to that. Cheers."

We clinked glasses, and I smiled at my friends. They weren't so bad, after all. And it looked like I'd managed to keep my secret hidden from Liam. Not that I had a secret. I just had a confusing mess of fucked-up thoughts in my head.

I'd be fine.

I just had to keep telling myself that.

TEN

ELLIOT

Curtis pulled back from me after just a few seconds of his lips against mine and gave me a small smile. The club lights played across his face as he eyed me carefully. "Uh, sorry. Couldn't help myself. Was that okay?"

I felt an answering smile tugging at my lips. He wasn't my usual type at all—well, my usual type was Ander, but in my efforts to forget him, I usually gravitated towards Ander-ish guys. Curtis had what I would probably call bad-boy-ish looks with his tattoos and the piercing at the top part of his ear. But this was what I needed. A clean break from Ander. And that began with opening myself up to new opportunities with guys who didn't share a passing resemblance to my best friend.

"You can do it again if you like." I leaned in, and he met me halfway. When he deepened the kiss, thoughts of my last kiss played on my mind, but I determinedly pushed them away. This was my fresh start. My clean break. And it wasn't *fair to Curtis if I was thinking about someone else while I was kissing him.*

When we broke apart, he placed his mouth to my ear. "Want to go somewhere a bit quieter?"

Did I? Could I? No. I wasn't ready. And this wasn't a drunken hook-up. This was someone that I'd met outside of a club, who was interested in me, and who I wanted to give a fair chance to. I slowly shook my head. "I...I don't think I'm ready for that. Yet. Sorry."

He stepped back, giving my arm a reassuring squeeze. "Hey. No problem. How about we start by exchanging numbers?"

In reply, I tugged my phone from my pocket.

That had been Thursday night. We'd texted back and forth a few times since then, and we'd arranged to meet for lunch on the following Wednesday in between lectures. So here we were in a little independent coffee shop, close to campus but out of the way enough that we wouldn't be interrupted by other students we knew. It had been my suggestion, and deep down, I knew it was because I hadn't wanted to chance running into Ander.

I groaned internally. Not again. While I was doing my best to keep all my focus on the cute guy who seemed into me, I couldn't help my mind going to Ander. He'd been off with me ever since the club, and that had been almost a week ago. Yeah, he still mostly treated me like he normally would, but there was an inexplicable distance between us. It felt like he was doing his best to keep everything between us at surface level. If there was something wrong with him, then I needed to get to the bottom of it. I couldn't stand the thought of my best friend hurting, especially if there was something I could do to help.

Curtis leaned back in his chair, eyeing me over the top of his flat white. "You're studying business, right? What made you pick it?"

I shrugged. The short answer was that I hadn't known exactly what I wanted to do, and business seemed as good an option as any. My parents had never pushed me towards a particular degree, let alone a career, and I thought that this degree would give me a good foundation for future business prospects.

The long answer...well, that involved the fact that I'd only chosen to come to this university because of Ander, and when he'd told me he was thinking of applying to study business...fuck, it sounded pathetic, but it had made my decision easy.

"It was as good a choice as any," I said eventually before taking a huge bite of my panini, hoping to stall any further conversation on this topic.

"Yeah, I get it. Same for me—I didn't know what I wanted to do either. I just wanted to play music, but my parents said I should have a backup plan. I agreed with them—it's not like gigging is gonna be my full-time career. I get to scratch the itch as a member of the 2Bit Princes, and we're happy with local gigs, playing covers and testing our original songs on whoever comes to watch us play." He paused, then shot me a contemplative look. "Hey. Want to come and check us out on Sunday morning? We get use of a studio on Sundays once a month, and we normally use the time to record our original songs so we can share them to our social media accounts throughout the month. We could grab lunch after?"

"I wouldn't be in the way?"

He shook his head. "Nah. There's a big room with sofas you can chill in. Cole might be there, but even if he isn't, no one will care."

"Okay." Swallowing hard, I finished my sentence. "Sounds good. I'll be there."

His smile was wide and genuine. "Looking forward to it. No pressure, okay?" He reached across the table and grabbed my hand, squeezing it once before letting it go.

We finished up our lunch, chatting easily about student life, keeping the conversation light, and when we were finished, I surprised myself by giving him a goodbye hug outside the coffee shop. It wasn't something I normally did. Maybe I was hoping for those elusive butterflies, and although they never came, I felt...hopeful. Curtis seemed like a great guy, and maybe, if I gave things between us a proper chance, he could be great for me.

———

A knock sounded at my bedroom door, and before I had a chance to reply, the door was opening. Ander's face appeared in the widening gap. "Coming?"

My fingers stilled on my laptop keyboard. "Where?"

He opened the door fully, moving into my room. "Next door. Movie night. Everyone's going."

A glance at my watch told me it was almost 8:00 p.m., and that meant I'd been sitting in front of my laptop for over four hours. "I'm not really in the mood for it right now. I've been working on this essay for hours, and I want to get it wrapped up tonight."

Stepping right up behind me, he placed his palms on my shoulders. I ignored the unexpected flare of heat. "E." He dipped his head to my ear, and his hands slid down my arms, lightly kneading my muscles. "You're all stiff. Take a break."

Fuck. I *was* stiff, if we were talking about the way my cock was rapidly responding to his touch and the way he was breathing in my ear like some kind of phone sex person.

"Please?" Sliding his hands back up my arms, he began to gently knead my shoulders. I bit down on my lip to stifle a sudden moan when one of his hands left my shoulder as he drew it up the back of my neck and into my hair, scraping his fingers across my scalp as he did so. "You're working too hard."

When I was sure I could speak again, I turned my head so I could meet his gaze. Distraction was my only technique. "Have *you* done this essay?"

He stared down at me for a long moment before he blinked, shaking himself. His hand slid out of my hair and back to my shoulder, a heavy warmth that radiated through my body. "Is it the one for Wilder?"

"Yeah." Forcing myself to move, I dropped my hands to my lap and then spun my computer chair so that his hands fell from my shoulders. Taking an unsteady breath, I pushed with my foot, allowing the chair to roll back from him. "It's due on Friday."

His brows pulled together. "I know it is. I've started it, and I have all my notes. I'll get it done on time, and so will you. But you've been shut away in here for hours, and it's not good for you."

"Even so, I don't feel like going anywhere. How about you go without me, and I promise you that I'll take a break for at least half an hour?"

"No deal." He shook his head violently, and I couldn't help the fond smile that crept across my face as I watched him. "I know that you'll carry on writing as soon as my back is turned. How about this—we go downstairs right now, and I'll make us both some food. Then you can get back to writing, and I'll go to movie night late. No one will care."

"Okay, fine." I climbed to my feet, stretching. Before I could overthink it, I crossed the small space between us and threw my arms around him. "Thanks for caring."

His arms came around me, and he held me tightly, burying his face in my hair. He sighed heavily, and then he released me, clearing his throat. "That's what best friends do."

Best friends. Yeah. It was.

Downstairs in the kitchen, we said a quick hi and goodbye to Charlie, one of our other housemates, who was heading out for the evening, and then Ander made me sit down at the kitchen table while he busied himself getting ingredients out of the fridge.

"Omelette okay? I need to go food shopping."

I couldn't help smiling at him. "Anything's okay. You know you can use my food too, right?"

"I know." He shot me a grin before grabbing a glass from the cupboard. "Already planning to." Ducking down, he opened the freezer door.

"Is there anything I can help with?"

"Nope." He straightened back up. When he returned to the table, he placed the glass down in front of me. "Just sit here and look pretty and crunch on some of these ice cubes."

My mouth fell open, making him laugh. He lowered his head to my ear. "I didn't forget the promise I made to you at the club."

"What promise?" My voice came out way too husky.

"To buy you a hundred bags of ice. This is ice from the first bag."

Was it my imagination, or had his voice also altered? It suddenly had a low, sexy rasp that was doing things to me that really shouldn't be happening.

The moment, if there was a moment, ended when he straightened up and strode over to the Bluetooth speaker on the kitchen counter. "I'm putting on some music because I'm not going to cook listening to you crunching ice."

"Fair enough." I tipped the glass up, letting one of the cubes slide into my mouth, quickly turning the inside numb with the cold. The sound of "All 4 Nothing" by Lauv started playing through the speakers as Ander began cracking eggs. It hit me all over again. Fuck, I loved this guy. Why had life been so cruel to give me only part of him? He was never going to love me the way I loved him.

For the millionth time, I reminded myself that I had to forget the way I felt about him. I'd had plenty of practice burying my feelings, so hopefully, I could still act normally around him and eventually move on, despite the way he'd been acting around me lately...which was all in my head, as I kept reminding myself.

When he slid my omelette in front of me, perfectly cooked and bursting with cheddar, juicy tomatoes, bacon, and spinach, he nodded to my now empty glass. "More ice? Do you want to come to my football match on Sunday?"

I blinked, taken aback by the sudden extra question he'd thrown in there. "Uh. No more ice, thanks. Sunday? What time?"

"Ten o'clock. It's a big one. Could make or break our season, to be honest. We're playing against Brighton, and a couple of their players used to be on a youth team with Travis and Liam." His voice dropped dramatically, taking on some kind of American-ish accent. "They're back, and this time, it's personal."

"I'll be—wait. No. Shit. I'm sorry, I can't come. I promised someone I'd do something with them on Sunday."

His mouth turned down, his eyes going all big and sad before he masked his expression. "Something with someone?"

My stomach churned. I hated upsetting him. "Yeah. I'm, uh..." Fuck, how hard was it to tell him? "I told Curtis I'd go and watch his band in the studio."

"Who's Curtis?" He inhaled sharply. "Is that the guy from the club?"

"Yes." The word came out as a croaky whisper.

Ander's shoulders slumped. "Oh." He lifted a hand, roughly dragging it through his hair. "Yeah. I mean. Yeah. You should go. Yeah. Uh. Have a good time." Shoving his chair back, he rose to his feet so abruptly that the chair wobbled on its feet. He headed to the kitchen door and then paused, briefly turning his head in my direction, although he didn't meet my gaze.

"You deserve to be happy, Elliot. I just want you to be happy."

Then he left.

ELEVEN

ELLIOT

The studio was close to Waterloo train station. To the left of the nondescript brown door, a series of named buzzers were mounted on the stone wall, and I pressed the one marked "Hopton Studios."

The buzzer sounded, and I pushed the door open, following the signs up to the second floor. I tried to ignore the heavy feeling in my gut that had been tugging at me ever since this morning—no, ever since Ander had invited me to watch his football match.

The sadness and disappointment on his face—it killed me. And I knew that most people would tell me it wasn't a big deal and I should put myself first...but the fact was, I wanted to be there for the moments in my best friend's life that were important to him—like he always was for me. But I'd made a promise to Curtis. Who I also wanted to be there for.

I ran my hand over my face, huffing out a breath. Fuck, why was I being so dramatic about this? I was blowing everything way out of proportion. There'd be other matches. I'd already watched Ander play more times than I could count. But there might not be another chance to do this with Curtis.

With that thought in mind, I entered the studio.

I found myself in a spacious room with big squashy leather sofas, a large coffee table, and a vending machine. Two huge speakers were set on either side of a long black desk with millions of buttons and knobs and lights, above which was a set of large glass windows. Through the windows, I could see into another room—or was it a sound booth? I wasn't familiar with the terminology—but it was where the band looked like they were tuning their instruments or whatever they did to get ready.

At the corner of the black desk, a guy sat in front of a computer monitor, tapping on a keyboard. He looked to be engrossed in whatever he was doing, and Curtis looked busy in the other room setting up his drum kit, so I headed over to the nearest sofa and flopped down on it.

My phone beeped three times in quick succession, and I tugged it free from my pocket to find three messages from Ander. I hadn't seen him before I left the house, so I'd texted him to wish him good luck for the match and to apologise for not being there.

ANDER:

No apology necessary. I understand and I don't expect you to cancel plans you've already made for me. Even though I'll be soooo sad that you're not there *crying emoji* *broken heart emoji*

Seriously though. Like I said before I want
you to be happy *heart emoji*

AND FUCK YES WE'RE GOING TO WIN

I sent a quick text back, although I doubted he'd see it
until after the match unless he happened to check his phone
at half-time.

ME:

I am happy, and I want to be there for you.
Good luck! You can do this

My phone beeped again, and I found myself smiling as
Ander's name appeared on my screen.

ANDER:

You're supposed to tell me how amazing I
am and hype me up for the game

ME:

Sorry, I didn't realise I'd been upgraded
from best friend to your personal
motivational coach. GO LSU! ANDER IS
THE GOD OF THE PITCH! HE'S THE BEST
PLAYER THAT EVER PLAYED ON THE
LEFT WING!

Enough?

ANDER:

No. Keep going

You don't need me to tell you how amazing you are. But I will, whenever you want me to. I know you're going to win and I'll treat you to dinner afterwards, ok? Or if you have plans, we can do it tomorrow. I want to celebrate my best friend knocking Brighton out of the competition *fist bump emoji*

ANDER:

Travis is glaring at me. Got to go. Yes to dinner. You're amazing too BTW *heart emoji*

The little red heart blinked up at me, and I desperately suppressed the feelings that were trying to crawl their way to the surface. This was Ander. It meant nothing. For him, flirting came as easily as breathing, and I would never be one to fall into the trap of thinking that something like this from him meant more than it did.

"Hey."

My head shot up from my phone screen to see Curtis grinning down at me. I returned his smile as I tucked my phone back into my pocket. "Hi. Nice setup you've got here."

"I can't take any credit. We just borrow the space." He glanced up at the windows where the rest of the band was taking their places. "We're about to start, but I'll introduce you to the others afterwards. I hope you like the music. If not, pretend you do."

I laughed. "I'm sure I will. I texted Cole after you'd invited me here, and he sent me the link to your YouTube channel. You guys are good."

He shrugged modestly, his eyes alight with humour. "We're not bad. Anyway, help yourself to the vending machine—it's free, and enjoy." Jogging away from me, he disappeared through the door to the right of the mixing desk, and I did as he'd suggested and grabbed a bottle of water from the vending machine.

The band started with a song I vaguely recognised— "Take Me Out" by Franz Ferdinand—before moving on to what must have been one of their original songs. A couple of minutes into it, the main door opened, and Cole entered the room, smiling when he saw me. "If it isn't my favourite cousin."

"Your favourite?" I raised a brow.

He threw himself down next to me, stretching out his legs in front of him, his knees poking out of his ripped jeans. "My favourite cousin who is also a student at LSU," he amended. I stuck my tongue out at him, and he returned the gesture, both of us reverting to the children we probably were deep down inside.

"Same to you," I told him. "Hey. They're good, aren't they?" I nodded towards the windows.

"Yeah. Hux, especially." His gaze slid towards his boyfriend, who was growling (quite sexily, I could admit) into the microphone.

Elbowing him in the side, I grinned at him. "You're not at all biased, are you?"

"Who, me? Nope."

My phone beeped, derailing me from my reply. I glanced down at the screen to see Noah's name, and the message preview had me thumbing open my phone so fast I almost dropped it in my haste.

NOAH:

Ander's injured. Not badly, so don't worry, but I thought I'd give you a heads-up

"I've got to make a call," I told Cole, quickly climbing to my feet and heading out into the corridor, hitting the Call button next to Noah's name.

As soon as the call connected, I began speaking. "What happened?"

"It was a bad tackle. Is that what it's called?" Someone else muttered something to him, and then he came back on the line. "Yeah. Ash says it was a tackle. He went down hard, and they took him off on a stretcher. I went and asked for you because I knew you'd be worried. It's a minor ankle sprain, and he needs to keep it iced and elevated, and he needs to use a compression thing and take ibuprofen as often as he's allowed. He'll be fine in a few days, but..."

"He's being dramatic?" I guessed, smiling despite my worry. "Acting like he's about to have his foot amputated?"

"Pretty much," Noah confirmed with a huffed laugh. "I also heard something about missing his moment of glory."

"Oh, Ander." My voice was far too soft and affectionate. But it was okay because it was Noah on the other end of the phone, and he knew all about my feelings for my best friend. "I'm on my way."

"Are you sure? I didn't want to interrupt you if you were doing something important, but I thought you should at least know."

"No, it's okay. He'd be there for me if I was the one injured, and I want to be there for him. I'll be there as quick as I can."

"Okay. See you in a bit."

When I ended the call, I headed back into the room and over to Cole. "Do you think the band will take a break anytime soon?"

He shrugged. "Dunno, why?"

"Um. I need to leave. Something's come up. Something important."

Although Cole and I weren't all that close—he'd grown up locally while I'd grown up in Bournemouth, and we'd only really seen each other a maximum of a few times a year until I'd come to LSU—he was well aware of Ander's best friend status, and he immediately made the connection. He rolled his eyes. "Let me guess. Is the 'something important' Ander?"

"Yes, it is." I couldn't hide the defensiveness in my tone. "He's been injured, and I want to make sure he's okay."

Cole sighed. "Of course you do. Okay, go. I'll make your excuses with Curtis. But listen, Elliot." He gripped my arm. "Don't fuck him around. He doesn't deserve to be your second best."

"I know, and it's not like that. Curtis is...he's a great guy." I smiled, watching him through the windows, head bent over his drum kit. "But Ander's my best friend."

"Just don't lead him on."

"I won't." Backing away towards the exit, I lifted my hand. "See you later."

As I left, I sent Curtis a text apologising for leaving

without saying goodbye and promised that I'd do my very best to make it up to him. Guilt sat heavy in my stomach, but I knew that if I didn't leave, I'd be worrying about Ander the whole time, and that wasn't fair to Curtis either.

I groaned. Why did this all have to be so difficult?

TWELVE

ANDER

"Does it still hurt?" Elliot's clear blue eyes were full of concern as he finished carefully moving my compression bandage into place.

Lying back on my bed with my back propped against the wall, I started to shake my head but then stopped. If I couldn't be honest with my best friend, who could I be honest with?

A strand of his hair fell into his eye, and before I knew it, my hand was rising, my fingers smoothing it back behind his ear. Wow. His hair was so fucking soft.

His gasp was audible, as was the expression of shock on his face, even though he quickly hid it. Shit. Why had I done that?

"My ankle hurts," I admitted, dropping my hand. Fucking sparks fizzed through me, despite the constant ache in my foot. What was all that about? Maybe it was a side effect of the pain.

When I chanced a look at Elliot, he had his teeth clamped down on his lower lip, and his cheeks were flushed.

"Where does it hurt?" Elliot's concern managed to override everything else, and I was grateful for it because I wasn't prepared to face the flash of raw emotion I'd seen on my best friend's face.

"It's just my ankle, and it'll be okay. The medic guy said it's only a minor sprain, and it'll heal quickly. I'll be walking normally in a few days."

Elliot raised a brow at me, and I didn't blame him. Usually, I'd milk it—get as much sympathy as I could. Now, though, I didn't feel like it for some reason.

"Hey, E?" My voice was so scratchy, even though I'd downed a pint of water.

His brows rose.

"You owe me dinner," I told him.

"Do I?" There was silence between us for a minute, and then his expression cleared. "I do, you're right."

"Can we just have a takeaway here?" Fuck, the way I was craving time with my best friend like I never had before...it honestly scared me. What was happening? Why was I looking at Elliot in a strange new way when there was nothing more than friendship between us?

The accident was making me emotional or something. That had to be it.

"Yeah, okay." His voice was soft. "What are you in the mood for? I'll order whatever you want."

"Uhhhh. Pide? The lamb one with the peppers? We haven't had it for a while."

He smiled at me. "I'll order now, and I'll get some

sides." Glancing towards my bedroom door, he frowned. "I'd better see if any of the others want anything. Levi's got Asher staying over tonight, and I think Charlie's in. Not sure about JJ."

There must've been something in my expression that gave away my thoughts because he huffed out a quiet laugh. "I'm not inviting them to eat with us. I just don't want anyone complaining when our order turns up and they don't get to have any."

Leaning my head back against the wall, I closed my eyes. "Okay." I heard the door open and shut, but I kept my eyes closed until I heard it open again.

Elliot entered my room with two glasses full of what looked like Coke with a ridiculous amount of ice. He placed the glasses down on my desk and then took a seat at the end of the bed. "Ash and Levi ordered. Charlie's already eaten, and JJ's out."

"Why are you sitting there?" I nudged his thigh with my uninjured foot. "Come up here."

He rolled his eyes but did as I suggested. "You're so bossy when you're feeling sorry for yourself," he informed me while stealing one of my pillows to shove behind his back.

"Me? Bossy?" I widened my eyes and let my jaw drop. "I'm injured. I might never be able to play again."

A smile curved over his lips. "There's the dramatics I've been expecting. You were far too blasé about your injury earlier. It was actually starting to worry me."

"You were worried about me? Really?" What the fuck was I saying? Obviously, he'd been worried—he'd cut his date short to come and see me. Fuck, *his date*. "Wait. What happened with your date?"

Elliot's gaze fell to his hands, and he studied them like they were the most interesting things he'd ever seen. "It wasn't a date. I was...I went to watch the band in the studio. Maybe..." His hands twisted. "Maybe it was a date. I don't know. I don't have much experience with going on dates."

His head rose and he faced me, his eyes blazing. "You're my best friend, Ander. Of course I'm going to come when you're hurt. Always. No question."

The feeling that went through me was uncomfortable. There was warmth—thinking about his words, that he was there for me, and he'd been worried enough to leave his date and come and find me. Then there was a weird sick feeling, thinking about the fact that he was on a date. The way I was reacting—it was clear to me that I'd been selfish, monopolising his time and taking it for granted that he'd always be there for me.

"I'm the worst fucking friend ever," I whispered. I hadn't even meant to say it, but now it was out there. Screwing my eyes shut, I pretended that I hadn't said it.

"Ander." Elliot's tone was cautious. "How are you the worst friend? Because you cut my maybe-date short? There'll be other dates. You didn't ruin anything for me."

Other dates.

The sick feeling was intensifying.

"I don't feel—"

"You've gone all pale." Elliot was suddenly gripping my arm, and then a cool hand was stroking across my forehead. "You're hot too. Lie down. Sleep if you need to; I can put the food in the fridge when it comes, and we can heat it up later." He carefully shifted me into a lying position. My stomach was fucking flipping all over the place, and my head was spinning.

I felt Elliot's weight leave the bed, and I reached out, encountering nothing but air. "Don't leave me."

"I'm not going to." There was a clinking sound, and then the bed dipped again. "This might be cold."

"Argh! What's that?" I recoiled as a freezing cold *something* pressed against my forehead.

"Ice cube from your drink to cool you down. There's no Coke on it, don't worry. I put it in my mouth first."

He put it in his mouth first.

He trailed the cube across my forehead, his fingertips grazing my skin, and I shivered.

Fucking hell, why was my dick suddenly taking an interest? Why? Why in the actual fuck? I was lying here injured, and there was a cold-as-fuck lump of ice being pressed on my head instead of floating around in my drink where it belonged. There was something seriously wrong in this scenario.

"Nrgh," I groaned.

"What was that?" Elliot's voice was full of amusement. "Was that even English?"

"It's *cold*," I hissed, shifting on the bed to hide the growing bulge that I knew he was going to see if he happened to look down at my joggers. A small jolt of pain shot up my leg from my ankle, and I hissed again, except this time, I was actually hurting. It had the bonus effect of deflating my hardening cock, though, so I guess it wasn't all bad. What the fuck was up with my body lately? All these weird reactions. I needed to get back to normal ASAP.

Distantly, I heard the doorbell, and then a couple of minutes later, Levi shouted up the stairs.

"Elliot! Food!"

The iciness disappeared, and I finally opened my eyes again to see Elliot crunching on the cube, smiling around it. He indicated towards the door with his thumb and then shifted off the bed. Without another look at me, he disappeared out of the door.

I scrubbed my hand across my face, sighing loudly. I needed to get a grip. Moving slowly to the side, I picked up my phone to give me something to do. Something normal. It buzzed in my hand as I gripped it, and when the screen turned on, flashing up a message preview, I saw:

CURTIS:
No probs. Are you free...

Shit, this was Elliot's phone, not mine. And I couldn't read the rest of the message because it would be a gross invasion of his privacy. But maybe I could dig for more information.

When Elliot came back in with a large bag with fucking delicious smells coming from it, I smiled at him. "You had a message."

He hummed in acknowledgement but didn't say anything else, busy pulling containers from the bag and placing them on my desk. I watched his hands as he opened the boxes, peering inside to check whose order was whose.

His hair flopped into his face, and I had a sudden urge to brush it back. Again.

I ignored the urge. Again.

When he brought the cardboard box containing my pide over, along with a bunch of napkins, I opened my mouth to speak but then paused at the expression on his face. He looked a little pissed off. What had happened in the five minutes he'd been gone?

"Thanks for the food," I said instead of questioning him about the message, carefully pulling myself into a seated position.

"You're welcome." Taking a seat at my desk, he opened his own box and began to eat, all without having made eye contact with me.

"E? What's wrong?"

His gaze shot to me, his eyes widening. Swallowing his mouthful of pide, he shook his head. "Wrong? W-why would you think something's wrong?"

I shifted on the bed. "Maybe the fact that you seem pissed off and you won't look at me?"

"I'm looking at you now. There's nothing wrong," he insisted, returning his attention to his food.

"Okay." There was no point pushing it if he didn't want to tell me, and to be honest, it could all be in my head. It was fucked up enough at this point with my weird reactions and thoughts, so it wouldn't surprise me if I was now imagining things about my best friend too. "Here, want your phone?"

He nodded, and I leaned over, passing it to him. I watched as he held a piece of pide in one hand, the other thumbing open his phone and scrolling to his messages.

Taking a bite of his food, he licked his lips, a smile tugging at the corners as his gaze scanned the message. When he began tapping on the screen, his smile widened, and my stomach flipped. Not in a good way.

Gritting my teeth, I refocused on my food.

Fuck. It was too quiet in here.

"I'm gonna put something on." I went to move, but Elliot immediately rose to his feet, glaring at me.

"Don't you dare move—you need to rest. I'll get the laptop." His glare disappeared, which I was glad about because I fucking hated it when he was angry with me.

"Sorry," I muttered, and he immediately softened, crawling onto the bed next to me and squeezing my arm lightly.

"Sorry for snapping," he said. He reached for my laptop, setting it up between us, and then retrieved his food from my desk. "What are we watching? You're the invalid."

"Hmmm. Well...it *is* Super Sunday, and Man United are playing Bournemouth at two, and Bournemouth is our home team, so we should support them..." I batted my lashes at him, and he rolled his eyes.

"Of course. How could I forget." His tone was flat, but he was smiling again. "If that's what you want, we'll watch it." Leaning forwards, he scrolled through my apps and pulled up Sky Sports.

"When the match is finished, you choose something. Anything. Even the anime you and Noah are obsessed with."

"I'm not obsessed with it. Noah is, and now Liam." He hesitated. "There was a show I wanted to try. It's about a guy with a twin who ends up in a coma, so he pretends to be him to infiltrate his gang and find out who put him in the coma."

The way his face lit up as he spoke made me so fucking happy. "We'll watch that, then."

"There's some romance in it."

"Elliot, this isn't news to me. It's like you think I don't know you or something. Unless it's anime, I know you'll always pick shit with some kind of romantic element to it." I nudged his arm. "Your soft romantic heart needs the fluffy shit to balance out the things I make you watch."

"This is true." He laughed. "Okay. We'll try it out after the football match. By the way, it's subtitled."

"That means I actually have to concentrate on the screen?" Giving an exaggerated sigh, I shifted closer so that our sides were pressed together from shoulder to ankle. "I suppose it's a sacrifice I'll make, just for you."

"Ander?" His gaze dropped back to his food, and he breathed out heavily. "I...I saw Travis when I was downstairs getting the food. He came over to ask how you were doing. He, uh, he said that some of the girls in number 5 were interested in"—he made finger quotes in the air— "nursing you back to health."

"Why do I need girls when I have my own personal servant right here?" I shot him a wide grin. "Ready to wait on me hand and foot."

His face immediately brightened, and he shoved at me, returning my grin with one of his own. "Hey. Don't push your luck, Ace."

"Ace. You haven't called me that for a while."

"Well, yeah. We're not kids anymore. That was when we thought it was really cool to have nicknames. Why we chose each other's, I'll never know. We had strange ideas about what constituted cool back then."

Raising my brows, I smirked at him. "I still like mine. Want me to bring your old nickname out of retirement, E-Zee?"

"Don't you dare! I swear, if anyone hears that name, I will tape your mouth permanently shut, and you'll have to be fed through a feeding tube." Elliot glared at me, trying to bite back a smile.

"I fucking love your murderous side."

"Shhh. The match is about to start."

Both of us laughing, we turned our attention to the laptop screen.

THIRTEEN

ANDER

A piercing whistle interrupted my concentration, and I growled out loud, ready to tear Travis a new one for throwing me off my game. I was just about to beat Liam's high score—didn't he realise how much of an achievement this was? It had been over a year in the making.

"Who are you dressed up for?"

Travis' words eventually penetrated my brain, and I tore my gaze away from the screen, but not before seeing my character die—fuck you very much, Trav. "Noob," I muttered under my breath. But then the game was forgotten, my mouth falling open as I turned my head to see what had Travis so distracted.

Elliot was standing in the doorway next to Noah, a flush on his high cheekbones, his light eyes sparkling as his mouth twisted into a shy smile. His hand lifted to his hair but then dropped, and I guessed it was because he didn't want to risk messing up his perfectly styled waves. My gaze raked over his body—a pale blue shirt, perfectly fitted to his lean torso,

103

the top two buttons undone and the sleeves rolled up. The shirt was tucked into a pair of tight, deep blue jeans that made his legs look a million miles long, and he was wearing a pair of polished black leather Chelsea boots that I'd never seen before.

My heart rate kicked up, and my game controller suddenly felt damp under my grip. Why were my palms suddenly sweaty?

"I— What?" he stammered, flushing more deeply as everyone's attention focused on him. "I just came over to borrow Noah's shoes. Uh, thanks, Noah. See you guys later." He ran for the hallway, lifting his hand in a half-hearted wave as he did so.

When he was gone, there was total silence in Travis' lounge, everyone exchanging sideways glances. Then Preston cleared his throat, glancing over at Noah. "Date?"

Noah shot me a look out of the corner of his eye as he took a seat on the sofa next to Liam. Liam ran his hand over his thigh in a soothing gesture as Noah nodded slowly, turning his attention to Preston. "He borrowed my shoes." He gave me another quick look, biting down on his lip. "For a date. Yeah."

My brain helpfully reminded me that this was my best friend, and I wanted him to be happy. Swallowing hard, I nodded firmly. "Yeah. He's going out with Curtis, right? Should be good. Hey, Liam? You gonna play me or what? I was about to smash your high score before Trav interrupted me."

Thank fuck, Liam took the hint. He snorted, picking up Travis' discarded controller. "You think you can beat my high score? The record I've held since October last year? Keep dreaming, mate."

I was vaguely aware of Travis getting up and leaving the room, muttering something about going next door to see his girlfriend. Noah and Preston fell into a discussion, their voices too low to make out, but I threw all my concentration into my game with Liam.

I didn't think about Elliot going on a date with Curtis.

Not even once.

Except...that was a lie.

The wind sent a paper bag skittering along the ground, briefly touching the toe of my Converse before fluttering away. I dug my hands farther into the pockets of my jacket, hunching my shoulders. It was so cold out here by the river tonight—every time I breathed out, there was a cloud in front of me, and my fingers and toes were starting to go numb. And what was I even doing on the north side of the river, well away from the LSU campus and my house?

The answer wasn't even an answer.

A sigh came from next to me. "Mate, shouldn't we get back? I don't wanna rush you, but we've been walking for a while now, and it hasn't been long since you sprained your ankle. Not to mention, it's fucking freezing, and my boyfriend's waiting for me in his nice, warm bed."

I glanced over at Liam. "I know. We'll cross back to the south side at the next bridge, okay? I'll pay for us to get a cab back to the Mansions if you want."

He nodded, his mouth twisting as he gave me a hesitant smile. "Okay. Do...do you wanna talk about this?"

I repeated the words that I'd said so many times in my head tonight I'd convinced myself of their truth. "I just got a bad vibe from Curtis, and I'm worried about Elliot. His location showed him somewhere along here. I just want to make sure he's okay; you know I'd never forgive myself if anything happened to him."

Liam nudged my arm. "I get it. You're overprotective." He paused. "I'd be the same with Noah."

"W—what? Oh, fuck off. It's not like you and Noah. Elliot's my friend, not my boyfriend."

"Obviously." Liam's voice was heavy with sarcasm. "He *is* on a date with someone who you think is sus, though, and that's why we're acting like stalkers. I mean, he's the person you care most about, right? He's your best friend, and you're looking out for him, even though it's a bit creepy to be following him around London. Now you've made me an accessory to your stalking crime."

I'd been unconsciously gritting my teeth as he spoke, but I made an effort to unclench my jaw. "Yeah, okay, I know. But yeah, he is. My best friend."

"He—" Liam stopped talking, gripping my arm and yanking me back into the shadow of a pillar. A chill went down my spine as I followed his gaze, already knowing what I'd see.

Elliot was exiting a restaurant up ahead—a large, glass-fronted building, the darkened interior decorated with hundreds of sparkling fairy lights. Curtis appeared next to him, and my stomach lurched as they stopped outside the

106

doors, staring at each other. Curtis leaned closer, saying something that made Elliot smile.

"Ander! What the fuck are you doing?"

It took me a second to realise that Liam was actively holding me back from going over to them. Taking a deep, measured breath, I relaxed my body against his hold, and he eyed me for a moment before releasing me.

"Seriously, mate. What was all that about? I know you're worried, but they're only talking." His gaze flicked to Elliot. "Hugging," he amended.

As I watched, frozen, Elliot and Curtis wrapped their arms around each other, the hug lasting way too fucking long, in my opinion. Did Elliot really want to be with someone so clingy? Wait, was Elliot the one who wanted the hug to last? Did he like long hugs? How did I not know this? As his best friend, I should know.

Finally, they pulled apart, and Elliot said something to Curtis. He nodded and then began walking in our direction. Shit.

Liam and I stepped farther into the shadows as Curtis passed us, but my gaze remained on Elliot. He'd shoved his hands in his coat pockets and begun walking away, a slump to his shoulders and his head hanging low.

There was no way I could hold myself back any longer. Before Liam could make a grab for me, I lunged forwards, jogging towards Elliot. I heard a muttered "oh, fucking hell" come from behind me, but I paid Liam no attention.

"Elliot!" I called as I got closer.

He spun around, his eyes widening as he saw me, and

my stomach lurched again as I took in his stricken expression.

"Ander? What are you doing here?"

Ignoring his question, because there were more important questions to answer, I stepped into his space, cupping his jaw. His eyes were red-rimmed, and tears were glistening on his lashes. "Did he hurt you?" I growled, carefully wiping away a tear that was tracking down his cheek. "I'll kill that fucker if he hurt you."

"Did who hurt me?" Confusion entered Elliot's gaze, temporarily chasing away the sadness. "What are you doing here?"

"I felt like a walk, and I dragged Ander with me. We were just about to head home." Liam's voice sounded close to my ear. Fuck, I'd forgotten about him. When I glanced over at him, he gave me a pointed look that said *you owe me.*

Elliot stared between us, clearly unconvinced, but then he sighed, taking a step back from me and rubbing his hand over his face. "Whatever. Can you just...I'll see you back at the house, Ander. Liam, see you soon, I'm sure."

He turned on his heel, and I reached out to grip his arm. "Wait. Did he hurt you? We saw you with that guy, and now..." I took a step forwards, lowering my voice. "You're obviously upset, E. What happened?"

"He did nothing. It wasn't *him*—he didn't hurt me." His voice wobbled, and it sent a shooting pain through my chest. "Please could you just leave me alone now? I'll see you at home."

"I'm not leaving you alone in this state."

"I can't do this with you right now," he whispered. "Please just let me go."

Liam cleared his throat. "Look, guys. It's late, it's fucking cold, and I don't know what's going on here, and I don't need to know. But Ander's right, Elliot, and I'm mostly agreeing with him because Noah wouldn't be happy if we left you here like this, not because I think that he has a right to know your private business. Even if he is your best friend," he added with another pointed glance at me.

Elliot folded his arms across his chest and gave me a death stare that made me bite back a smile despite the situation because he looked so fucking cute pouting his lips like that. "Fine. I'll get a cab. Alone."

"No." I immediately shook my head. "We—"

Liam's hand covered my mouth, muffling the rest of my words. "We'll wait with you while you get a cab, and then we'll get our own. Ander, no more talking."

I yanked his hand away, and now I was the one fucking pouting like a child. "Fine."

"Fine," Elliot repeated, and then we all glanced at each other, and just like that, the tension dissipated as we all cracked a smile. "Has anyone ever told you how annoying you both are?" he asked as we headed for the road to flag down a black cab.

"Yeah, Noah's told me plenty of times." Liam grinned at him, relief in his expression. He lifted his arm as a cab came into view. "Here you go, Elliot. Ander and I are gonna walk for a bit, and then we'll head back."

We are? I raised a brow at him, but he shook his head at me.

Elliot climbed inside the cab without a backwards glance, the smile that he'd briefly worn instantly dropping. Fuck, what was wrong with him? He was clearly upset, but he didn't want me there. As soon as the cab started back up, he finally met my gaze, and as he did so, the cab's interior light illuminated his eyes. Eyes that were filling with tears again.

"*Fuck*," I whispered, staring after the cab as it disappeared out of sight.

"Give him space. Don't push him. He's your best friend, but that doesn't mean you're entitled to know everything about him," Liam helpfully reminded me as he began walking back down to the riverside.

"I think I preferred it when our main topic of conversation was girls, not you giving me pointless advice."

"You can still talk to me about girls, you know. Just because I'm in a relationship with Noah doesn't mean that we can't be like we used to be. I mean, yeah, I'm not gonna be your wingman anymore, and I won't be able to reciprocate with the hot-girl talk because I'm only interested in one person now, but you're my friend, and yeah, you know. We can talk."

I sighed, shoving my hands deep into my pockets. "I don't want to talk about girls."

"Boys?" he ventured, keeping his gaze fixed on the path ahead.

"Or boys. I think that my experiment was a failure. I'll keep an open mind, but I haven't found anyone I want to kiss or do anything else with."

We reached a bridge that would allow us to cross to the

south side of the river and stepped onto it. Liam stopped, glancing down at his phone screen. "Have you even been looking?"

"I went to that club," I reminded him. "Danced with JJ's friend, but, nah, nothing."

"You wanna walk all the way back, or should we get a cab from here? It's going to take us about twenty-five minutes if we walk. Is your ankle up to it?" He tapped on his phone screen. "I can get an Uber, or we can keep walking and flag down a black cab if we see one."

"Yeah, keep walking and flag one down," I said. "My ankle's fine. No pain at all."

"You're overthinking it." Leaning into the road, he waved his arm. "There's a cab. Come on, let's get it."

"Overthinking what?" I climbed into the taxi behind him and closed the door.

"The Mansions, please, mate. By LSU," he instructed the cabbie, then turned back to me. "Overthinking the kissing thing. Just because you haven't found anyone you're into yet, doesn't mean you won't. Let the opportunities come to you. I don't need to remind you that you don't exactly have to work for it. How many girls have you pulled this semester already? Be your usual self, and people will come to you." He shot me a grin.

"You're right." Relaxing back against the seat, I blew out a heavy breath. "Fuck, mate, it feels like you being with Noah has made you so much wiser. How did that happen?"

A smirk appeared on his face. "Maybe it's all the dick sucking. Supposedly, semen boosts the brain."

"Semen boosts the brain?" I raised my brows, unsure if

111

he was joking or not. An image flashed in my mind...me, on my knees in front of a pair of legs, a hand in my hair... I coughed, shifting in my seat.

"It's got protein in it, so maybe." He shrugged, his eyes alight with amusement. "It's a good enough excuse as far as I'm concerned."

"Yeah, I don't want to know what you get up to with Noah. I've already told you that." I shook my head at him.

"I'm not going to give you any details, but if you ever need any dick-sucking tips—"

"I don't."

"You might." Still smirking, he glanced out of the window. "Oh. We're here."

I leaned forwards in my seat, addressing the cabbie. "Anywhere here's good, mate. Cheers."

When we'd exited the cab and were standing on the pavement between our respective houses, Liam turned serious again. "Don't push it with Elliot. Give him some space, yeah?"

I nodded. "Yeah."

FOURTEEN

ELLIOT

This weekend had come just at the right time. After everything that had happened, I needed a break from my life, badly. Ander was with me, which was less than ideal, given the circumstances, but at least we had a buffer of family and friends. We were back at home in Bournemouth for the weekend, celebrating my cousin Dee's twenty-first birthday. Ander had an insane crush on her for about a year when we were fifteen, which she'd found hilarious. He'd managed to get over it, eventually, helped by the fact that she'd announced to everyone that she was a lesbian about six or seven months into his crush, and he finally realised that meant he'd never have any chance with her. Now they were friends who liked to tease each other mercilessly.

Dee had hired out the upstairs part of Cloud, my favourite bar, and it was packed with her friends and various relatives. I was standing at the bar with Ander, waiting to be served, when she came running over.

"Cocktails! Have a screaming orgasm, they're fucking delicious!" she shouted drunkenly, waving the bar menu in my face. My cousin was tiny, with hair in a pixie cut that seemed to change colour every time I saw her. This time, it was a pastel pink.

"I'd love a screaming orgasm with you." Ander smirked at her, and she rolled her eyes, smacking his arm with the menu.

"Still a lesbian."

"I can verify that." Another girl sidled up next to her, slipping her arm around her waist. She was also petite and ethereal-looking, with long blonde hair and huge eyes framed with long lashes. "Hi. I'm Faye, Dee's girlfriend."

"Faaaaye. Babe. This is my cousin Elliot and his best friend, Ander, who used to be obsessed with me and still harbours a delusion that I'll turn straight for him." Dee grinned at us both.

Ander laughed, blowing her a kiss. "I know it doesn't work like that, Dee-Dee, but I know you'd miss my flirting if I stopped now."

"Is he always like this?" Faye asked in a stage whisper as Dee returned Ander's gesture with her middle finger.

"Always," I confirmed. "The diagnosis is that it's a permanent condition."

"Poor thing." She pulled a sad face.

"Elliot! I haven't seen you for so long!" My aunt Sadie was suddenly in front of us, yanking me into a hug so tight I could barely breathe. When she released me, I gasped for air, then laughed as she proceeded to do the same to Ander, making his eyes widen dramatically.

114

"Okay, Mum. Time to lay off the Aperol spritz." Dee placed a hand on my aunt's arm. "Look, Jean's waving to you."

Jean was my mum. She wasn't a drinker or a partier, but glancing over at her, sitting at a table with a large number of empty glasses, waving madly at my aunt, I could see that she'd already indulged in two or three too many cocktails. I groaned under my breath, and Ander nudged me, following my gaze.

"Do we need to stop drinking to make sure she's okay later?" His mouth was almost touching my ear, his breath warm on my skin, and I suppressed a shiver.

I turned my head slightly, and his face was so close to mine. With a shaky inhale, I met his eyes, a kaleidoscope of greens and golds and browns that I wanted to get lost in. "No. My dad's picking her up after his shift finishes."

"Okay. Need a break from the drunk people you're related to?" he murmured, and was it my imagination, or was he even closer now?

"Yeah." My mouth formed the word, but I didn't make a sound.

Ander took a step back, giving me a soft smile. "Come on, then. Let's go downstairs for a bit."

When we were seated in a booth on the ground floor level in the main bar, Ander rested against the padded backrest, rolling his head to the side to face me. "Now I can speak to you without shouting." It was still loud down here, but thanks to the position of the bar's speakers and our location tucked away in a corner, it was easy enough to hear each other.

I fished out a cube of ice from my drink, sliding it around in my mouth, suddenly nervous. Ander had given me space all week, which had surprised me, but I knew that he wouldn't let it go forever. I knew that he wanted an explanation for why I'd been upset when I'd seen him that night, and I also knew that I wouldn't be able to give it to him.

Crunching down on the cube, I glanced away from his intense gaze, inhaling sharply at the sight my eyes landed on. The remains of the ice slid down my throat as I groaned. "Fuck. Not again."

Ander moved closer, instantly alert. "What? What's wrong?"

"Look straight ahead," I muttered under my breath. Sliding into the booth directly across from ours was Gary, the guy that had come on to me last time we were in this same bar.

"Fuck that twat," Ander whispered harshly. "He'd better not come over. I can't even pretend to be your boyfriend this time."

"Why not?" The words fell from my mouth without thought, and I instantly wanted to take them back because that would lead to Ander asking me—

"Because you have a boyfriend? Don't you?"

Picking up the beer mat in front of me, I began playing with it, slipping it through my fingers. "Uh. No, I don't."

"What about Curtis? *Oh.* Was that why you were upset?" His voice was so soft and gentle it killed me.

Yes, but not for the reason you're thinking. I was upset because I'd realised that I was doomed to love Ander. I couldn't have something with Curtis, and I knew that I had to break things off before we even got started. Ander owned my heart, and while he held it, I couldn't give it to anyone else. Then when I saw Ander, after turning Curtis down for good and making it clear that there could only ever be friendship between us, it had all been too much for my heart to take.

Why did I have to love someone who couldn't love me back?

"We decided we were better off as friends," I said eventually, hoping that he'd take the hint and not probe any further. The only upside of the situation was that Curtis had shared my view—he'd almost been relieved when I brought up the subject, immediately letting me know that he'd planned to say the same thing and I'd beaten him to it.

"Oh." Ander was quiet for a moment, an unreadable expression on his face. When he opened his mouth again, he spoke carefully. "How do you feel about that?"

I shrugged. There was no way to explain without letting him know how I felt about him, and that wasn't going to happen. "It is what it is."

"I'm sorry, E." Moving so he was right next to me, he slid his arm around my shoulder in a conciliatory gesture. "It'll happen. You'll find someone who makes you happy. Anyone would be lucky to have you."

A sigh fell from my lips as I tipped my head back against the booth, trapping his arm in place. "If only that were true."

His hand came up, and he gripped my chin, turning my head to face him. When I met his gaze, his eyes were dark and serious. "Elliot, you're a catch. You're clever, you're interesting, you're a really fucking nice guy, and..." Pausing, he swallowed, and my eyes traced the movement of his throat working. "Objectively speaking, as your best friend, I feel the need to remind you that you're very good-looking."

A startled laugh burst from me. "I'm distinctly average, and I'm more than fine with that, believe me. But thanks."

He shook his head violently, his eyes narrowing. "Stop it. You're sexy as fuck, and we both know it."

My heart was racing. Were his cheeks flushing? Clearing his throat again, he released his grip on my jaw, dropping his gaze to his drink. "I mean, as a hot-as-fuck man myself, I can recognise true hotness in other people."

I honestly didn't know what to say. In my panic, my gaze bouncing all over the place, I accidentally caught Gary the sleaze's eye. He leered at me, and I groaned. "Look who's noticed us here."

Ander's gaze immediately snapped to mine and then to Gary's. Making a noise under his breath that was almost a growl, he used the arm that was around me to pull me closer. He dipped his head to my ear, and I felt his lips brush over my skin as he murmured softly, "Operation 'pretend to be Elliot's boyfriend' is underway."

Raising his head, he looked at me. Time seemed to stand still as our gazes held, breathing in each other's air.

"Elliot," he breathed, angling his head forwards—

"Oh, my! What do we have here?" A loud, slightly slurred voice ripped us right out of our bubble, both of us jumping away from each other as if we'd been electrocuted.

My mum and my aunt were standing in front of us, both with identical expressions of open curiosity.

Shit.

Ander was the first to recover. "Jean! Sadie! Take a seat." He practically yanked my aunt down into the booth with us, my mum having no choice but to follow suit since she was hanging off my aunt's arm. As soon as they'd collapsed into the booth, he was ducking forwards, his voice lowering. "Listen carefully. There's a man sitting in the booth across from ours—no, don't look until I've finished speaking—who has taken an unhealthy interest in our Elliot. I'm his boyfriend—" He accompanied the word with an exaggerated wink and nudge. "—and my presence is letting him know that Elliot is unavailable."

Their faces cleared, and they exchanged looks that could only be described as gleeful. Oh, *fuck* no.

"Say no more." My aunt returned Ander's wink. She raised her voice to a level that I was certain foghorns would struggle to achieve. "Oh, we're just so delighted to have Ander as part of the family, aren't we, Jean? We were all so happy when we found out that you were Elliot's *boyfriend*."

"Yes, Sadie. We were *so* happy. It was a dream come true! Ander is *such* a lovely boy, so polite and handsome."

This had to be a nightmare. Imagine the worst soap opera actor ever, then imagine them being a hundred times worse. That was how bad my mum's acting was. As if that wasn't bad enough, she accompanied her little speech with a series of winks and smiles that I genuinely had no words for.

I buried my face in my hands. Next to me, I could feel

Ander's body shaking with suppressed laughter. *Bastard.* His hand made soothing circles on my back, though, and when I finally felt able to raise my head, my cheeks hot, he moved it back to my shoulder, continuing the soothing motion with his thumb.

"I'll get rid of them," he whispered with a grin, leaning into me again.

"Boys, we need to celebrate this occasion. Champagne all around, I think!" my aunt announced, already flagging down one of the bar staff and asking for a bottle and four glasses. I couldn't help the wry smile that twisted my lips, and this time, it was my turn to lean into Ander.

"Looks like we're stuck with them for now." As I spoke into his ear, he tilted his head, and suddenly, my lips were brushing across his soft skin.

We were so close that I both felt and heard his breath hitch. His grip on my shoulder tightened briefly, and his eyes fluttered closed for a second.

What?

I was fascinated. Very, very fascinated. I wanted it to happen again.

"I hope they don't blow our cover," I whispered, keeping my head exactly where it was so that my lips continued to touch his ear.

A noise came from his throat that almost sounded like a whine. He grabbed his pint, tipping it to his lips and downing the rest of the contents. Slamming the glass back down on the table, he turned to look at me, and his eyes were dark and unreadable.

"We'd better make it convincing, then, hadn't we."

I held my breath as he slid his hand across the table to cover mine.

His touch set me on fire.

Threading his fingers through mine, he moved both of our hands down, off the table, and onto his thigh.

My hand was on Ander's thigh.

I could feel his muscles shifting under my grip as I dared to run my thumb over the denim of his jeans. He was so quiet next to me, his hand moving from my shoulder to the back of my neck, where he brushed over the short strands of hair there. I shivered at his touch.

"Such a lovely couple!" My aunt's exclamation cut through the haze of *lustwantneed* that had descended over me. Blinking a few times, I reminded myself that none of this was real. We were playing a game. That was all.

I caught my mum's eye. Her expression was thoughtful and far too lucid for someone who was as tipsy as she'd been acting. When her lips curved into a smile that I knew from experience meant she was up to no good, I steeled myself for whatever was about to come out of her mouth.

"They *are* a lovely couple, aren't they? It's a shame that Elliot's dad isn't here to see this. We'd better take a photo for him." She brandished her phone, her smile widening, looking increasingly shark-like. "Smile for the camera, boys. Now, get closer. Elliot, lean into Ander more...yes, hold that pose." She snapped a series of pictures while I warred between wanting to burrow into Ander's warmth and run far, far away from this situation.

"I think we should have one of them kissing, Jean." My aunt winked, clinking her champagne flute against my mum's. She then gave a very unsubtle glance towards Gary, who thankfully wasn't paying us any attention. "That would certainly convince *everyone* that this relationship is the real deal."

Ander froze at my side, and then he slowly turned to face me. His gaze was searching, but whatever he saw on my face made his expression clear. *It's just pretend*, he mouthed, and I gave a small nod, leaning in at the same time as his hand slid up from my neck to cup the back of my head.

It was the softest, quickest press of lips, but it sent sparks fizzing through my entire body. I slammed my eyes closed because there was no way I could look at him and hide the way I felt, not after that.

"Our work here is done."

I dared to open my eyes to see my mum tugging my aunt up and out of the booth. She shot me a look as they disappeared around the corner, and I knew exactly what she was trying to convey.

She knew that I wanted Ander, and she wanted me to go for it.

If only it were that easy. But nothing about Ander Loveridge was fucking easy.

Lost in my thoughts, it took me a few minutes to notice that Ander had remained still and silent at my side. I chanced a look at him, noticing the way he was staring into the distance, his bottom lip tugged between his teeth, a frown pulling his brows together.

"Ander, is everything okay?"

He didn't even appear to have heard me.

"Ander?" Shifting to face him fully, I squeezed his thigh gently. "Hey, what's wrong?"

His head turned, and he blinked slowly. Releasing his lip from between his teeth, he slid his tongue across it, leaving it full and glistening and so, so tempting.

Tearing my gaze away from his lips was a struggle, but when I dragged it up to his eyes, my heart stuttered. Fuck. *He was looking at my mouth*. I wasn't imagining it. What did it mean?

"Ander," I whispered.

His eyes met mine, and they were so dark.

"Pretend with me," he rasped, low and hoarse, and then he kissed me.

FIFTEEN

ANDER

This was what I'd been searching for. Except it was more because this time, I wasn't doing it as a favour to a friend. I was kissing Elliot for one reason only. *Because I wanted to kiss him.*

His lips parted, allowing my tongue entry, and I slowly traced it across his lips, then slid it against his. He moaned softly, the sound going straight to my cock, which was already half-hard, thanks to the proximity of his hand to it. But at that moment, all I was interested in was having my mouth on his for as long as he'd let me.

Fucking hell. The way he kissed was so addictive. He was already deepening the kiss, his free hand coming up to my face, his fingers stroking over my skin. We kissed for what felt like hours, everything else sliding into insignificance. There could've been a fire alarm going off, or even an alien invasion, but the only thing that mattered to me was Elliot's mouth on mine.

When he finally pulled back, my heartbeat was going

fucking crazy, and I couldn't catch my breath. All I could do was stare at his kiss-swollen lips, wishing I could kiss him again.

He sighed, swiping his hand across his face. "Ander...we shouldn't have done that."

I knew he was right. It wasn't fair of me to kiss him that way, especially when everything with Curtis had only just happened. Fuck, his face from that night still haunted me. I hated seeing him so upset.

"I know. You're right," I said eventually, and it was the hardest sentence to force out because I had a sneaking suspicion that I might have less than platonic reasons for wanting to kiss my pretend-for-the-night boyfriend.

That was a thought that needed a lot of caution and a lot of time to process. If I was developing feelings for my best friend, then I could end up irrevocably fucking up the most important relationship in my life if I took a wrong step.

But the only thing on my mind at that point was kissing him again.

And getting those legs wrapped around me.

And dropping to my knees and sucking his—

Fuck.

Fucking fuck. This was worse than I'd realised.

While I was having my fucking existential crisis, or whatever it was called, Elliot was watching me silently, his gaze inscrutable. Was he pissed off that I'd kissed him? Worried that we were fucking up our friendship? Relieved that we'd stopped? I couldn't get a read on him.

He took a deep breath, exhaling slowly through his

nose, and then his eyes met mine. "Fuck it," he muttered, grabbing my hand. "Come on."

I let him lead me through the bar until we were outside. The sudden cold was a shock to my system, especially combined with the winter sea breeze, which felt like hundreds of tiny ice needles stabbing at my skin. Elliot didn't stop, dragging me around the corner of the building, where immediately we were more sheltered. The wind dropped, and I took a breath.

"Ace," he murmured, and then he was crowding me against the wall, and his lips were on mine again.

There was no one here to see. No one to put on a show for. Just me and him and the sound of the waves crashing against the shore.

"Fuck, E," I groaned, widening my legs and allowing our thighs to slot together. The feel of his hardness against me was something that had been a curiosity the first time, but now it stoked the embers into an inferno in my body. Pressing harder into him, my cock throbbing, I rolled my hips, making him gasp. Fuck. I didn't want to stop. Warning bells were blaring, but I ignored them. I just...I just wanted to know what he looked like when he came. The sounds he made.

Our kisses turned desperate, and our movements sped up. It was fast, it was frantic, and then it was suddenly over as Elliot yanked his body out of my grip with a pained cry.

Shit. What had I done? I'd just fucked everything up, hadn't I?

"Elliot. I'm—"

"Don't say it." His voice was thick with unshed tears,

and I forgot all of my issues. All I cared about was making sure he was okay. But he was already pulling away from me, staggering backwards, putting distance between us.

"E. Come back here."

"N—no. I need to go. I need...I need space. *Please.*" Tears were already gathering on his lashes, and it instantly made me feel like the world's biggest asshole. I'd pushed things too far, and I'd made my best friend cry.

"Okay." I held up my hands, my heart fucking breaking at the look on his face. "I'll give you as much space as you need."

'Th—thank you." His voice cracked, and then he was properly crying. He stared at me, stricken, and then he turned on his heel and fled.

I slumped back against the wall, attempting to swallow around the lump in my throat.

Fuck.

———

"Ander?"

I paused my creeping movements through the darkened hallway of my parents' house. I'd hoped to make it upstairs undetected, but it seemed like my dad had other ideas. As if this night couldn't get any more difficult.

"Hi, Dad."

"Come here."

It wasn't a question but a request. Sighing, I made my way through the open kitchen door, blinking at the sudden brightness as I sank into the chair opposite my dad.

He eyed me over the top of his glasses, his hand wrapped around a steaming mug of what smelled like hot chocolate laced with Baileys.

"I had an interesting text from Jean earlier," he began, and I groaned.

"Dad, no. That wasn't what it looked like."

"No?" He raised a brow, taking a delicate sip of his drink. "I didn't see a picture of my son, smiling and happy with his best friend?"

"Oh. Well then, yeah. That was exactly what it looked like." If only I could've turned back time to that moment and stopped everything that had happened since then.

"I also saw another interesting picture. You appeared to be kissing Elliot."

Lowering my head to the table, I closed my eyes. It didn't make it any easier. "Yeah. It...I was helping him out. He had a, uh, a situation."

"Mmhmm. So I heard. Funny thing, though." There was a pause, and I wished for a meteor to hit the house. Not enough to cause any devastating damage, just enough to get me out of this fucking conversation. "I happen to know my son rather well, and that was not the look of someone who was helping a friend out."

"Dad, please," I whispered.

"Ander." His voice softened. "If you like Elliot as more than a friend, it's okay. You don't have to hide it. I hope you know that."

My head flew up. "But I *do* have to. I've ruined everything tonight, Dad. Every-fucking-thing. He didn't even want to speak to me when he left. He asked me to give him space, and I'm so fucking scared that I've lost my best friend."

In an instant, my dad had rounded the table, and his arm was around me, a warm, steadying weight. It spoke volumes that he didn't even call me out on my use of the F-word. "Your friendship is stronger than that. Nothing is irreparable when it comes to the two of you. Give him time and space, and be ready to listen to him when he's ready to talk. Really listen to him, Ander. Don't just hear what you want to hear."

"Okay." My voice came out so fucking small.

My dad squeezed my shoulder. "That's the spirit. Now, what do you say to a little nightcap? Your mum's asleep, and what she doesn't know won't hurt her."

"You do realise that I've been old enough to drink for almost two years now?" I rolled my eyes, feeling more like myself again.

"Yes, but she still sees you as her little boy. Let's not shatter her illusions now, hmm?"

"Okay. But you'd better put double in my drink. I need it."

He patted my arm, giving me a warm smile. "Coming right up."

Upstairs in my childhood bedroom, I collapsed back on my bed, my head slightly fuzzy from the drinks I'd consumed. Turning my head to the left, I stared at the framed photo of Elliot and me that stood on my bedside table, a small smile tugging at my lips as I thought back to that day. It was early summer when we were fifteen, and we'd gone down to the seafront after school with a group of our mates. Away from the pier, on the quieter part of the beach, there was a cluster of small rowing boats pulled up on the sand. I'd jumped into one of the boats, dragging Elliot in with me, and then leapt onto the wooden seat. I'd thrown my arms around his neck, hugging him from behind, and one of our friends had taken a photo of us both laughing, Elliot's arms thrown out to the sides in an attempt to keep his balance with my body weight on his back.

My thumb traced his bright, beaming smile as I sighed. I almost wished that I could rewind time, to go back to those days when we were nothing more than two teenagers without a care in the world.

Or even rewind time to yesterday so I could make different decisions, and I wouldn't have to see that look on my best friend's face.

Would that be enough? Or would it be better to rewind back even further, to the night that I'd suddenly thought it was a good idea to pretend to be his boyfriend and we'd kissed for the first time?

Fuck. That night had set off a whole chain of events that sent my life down a totally unplanned path, and now everything between us was strained and messed up.

Sighing again, I stripped down to my boxer briefs in short, jerky movements, my frustrations rising to the surface. But when I was under my duvet, something else happened.

I remembered. Clearly remembered.

Hot breath against my skin. Open-mouthed kisses. Desperate pants in my ear. A hard length against me.

My cock was completely on board with my derailed train of thought, thickening inside my underwear and tenting the fabric.

Fucking fuck. This was not good. But then, if I thought about it... How long had it been since I'd been with anyone? A lot longer than usual, so it wasn't surprising that my dick was hoping for some action. My hand was a poor substitute, although, let's face it. I was a master masturbator. Pro level if there was a wanking championship.

Wait. *Was* there a wanking championship? I'd have to google it later.

But now I had more important things on my mind. I shoved down my underwear and wrapped my hand around my aching cock, stroking up and down. My hips jerked upwards as my memory supplied me with images from earlier tonight, and I came ridiculously fast, painting my abs with my cum. Rolling to the side to grab some tissues from my bedside drawer, I groaned as I thought about the fact that I'd just come harder than I could remember doing in a long time, and it had been to thoughts of what I'd done with my best friend.

This whole situation was getting way out of hand, and I didn't know where I stood with Elliot anymore. He'd said he needed space from me, but what if it ended up driving us further apart?

SIXTEEN

ELLIOT

"And that was it. I ran...and I feel like I've been running ever since." Gulping in a much-needed lungful of air, I continued, my words gasped between breaths. "I was...too much of a coward to even travel back in the car with him...I caught the train instead."

Noah glanced over at me, a light sheen of sweat glistening on his face as the sun's rays fell across him. "That's a lot...to process," he panted, slowing his pace to a walk. "Let's walk for a bit."

My lungs burning, I matched his pace, grateful for the reprieve from what had turned out to be a punishing early morning run alongside the River Thames. It was sunny, but it was so cold that it hurt to breathe, and every step had been a struggle, even after we'd completed our warm-up.

"So," Noah spoke again at around the same time it stopped hurting me to breathe. "He kissed you, unprompted. Then you took him outside, kissed him, and you both humped each other, then you ran away?"

"We didn't hump. That makes us sound like...I dunno. Whatever. We got ourselves off, using each other's bodies. Or we started to until I panicked and left."

"Yeah. Exactly what I said, and your phrasing was worse." There was a tiny smirk on his lips, and I gave him a half-hearted glare as I uncapped my water bottle.

"It wasn't like that. We were making each other feel good."

"No need to explain. You've painted a graphic enough picture already." Noah was openly grinning at me now, and despite myself, I could feel my own smile tugging at my lips.

"Whatever. The point is, I think he probably just got caught up in the moment. Two reasons—he kissed me at the table when sleazy Gary was still in full view, and the other reason is that I knew he wanted to experiment with guys. I was there and available. Then I made everything a hundred times worse by practically dragging him outside, forcing a kiss on him and carrying on until I, y'know. Ran. If I'd let things go all the way, it would've been even worse, and I can't imagine it getting any worse than it is right now."

Noah stopped walking, leaning against the railings that ran alongside the path, the only barrier between us and the river. "Okay, let's look at this objectively. Maybe he did kiss you because he wanted to ensure that Gary knew you were taken." He threw me a look that clearly said, *I doubt it.* "Your second point—you're his best friend. He's not going to use you as an experiment. I mean, yeah, I guess maybe he might, but there's no way on this earth that he would just dive in and do that without talking to you about it first. I know we haven't known each other for that long, and I don't know Ander very well yet, but it's obvious to anyone with eyes that he cares about your friendship a lot."

Taking a large gulp from my water bottle, I leaned back against the railings next to him. "Say you're right about that. What about the fact that I dragged him outside and we did those things?"

"What about it? I wasn't there, but it doesn't sound to me like you forced anything. He never said no, never tried to get away, right?"

I nodded slowly.

"Well, then. That should tell you something."

"But you didn't see his face." My voice came out low and defeated. "I saw the regret written all over it after I pushed him away. It was clear to me that he wished we'd never even kissed in the first place, let alone take things as far as we did."

Noah's shoulders slumped, his sunny optimism finally wiped away, and I felt even worse because now I'd brought my friend down too.

"I guess there's only one thing you can do," he said eventually. "You need to talk to him about it. There's no point in guessing how he might feel. The only way to know is to ask."

"But what if I ask him and he doesn't tell me the truth?"

Noah didn't have an answer for that.

"You dropped your pen." Straightening up and holding his hand out, Ander gave me a smile that I'd never seen before.

It was fake. So fake that he shouldn't even have bothered because his insincerity was blatantly obvious to anyone with eyes. I shouldn't have kissed him again. It had been a huge mistake, as evidenced by the way we'd been tiptoeing around each other ever since. A kiss wasn't worth fucking up our friendship.

"Loveridge! Eyes on the slides," Dr. Wilder hissed from the front of the room, next to the interactive whiteboard, his mouth twisting in displeasure.

"Fuck me, this wanker needs to get laid," Ander muttered under his breath. When he turned back to me, his smile had turned conspiratorial, softening around the edges, morphing into a genuine expression.

"Yeah," I agreed quietly, curling my fingers around my pen as I tugged it from his grip. The lecture theatre was full, and I didn't want to draw any unwanted attention to Ander and me, but at the same time, a part of me wanted him to acknowledge me—no, *us*. Acknowledge what had happened between us in Bournemouth.

"E. I'm—"

"Fuck, yeah. We made it." Liam was suddenly sliding into the seat to my left, closely followed by Preston.

"Cutting a bit fine, aren't you?" I glanced over at them both, speaking in a whisper so we didn't draw any more attention to ourselves.

"Montgomery! Holmes! The lecture starts at 10:00 a.m. sharp, not 10:08! Learn to tell the time!"

"My apologies, sir. It won't happen again." Preston actually sounded sincere, and it had the surprising effect of making Dr. Wilder's anger deflate. He gave a brisk nod of acknowledgement and returned his attention to the whiteboard.

Settling back into my seat, I attempted to follow along with the discussion on global sustainability issues, but it was a lost cause. I was too aware of the person sitting next to me.

I flipped to a blank page in my notebook and began to write, shielding the paper with my arm so that Liam didn't see.

I hate this. Please tell me we're OK.

Then I cleared my throat and inclined my head slightly. Ander's gaze shot to me straight away, and I subtly tapped the edge of the page, drawing his attention to the words I'd written. I fixed my gaze on the whiteboard, seeing his hand moving out of the corner of my eye. When he gave a small cough, I glanced down to see his notebook at the edge of his table.

Same for me. We're OK if you're OK. Are you OK?

He'd underlined "Are you OK?" twice, and it was a question that I couldn't really answer. But I quickly wrote "yes" on my page and then dared to look at him. He gave me a relieved smile, which I couldn't help returning, some of the weight lifting from my shoulders. *Coffee afterwards?* he mouthed. I nodded straight away, and his smile widened.

After that, I was actually able to concentrate on the remainder of the lecture, and when we exited the lecture hall, Ander slung his arm across my shoulders in the same casual, friendly way he'd done hundreds of times before, although there was a little more hesitance than normal.

Things were back to normal.

Except they weren't, not now I'd experienced what it was like to touch, to taste, to feel his hot breath against my throat as he ground his hard dick against mine. I did my best to lock those memories away. We were friends, and everything was as it should be.

When we were seated on the sofas in the student union with Liam and Preston, plus Mike and George, another couple of guys from our course, the talk turned to the weekend. The thing that I was trying to forget about.

"Ander, I owe you one." Mike grinned at Ander. "I had a fucking great weekend. Maya was amazing in bed. Ten out of ten for the recommendation, man. I didn't know anyone could be that flexible."

I gripped my coffee cup tightly, ignoring the unwanted sting of jealousy as they spoke about one of the girls who lived next door to Liam and Preston and who I knew for a fact that Ander had slept with at least once.

Ander smirked at him. "Yeah? All I did was show her a photo of you and give her your number."

"Whatever, I owe you. She kept me satisfied allll weekend. Did you know that your dick can actually get inflamed from too much fucking?"

"Gross, man. We don't wanna know." George pulled a face while the rest of us winced at the thought.

"You're just jealous that I got some and you didn't."

"I got some." Liam's face was smug, and it made me smile because he'd gone from someone in deep denial about his feelings to someone who dropped Noah into almost all of his conversations. "I had a great weekend. This one was away visiting his boyfriend—" He pointed towards Preston with his thumb. "—Trav was over at Kira's the whole time, and so was Damon now that he's seeing Flick, and believe me when I say that me and Noah made the most of having an empty house."

"Our house would've been empty too," Ander mused, taking a sip of his mocha. "Wonder if JJ decided to make the most of it. I need to have a word with him because if he fucked someone in the communal areas, he's paying for a professional cleaner."

"How the fuck did you all end up with empty houses? Ours is so bloody busy we never get any peace," George muttered.

Ander shrugged. "It just worked out that way. Me and Elliot were away celebrating his cousin's birthday, Levi was somewhere with Asher for the weekend celebrating...fuck, what was it now? Might've been the anniversary of them becoming boyfriends or saying they loved each other, I don't know. Some romantic boyfriend shit that none of the rest of us needs to know about. And Charlie was also away—think it was his sister's wedding?"

"Next time you're all away, let me crash at your place. I'll pay you." George put his hands together in a begging motion, and Ander snorted.

"I doubt it'll happen."

Preston leaned forwards in his seat. "How was Bournemouth, anyway?"

Ander and I both froze, and Preston's eyes widened at

the aura of panic that I was most definitely telegraphing. He grimaced and then, recovering quickly, said, "Uh, I mean, is it nice? I've never been, and I'd like to take Kian away somewhere, maybe after Christmas."

Collapsing back against the sofa, I hid my face behind my coffee mug as Ander replied, and soon the others were interjecting with their own ideas about where would be a good place to take someone for a weekend away. The topic moved on to what everyone was planning to do for the Christmas break, and what could have been an awkward conversation was forgotten.

I wished that other things could be forgotten just as easily.

SEVENTEEN

ANDER

"You need to sit this one out. I want you at full fitness for the game against Croydon." Folding his arms across his chest, my football coach stared down at me, his mouth set in a hard line.

All I'd done was go down a bit hard in training and felt a bit of a twinge in my ankle, which I'd made the mistake of mentioning to Travis. He of course mentioned it to Bryan, who immediately pulled me out of the training match. Now here I was, sidelined for the foreseeable future.

"Can I at least be on the subs' bench?" I tried.

"No. I want you match fit for Croydon. We need your defence skills." With that, he strode off, and I was left slumped at the side of the pitch, gritting my teeth.

Eventually, I picked myself up from the floor and made my way into the changing rooms, showering and grabbing my stuff from my locker. Hands shoved in my royal blue LSU hoodie pockets, I headed away from the football pitch and across the campus to the student union. Might as well work on my essay while I was here. The library was the obvious place, but I preferred to be comfortable, so the student union sofas were my goal.

When I entered the building, my day instantly became worse. Every single sofa was occupied.

For fuck's sake. I didn't feel like going home yet...and I didn't want to think about why I was avoiding hanging around the house lately. The library it was, I guessed.

"Ander, right?"

I was pulled out of my thoughts by a soft voice, my eyes meeting that of a girl who was occupying my preferred sofa —the one in the corner next to the power outlet on the wall, with a coffee table just the right height for resting your legs on.

Instinct took over, and I turned on the charm. Honestly, it was automatic. "Yeah, that's me. And you are...?"

The girl smiled, a light blush coming to her cheeks. She was very pretty, with long, tumbling red waves and deep green eyes and a fit body that was showcased by a tight cream jumper and even tighter jeans. "I thought so. You're on the football team, aren't you? I'm Daisy. Pete's twin sister."

I racked my brain as I returned her smile. Who the fuck was Pete?

Lucky for me, she kept talking. "Pete had try-outs for the football team, but he didn't get a place on the first team. He's on the second team now, but he's hoping to get a place on your team. The coach said he was going to trial him—" She cut herself off, her blush deepening. "Sorry. You probably don't want to hear all this. I'm rambling. Pete says I ramble when I'm nervous."

Now I was smiling for real. "It's nice to meet you, Daisy. Is this seat free?" I pointed towards the space her huge backpack was currently occupying, and she nodded quickly.

"Yes, yes, of course. I'd be honoured, really."

As I lowered myself into the freed-up space, a thought hit me so hard that it left me reeling. This girl was obviously into me, if the blushes and shy glances were any indication —and believe me, I *knew* when girls were interested. I could read all the signs. As we'd already established, she was gorgeous, so there was nothing stopping me from making a move.

Except...*I didn't want to.*

It wasn't about attraction, because yes, I did find her attractive. But for once, I wasn't interested in taking it any further. And that had nothing to do with my recent revelation that I might be interested in experimenting with men. I was still very much an equal-opportunity player.

So what was stopping me?

"Ander."

The very person consuming my thoughts appeared in my field of vision, my name slipping from his lips on a breath, as if he hadn't meant to say it. The way he slammed his mouth shut straight away, his posture stiffening, was also a good indication.

"Elliot." For some reason, my mouth was dry, and fucking hell, had his eyes always been that blue? "Want to join—" Just in time, I remembered that Daisy was sitting next to me "—uh, us?"

143

He ran his hand through his wavy hair, his lashes lowering as his gaze flicked from me to Daisy. His hair looked so fucking soft. Maybe I should borrow his shampoo.

"Uh." A frown pulled his brows together as he eyed Daisy. There was something in his expression that I couldn't read. "Thanks for the offer. There's not much room, though. I'll see you back at the house later."

"Oh. I could sit on you?" Daisy shot me another smile, and then her entire face flushed as she realised what she'd just said. "I'm so sorry! That was completely inappropriate. Um, your friend could sit on the arm of the chair?"

A tiny, reluctant smile tugged at Elliot's lips, and it warmed me all over.

"Okay. I'll sit down if you insist." He went for the arm of the chair, but I lunged forwards and threw my arm around his waist, and suddenly, I had a lapful of my best friend.

His shocked intake of breath made me laugh as I tugged him into place, keeping my arm around him so he didn't get any ideas about moving.

"Daisy, meet my best friend in the world, Elliot. E, meet Daisy. Her brother's on the LSU second team, but we might end up playing together on the first team from the sound of it."

Elliot was kind of frozen above me, so I dug my fingers into his stomach. He jumped a mile, his head swinging around to shoot me a savage glare, which only made me laugh again.

"It's nice to meet you, Elliot," Daisy said sweetly.

"What are you guys studying? Ander and I didn't get that far."

We fell into an easy conversation, and bit by bit, Elliot relaxed against me. After a while, I noticed that I'd been absentmindedly stroking my thumb across his stomach, but he hadn't said anything, so he probably hadn't noticed.

Was his skin as warm as it seemed to be through the fabric of his thick jumper? Was he *too* warm? Did he need to cool down? It was suddenly imperative that I found out the answer.

As slowly as I could, I moved my hand lower and dipped my fingers under his jumper. He had a T-shirt on underneath, so I carefully eased it up. And then I was touching his skin.

He jerked against me, and my heart fucking stopped for a second, my breath catching in my throat. He *was* so warm. But was he *too* warm?

I needed to feel more.

Carefully, I spread my fingers, flattening my hand against his stomach. I felt his abs tense beneath my touch, so I moved my thumb in the same stroking movement I'd been doing earlier, hoping it would reassure him. My own stomach had a weird feeling, like I'd get from the drop of a roller coaster, but I ignored it in favour of making sure that he knew that this was okay, that I was here and looking out for him.

There was a muffled noise from his throat, and then he rubbed his hand across his face shakily, shifting on my lap. "Uh. Sorry. Tiredness catching up with me," he said hoarsely, focusing on Daisy, and she gave him a sympathetic smile.

"There's a lot more work in the second year of uni, isn't there? Or so I've heard."

My free hand had somehow made its way to Elliot's arm —no, wait, to his hand. His *hand*? What the actual fuck? Why was my hand covering his, lightly pressing it into the leather cushion of the sofa?

"So much work," I agreed, taking the opportunity to lift my hand from Elliot's and raising my arm into the air in a stretching movement, hopefully before anyone noticed. I added a deliberate yawn, just to make sure. But I kept my other hand exactly where it was, splayed across his abs. It was probably safe to leave it there because Elliot's arm was in the way of Daisy's view. "But not as much as next year."

Daisy groaned. "Don't tell me that. I'm already having nightmares about my dissertation."

"At least you've got far enough in the thought process to have nightmares about it. I haven't even thought about what I'm doing yet," I joked, shuffling in my seat and hooking my chin over Elliot's shoulder. My free hand was now popping the PopSocket on the back of my phone up and down, over and over, the movement calming me.

"I should take a leaf out of your book." Climbing to her feet, she indicated towards her bag and laptop, open in front of her on the coffee table. "I'm just going to go to the loo. Can you keep an eye on my stuff, please?"

"Of course," Elliot was quick to assure her. But the second she was out of earshot, he spun around, and suddenly, I was very, very aware of our proximity and how close his face was to mine. "Why am I here? Are you getting her number, or do you already have it? Wait, why aren't you at football training?"

"Whoa." My head was spinning from his rapid-fire questions and not at all from the minuscule distance between us.

We'd kissed.

Done more than that.

Fuck you, brain. This was not a time to be remembering how fucking good my best friend—

No. No, no, no.

"I don't know why you're here, but I'm glad you are," I said honestly. "My day's been shit if you want to know the truth. I got sidelined in football, just a tackle that was nothing, but the coach and Travis took it seriously. They made me leave the training session, and I'm not allowed to play the next game."

His eyes widened, concern filling his gaze. "Ace. I'm sorry."

My stomach did that dipping thing again, like I was on a roller coaster. "It's not your fault."

Raising his hand, he curled it around the back of my neck, his touch grounding me, like it had so many times before. "Still, I'm sorry. I know how much it means to you." He swallowed hard, staring at a spot behind my ear. "What...what about Daisy's number?" he whispered hesitantly.

Beneath my palm, his stomach tensed again, and all I wanted to do was to make sure that the person I cared most about in the world knew how important he was to me.

Without even pausing to think about whether it was a good idea or not, I angled my head forwards, my nose brushing against his. "I didn't get her number. I don't...I don't think I will."

Our eyes met, so close, and my heart stuttered again. I was free-falling, and I didn't know where I was going to land.

"Oh," he breathed.

"Oh," I repeated.

EIGHTEEN

ELLIOT

S omehow, I'd ended up next door at number 3, squashed into the lounge with a combination of people from numbers 1, 3, 5, and 7 and an assortment of various friends. Drinks were flowing, and the only reason anyone had given for drinking so much on a weekday (other than the fact we were students and therefore never really needed an excuse) was that it was the annual LSU Kiss an Eel Day—aka KED. It sounded ridiculous, like some weird, made-up thing, but it was, in fact, real. Long story short, the site on which the university was built had originally been a fish market where the jellied eels were so popular people would come from all over London to buy them. Apparently, people used to *love* jellied eels. Thankfully, our palates had improved since then...mostly. Not that I was shaming anyone who liked jellied eels, but would I personally eat them? Absolutely not. No way.

Anyway, the legend was that if you kissed the eel statue that used to stand in the centre of the market on the date that the market was founded, you'd have good luck for the rest of the year. So, after the market had closed and LSU had bought up the land, they decided to honour the tradition by claiming it as KED. There was even a bronze statue of an eel in the foyer of the arts building, which some insane students would queue up to kiss every KED.

I did vaguely remember the day being celebrated the year before, although from what I could recall, I'd been stuck in bed with the flu, and Ander had spent the entire time looking after me, both of us watching endless episodes of *The Great British Bake Off*, one of my comfort reality TV shows.

"Let's play never have I ever," someone shouted, and I dipped my head to my cup of the unidentifiable greenish-blue drink that Travis' girlfriend, Kira, had given to me, in an attempt to avoid being dragged into anything. I wasn't in the mood for playing games—wasn't in the mood for anything social, if I was completely honest. In the back of my mind, I knew that my feelings were mostly to do with the fact that things between me and Ander were weird at the moment. Really, really weird. And with things being the way they were and the knowledge of Ander's flirtatious behaviour at parties, I would rather have just stayed in my bedroom and binge-watched TV.

But every single one of my housemates had ganged up on me and forced me to come, so here I was. Except now Levi had disappeared, probably to call Asher or something, and Charlie was nowhere to be seen, so of my housemates, only JJ, Ander, and I were left in the lounge.

"Elliot! You're playing." Before I had a chance to

process anything, JJ was forcibly dragging me into the loose circle that had formed around the centre of the room. "Sit."

He pushed down on my shoulders, and I found myself sprawled on the floor, sandwiched between him and Finn, a guy from the football team. Directly opposite me was Ander with a pretty girl on one side of him and Noah on the other.

Great.

When everyone was in place, JJ began. "I'll start. Never have I ever...had sex in a public place."

At least two-thirds of the people playing raised their drinks to their lips, including JJ himself. Were you supposed to pick something you'd actually done when it was your turn? As for me, I was frozen for a second—what counted as sex? Playing it safe, I lifted my drink. I was pretty sure that oral and handjobs in a club counted, and then there was everything that had happened with Ander around the back of Cloud...that was a sexual act, right? Even if we hadn't finished?

From across the circle, I felt Ander's gaze boring into me as he took a large gulp.

I suddenly found it hard to swallow.

"Never have I ever had a threesome." The next person was up, a girl who was shooting hopeful sideways glances at both Ander and Liam, although she was barking up the wrong tree with Liam. Liam caught her look, and he huffed, getting up from his spot on the floor and moving to where Noah was sitting. He squeezed in next to him, dropping a kiss on the side of Noah's head and curling his arm around his waist. Noah smiled at him, and for a second, they were lost in their own little world. I wanted what they had so badly, and I couldn't have it. It hurt more than I wanted to admit.

Ander drank again. I didn't. It was a reminder of just how different our experiences were.

We moved on, and I chased away my darkening thoughts by focusing on the next statement made by one of JJ's friends. Were they friends? Whatever they were, he was someone who was giving JJ looks that suggested he wanted more than friendship at that moment in time. "Never have I ever slept with anyone who was more than five years older than me."

Only a few people drank, which I guessed wasn't all that surprising since we were in uni, and from what I'd seen, the majority of people seemed to be fucking around with fellow students. JJ drank, flipping his middle finger at his maybe-friend, and then laughed once he'd downed the remainder of his drink.

"Still jealous, Bo? You know I prefer my men a little more seasoned than us. Although, if you ask nicely..." He trailed off, licking his lips suggestively, and Bo slithered over to him. I averted my eyes, catching Ander's in the process, and I flinched, quickly looking away. Not before I saw the naked hurt in his expression, though.

"My turn. Never have I ever fancied someone here at this party," one of the girls said, and almost everyone around the circle drank. Quickly raising my cup, I took a sip. No one would know who it was. The house was packed with people, and anyway, I'd flirted with Noah back when we'd first met, so as far as anyone knew, I could've been thinking of him.

I sucked in a breath when JJ's voice rang out loud and clear. "Never have I ever liked my best friend as more than just a friend."

It seemed like silence fell across the room, although maybe it was the fact that my heart was beating so loudly I couldn't hear anything else. JJ was staring across the circle, not even looking at me. Why the fuck had he asked that question? I fixed my gaze on Noah, and he nodded once, encouragingly.

My hands shaking, I picked up my drink.

Across from me, there was a long pause, and then something moved.

Another hand, mirroring my own.

My eyes met a pair of hazel ones as I lifted the cup to my lips.

I drank.

So did Ander.

———

Ander drank.

Ander drank.

Ander *drank*.

Ander drank.

However I phrased it in my head, it still made no sense. Now I was in my bedroom, hiding under my duvet, where I'd fled as soon as I'd put down my drink. I was the very definition of a coward.

There was a loud crash, and I shot out from under the

duvet to see a figure silhouetted in my now open doorway, the door itself shaking after smashing into the wall.

No. Why hadn't I locked the bloody door?

I threw the duvet back over my head. If I hid, the monster wouldn't see me, and they'd go away. Right?

The duvet was suddenly ripped away from me, and I squeezed my eyes shut, curling into a ball.

There was a soft chuckle from above me. "Out of the two of us, I would've put money on me being the dramatic one. Anyone would, I think. But here you are, acting like you did after we watched *A Quiet Place.* Remember how you hid under the covers and wouldn't let me leave in case those creature things came to get you?"

"Hey, that film made me jump!" I dared to crack my eyelids open, just a bit, enough for Ander's face to come into focus. There was a soft smile curving over his lips.

"I know it did." His smile disappeared as he sank onto the edge of my bed. "E, please can we talk?"

There was no getting out of this. Slowly, I straightened out my body and moved into a seated position, my back against the headboard of the bed. I kept my gaze trained on my knees—it seemed like the safest place.

"What do you want to talk about?" I asked as if I had no clue why he was here in my room.

I could feel his eyes boring into me for a long, long moment before he took a deep breath. "A few things, beginning with what happened last weekend and ending with what happened tonight. Maybe other things, but that's probably enough for now. I think it covers most of our...uh... issues lately."

Swallowing hard, I nodded. "O—okay."

"Okay," Ander echoed. He shifted a little closer so his thigh was almost brushing mine. "Let's start with the—no, let's start with tonight. We both drank at that question."

"Yes." Fuck, why did I sound so hoarse?

"Were you being truthful? Did you ever like me as more than just a friend?"

The shakiness of his voice gave me the confidence to reply, even though it was a whisper. "Yes."

His body shifted again, and then he was next to me, his back against the headboard. "*Fuck.* Me too."

My heart skipped a beat at his words. I'd seen him drink earlier, but it was one thing when we were in the middle of a game and a completely different thing when it was just the two of us, with no one else to hear our words. "W—when did you like me?" I needed to know. *Now.*

"Uhhh." Rubbing his hands over his thighs, he stared down at my duvet, hiding his expression from me. "Now?"

Now?

Now.

I closed my eyes and let the truth fall from my mouth. "Same for me."

There was a harsh intake of breath, and then a warm hand was cupping my cheek, turning my head to the side.

Then Ander's lips were on mine, and I was lost.

NINETEEN

ANDER

Kissing Elliot felt so fucking *right*. This wasn't like the night in Bournemouth. This was us admitting that we liked each other in a completely new way, as something more than friends. This was...fuck, why was I even *thinking* right now when Elliot's soft lips were pressing against mine insistently and he was pulling me closer?

The hot slide of his mouth was sending goosebumps all over my body. I kissed him harder, my mind emptying of thoughts as he kissed me back with just as much enthusiasm, licking into my mouth, tiny noises falling from his lips that made my cock throb.

"You're so fucking good at this," I panted, pushing him down so that he was reclined beneath me. There was a flush on his high cheekbones, his lips were red and swollen, and his pupils were blown wide. How the fuck had I never noticed just how hot he was before? I mean, yeah, I'd always thought he was good-looking, but now it was different...he was making my heart race, and my stomach had that same free-falling feeling that I kept getting around him. And now my cock was tenting my joggers, making it obvious to us both just how into him I was.

His tongue swiped across his lips, and I groaned. I had to taste him again.

As we kissed, his arms went around me, his hands tentatively moving over my back like he wasn't sure about touching me. That wouldn't do.

"You can touch me." I lifted my head, looking down at him as he lay beneath me, his breaths unsteady, just looking back at me. I did what I'd been wanting to do for a while and slid my hand into his hair, and yeah, it was as soft as it looked. Softer, in fact.

My fingers explored further, down the side of his face, and I stroked my thumb over his jaw. "You're so gorgeous."

"This doesn't feel real," he whispered. "I never imagined that you'd like me back."

"How long have you liked me like this?"

"Please don't ask me that, Ander." The agonised look that suddenly came over his face was enough to stop me in my tracks. Satisfying my curiosity wasn't important enough to push him to reveal anything that he didn't want to.

"Okay." I lowered my head again, lifting my thumb and pressing a kiss to the place on his jaw where it had been resting. Pausing, I thought about my next move. I'd normally just go with the flow, but this was my best friend, not a one-night stand, and I needed to know what he wanted from me. I kissed him in the same spot again and then kissed across his chin and back to his lips. "What do you want, E?"

He fucking trembled beneath me. "I want...I don't know...*you*. Just you."

A protective, possessive instinct burned through my body as I stretched myself on top of him, our thighs entwined, and wrapped my arms around him. It was a feeling I'd never had before, but it made me want to give him everything and to make sure that no one ever hurt him.

"Let's start with kissing and see how we go, yeah? No pressure," I reassured him. "You might have to show me what you like."

"I don't know what I like. I—I've never..." Twisting his head to the side, he buried his face in the pillow.

What? How the fuck was that even possible? I know we had an unspoken agreement to not discuss our sexual conquests, but Elliot was— "How is that possible? You're...*you*."

"Urgh," he mumbled from the pillow. "I've done some things, okay? A few handjobs and blowjobs in clubs, mostly. Kissed guys. But nothing more."

"Not even with *Curtis*?" I growled.

His head shot back around to mine, a tiny smile tugging at his lips. "What was that voice? Why did you just say his name like that?"

Now it was my turn to hide my face, and I ducked my head down to his throat, nipping at his skin. "I don't like him."

"Any reason in particular? Have you even met him?"

As much as I disliked the way this conversation was going, it had the bonus effect of chasing away Elliot's obvious embarrassment—which, by the way, he shouldn't even be feeling. So fucking what if he hadn't had much experience? It made it even better, in my opinion. And yeah, as a self-certified player, I was aware of how hypocritical I sounded.

"I don't need to know him to know he's not good enough for you," I muttered, my thoughts returning to Curtis. The image of him kissing Elliot in the club was forever burned into my retinas. "No one is."

Elliot's arms tightened around me, and he smoothed his hand across my back. "No one?"

"No one. Not even me. You're too fucking good for me, but I'm too selfish to stop this from happening. Unless you want me to stop."

There was a long pause, and I didn't dare to move. When his hand moved up to the nape of my neck and into my hair, tugging it so that I had to lift my head to meet his gaze, he shook his head. "I don't want to stop if you don't want to stop. As long as we promise that we won't let it fuck up our friendship."

"We won't," I promised. My head was spinning, thinking about how our relationship had turned on its head so fast, but it didn't feel wrong. Nothing about this felt wrong.

He smiled at me then, and that free-falling feeling was back. Fuck, I wanted him so badly. My dick, which had deflated somewhat with the mention of other guys and the person beginning with a C who I wouldn't speak of again, jerked, hardening again as I ground my thigh into his.

Tugging his plush lower lip between my teeth, earning me a sexy-as-fuck moan, I rolled us both over on the bed, dragging my hands down his back and onto his gorgeous round ass. "Enough talking."

Now he was on top, I let him control the pace, feeling the press of his erection against my thigh, something that turned me on more than I could've ever thought possible. I'd never even thought about it before...not until that first night we'd kissed.

"I wanna see your cock."

"What?" Elliot froze on top of me. Fuck, why did I just blurt it out like that?

Time to do damage control. I rolled us again, reversing our positions. Moving my mouth to his ear, I ran my teeth across his lobe, sliding my hand down his side at the same time. "I said you're wearing too many clothes."

"Ander." He arched into my grip as I tugged up his T-shirt and jumper in one go, letting me see all the smooth skin of his torso that I wanted to kiss all over. Why had I never felt this urge before? *How* had I never felt it?

"These need to come off too." My voice was so hoarse as I let myself drink him in. My fingers slipped down to the waistband of his navy joggers. "I want to see all of you."

I felt him swallow hard against me, his Adam's apple bobbing, and I had to lick it. The fresh, salty taste of his skin was so good.

"You first," he whispered, staring at me with dark, hungry eyes. The way he was looking at me... My cock was pounding, the brush of fabric against the head a torturous tease every time I shifted.

Moving into a seated position, I yanked off my hoodie and T-shirt, baring my upper body to him, and I watched in satisfaction as his pupils dilated even further. His erection was a rock-solid length against my ass, and suddenly, I didn't know if I wanted to fuck him or if I wanted him to fuck me. If he even wanted either of those things.

"Are you ready to see all of me?" I palmed my cock through my joggers, moaning at the friction, and he gasped, his hands gripping my thighs so hard that I knew there'd be finger-shaped reminders of this the next day.

"Yes. *Please*. I need it."

Sliding my hands down my torso, flexing my muscles because *fuck* yes, I wanted to show off for him, I rolled my hips. "I want to see you too."

He just groaned an incoherent word, and I took it as assent. Shifting my position, making his hands fall to his sides, I got rid of my joggers, then his, leaving him in just his boxer briefs, his erection straining against the black cotton. "Ready?"

His eyes met mine, his pupils blown so wide that only a thin ring of blue remained. It felt like time stood still when our gazes clashed, but he eventually broke the tension with a single nod. Sucking in a breath, willing my hands not to shake, I removed the final barrier between us and then moved back to straddle him again.

Now, I allowed myself to look properly.

And the sight was *so* worth the wait.

My best friend was completely. Fucking. Gorgeous.

I raked my gaze down his body. From that soft, wavy hair, now tousled from where I'd had my hands in it, over the planes of his face with those stunning light blue eyes framed with long lashes, his gorgeous mouth now reddened and swollen, making me want to kiss it, down the sharp jut of his jawbone, and lower still. His body was long and lean, pale and smooth and lightly toned, and then...there was his cock. Long, slim, with a slight curve, flushed and leaking at the tip, it made my mouth fucking water—and that was *not* a normal occurrence for me. In fact, it had never been an occurrence for me.

"What are we doing?" He lifted his hand, hesitantly tracing his fingers down my abs. A shiver went through my body at his soft, exploratory touch.

Instead of replying, I leaned down and kissed him, sliding my tongue into his mouth when he opened up for me. He pulled me into him, and suddenly, my body was lying across his, and then *fucking hell*, my cock was touching his. I could feel the hard length against mine and a damp patch on my skin where either his or my precum was smearing on my body. His thighs were spread on either side of mine, tense and packed with hard, lean muscle, thanks to all the running he did.

"Wow." Elliot's hushed whisper, breathed out against my lips, was somehow even better than any of the other sexy noises he'd made because he sounded exactly how I felt.

"Wow," I echoed, trailing kisses across his face and down his throat. Licking across his skin, I rolled my hips, and okay, yeah, this was different, but *fuck me*, it was good. He was moaning again, and a wave of possessiveness hit me. No one else should ever get to hear him make those noises. Just me. I could only blame that thought for what I did next, sucking a mark into the soft skin of his throat and

163

then lower still, knowing that my marks would be visible the next day, and it would warn everyone that he was taken—

Wait. He wasn't taken.

But even so, it would make anyone think twice about hitting on him.

The way his cock was rubbing against mine felt so good, and I knew that I could easily come just from this. And that would be something that we'd be doing in the near future, I'd make sure of it, but now I needed to taste a cock for the first time. And not just any cock. *Elliot's* cock.

I began kissing down his body, and he let me go, his cock now rubbing against my abs as I did my best not to drag my erection against his duvet. Because seriously, I was ridiculously fucking close to coming, and that would not do.

Raising myself onto my elbows when I reached my target, I stared up his body to his flushed face. "Can I suck you off?" Fuck me, my voice sounded like it had gravel in it.

He shuddered. "Y—yeah. But don't you want—"

"I want to suck your dick, E. You have no idea how much."

His mouth fell open, and he straight up moaned. "*Oh.*"

My cock fucking throbbed at that. I took his reaction to mean he was on board with the plan and tore my gaze away from his face to his cock. Lowering my head, I just breathed across the tip, watching his dick jerk, a bead of precum dripping onto his stomach.

"Fuck, that's hot," I murmured.

"Y—you really think so?" Elliot was panting above me, and I had a feeling that he wasn't going to last long. I dragged my finger across the precum on his belly, his muscles contracting under my touch.

"Yeah, I do." Lifting my finger, I sucked it into my mouth, and he groaned low in his throat.

"Fuck, Ace."

"Mmm." I savoured his flavour, different to mine—I had tasted my own. Who hadn't?—and the fact that it was *his* made it a million times hotter. My cock was leaking and throbbing, and I gave in, grinding down into his duvet.

Wrapping my fingers around the base of his cock, I angled it up so I had it lined up with my mouth, and then I licked across the head.

Elliot's hips arched upwards, and suddenly, a whole lot more of his dick was in my mouth than planned. Fuck. This was...I could *feel* him. Everywhere. Soft skin around that hard, hard length, pulsing and rubbing against the inside of my mouth, and as tears sprang to my eyes, I had a new appreciation for all the blowjob givers in the world. This was not as easy as it looked.

Easy or not, I shocked myself with the realisation that I fucking loved it. The way Elliot was going crazy, his hands coming down to grip handfuls of my hair, his whole body shaking with the effort of holding back rather than thrusting into my mouth, the sexy-as-fuck noises falling from his throat... Fuck, I was so hard, and he was turning me on so much that I really was going to come just from sucking him off.

"I'm close," he gasped, even though I'd barely got his dick in my throat, and I took that to mean that I needed to redouble my efforts to give him the best experience possible.

I licked across the vein on the underside of his length, releasing my grip on the base of his dick in favour of sliding my hand across his balls and then farther still, over his taint and between his ass cheeks. My hips ground down into the bed, my cock desperate for friction. When I pressed a finger against his hole, his entire body seized up, and then he was coming down my throat.

Fucking fuck. I was *swallowing his cum*.

The realisation tipped me over the edge, and I drew off his dick just in time, coming all over his duvet with a shout that I muffled with my mouth on his thigh.

We lay there for a while, the sound of our unsteady breaths loud in the room. Eventually, his death grip on my hair loosened, and his hands fell to his sides.

I raised my head. Conflicting emotions were playing across Elliot's face, and I couldn't have that. Lifting my body, wincing at the wet patch underneath me, I crawled up the bed until I was level with him, and then I lay my head on the pillow, resting my hand lightly on his chest. His heartbeat was racing underneath my palm, and he wouldn't meet my gaze.

"E. Hey, E. Look at me." I stroked my thumb across his hot, damp skin.

He took a deep, shuddering breath, closing his eyes.

"Please," I whispered.

TWENTY

ELLIOT

H is "please" seemed to echo around my bedroom. I swallowed hard, forced my eyes open, and then rolled my head to the left to meet Ander's worried gaze.

"I..." I didn't know what to say. I'd never experienced anything like this before. I'd never had any kind of sexual experience in a bed. I'd never come so hard in my life. I'd never done anything sexual with anyone who wasn't a random encounter at a bar or club or party.

I'd never been with anyone who cared about me like I knew Ander did.

And I'd never, ever dreamed that the boy I loved would do anything like this with me.

I was completely. Fucking. Overwhelmed.

To my horror, I felt my chin tremble, and I blinked rapidly, willing the impending tears away. But it was no use. I sniffed, and a tear rolled down my cheek.

"Elliot." Ander's voice was full of so much concern, I knew I was going to break down at any second. I threw my hand up to hide my face from him, but I wasn't quick enough. He pulled me into him, my head falling to his shoulder as his arms came around me. Stroking up and down my back, he kissed the top of my head. "Please don't cry. Whatever it is, we'll work it out. We can get through anything, okay?"

Wetness soaked into his skin, but he made no effort to move me. He just held me, continuing to stroke my back, pressing kisses to my head, so soft and gentle that a lump formed in my throat. I curled my arm around him, letting his warmth and his slow, steady breaths soothe me.

When I could finally speak, the first word out of my mouth was a mumbled "Sorry."

"There's nothing you need to apologise for." He was instantly reassuring, and I loved him for it.

"It's just..." Fuck, I had to give him an explanation, but I didn't know how to explain it. "I don't know why I was crying. It...it's just that it's never been like that for me before," I eventually said.

His soft "Me neither" had my head shooting up.

"How?"

A small smile tugged at the corners of his lips as he stared down at me. "For one, I never predicted our friend-ship going in this direction. And then there's the whole thing where I sucked your dick, and you made me come because it was so fucking hot."

"What?" I knew that my cheeks were hot enough to fry eggs on, and I buried my head in his neck.

"I liked it, E. Really liked it. I want to do it again. If

you..." For the first time, hesitation entered his voice. "Did you like it? Do you...do you want to do it again?"

"Yes," I admitted in a whisper. "I want to do it again. I want to do whatever you want to do."

"Okay. Then we will," he said as if it were that simple.

Was it that simple, or had we opened Pandora's box?

Only time would tell.

A shower and a change of sheets and clothes later, I was feeling a little better. Ander and I were sitting propped up against my headboard, wrapped up in my duvet with my laptop open in front of us. The soft glow of my bedside lamp, cycling through all the colours of the rainbow, threw out enough lighting to illuminate us both.

I couldn't believe I'd cried in front of Ander. I'd heard that some people cried after sex, but even so, I hadn't ever imagined it happening. And even worse, I hadn't got to touch him the way I'd always wanted to—to have him fall apart under my hands and mouth. Could I ever do that? He had so much more sexual experience than me, and that was a daunting thought. I'd never even been fully naked with anyone until today—changing in front of each other didn't count.

Then there was the fact that I didn't know if all of this was part of his curiosity about guys or if he liked me for real.

"Stop thinking so hard."

"Huh?" My head shot around to see Ander watching me with a small smile on his face.

He shifted closer to me so that his thigh was pressed against mine. "I know that you're thinking about what happened, aren't you?"

"Yeah," I admitted. Gathering my courage, I forced myself to say, "Can we talk about last weekend?"

"Okay." He took a deep, slightly unsteady breath, as if he was nervous, his gaze dropping to his hands. "In the bar... I, uh, I really wanted to kiss you right then. I used that dickhead guy as an excuse."

My heart skipped a beat, and butterflies unleashed themselves in my belly at his words, at the knowledge that he really had wanted to kiss me. *Me.*

"What about you? Did you want me to kiss you?"

I almost laughed at his question because, wasn't it obvious? I'd more or less thrown myself at him, dragging him out of the bar and then practically humping his leg while I attacked him with my mouth. "Did the way I dragged you outside not give you a clue?"

I'd expected him to laugh, but his mouth turned downwards, and suddenly, the butterflies were replaced by nausea. "You ran away from me. You took a train home so we didn't have to be in the same car together." Holding up a hand to forestall any protests I was about to make, he continued, "Just so we're clear, I'm not blaming you for any of that. You're allowed your space. But honestly, E, I've been going out of my fucking mind ever since. I was so fucking worried that I'd messed everything up between us."

He was worried about the same thing that I was?

"Me too. That...that was why I left. I panicked. I thought that maybe you were just caught up in the moment, or I was just there and available when I knew you wanted to experiment with boys."

His eyes flew up to mine, widening. "No. *No*. I wanted to kiss you because it was *you*. I told you; I like you, Elliot. Not just as a friend...but more than that."

"You did?" I knew he'd said he liked me, but honestly, I didn't think it had sunk in.

"Yeah. And you wanna know what I did later that night?"

I stared at him. A gleam had come into his eyes, and his lips were curving upwards.

"What?"

Leaning closer so his mouth was right next to my ear, his breath tickling my skin, he murmured, "I wanked myself off thinking of you."

A choked whimper burst from my lips, and I felt him smile against my skin. Bloody hell, my heart rate had just gone from 60 bpm to a million bpm, and my mind had emptied of every single thought except the fact that *Ander had got himself off thinking of me.*

My mouth opened and closed a few times, but I was honestly lost for words.

As Ander drew back a little, his smile widened even further. "I made you speechless."

"Show me what you did."

I clamped my hand over my mouth. Did I say that *out loud*?

"That was going to be my next suggestion." He was still

smiling, not making fun of me, and my embarrassment faded as I reminded myself that this was my best friend, and he'd never intentionally make me feel uncomfortable or upset.

Recovering a little, I raised a brow. "Go on, then."

"O-okay." The way he tripped over the word made me smile too. I guessed we were both nervous in a way, navigating this new dynamic between us. He reached for the laptop, closed it, and then placed it on the floor before pushing the duvet down, kicking it off us both so that it was bunched up at our feet. I glanced down and saw that his boxer briefs were already tented. I still couldn't believe that this was happening, that somehow, I turned him on this much.

"Ander." I reached out, daring to run my fingers down his arm.

"You too," he said, low and throaty, and I would've agreed to anything at that moment. I palmed my rapidly hardening erection through my underwear, biting down on my lip, and he groaned. "Fuck, yeah. Do it. You're so sexy, E."

"Same," I rasped, still disbelieving. Was this really happening? If this was a parallel universe where Ander was into me, I never wanted to leave.

He dragged his hand down his body, flexing his muscles again, and my mouth watered at the sight.

"You like that?" A sexy smirk appeared on his face.

"What do you think?" I slipped my hand under the band of my underwear, curling my fingers around my now fully hard dick. "You know what you look like."

"Yeah. But I like knowing that I have this effect on *you*. It's fucking hot. Look how hard you made me." He tugged his underwear off, his cock springing free, and I couldn't live on this earth for one second longer without knowing how he tasted. Ridding myself of my boxer briefs, I shifted down the bed as quickly as I could. Then I lowered my head and took his thick erection into my mouth.

Fuck. *I had Ander's dick in my mouth.* I moaned around his length, and he muttered out a string of swear words above me, one of his hands coming up to grip my shoulder, the pads of his fingers digging into my flesh, and the other clamping down on his thigh.

"E, wait." His words were a wrecked moan, and it was so hot. "Wait."

Reluctantly, I raised my head, licking my lips, savouring the taste of his precum.

"Fucking hell. You're gonna kill me," he ground out, staring at my mouth. "Come up here."

I couldn't deny him anything, so I went to him. He immediately yanked me into his arms, his mouth coming down hard on mine as he pulled us both down to the bed, rolling us over so I was pinned underneath him.

"Want you so much," he panted against my mouth. "I was gonna come in about two seconds if you'd carried on sucking my cock, and I don't want it to be over so soon."

Before I had a chance to reply, he covered my lips with his again, and I lost myself to the hot glide of his mouth against mine, the way our bodies were grinding against each other as we found a rhythm, our cocks sliding together in a way that had me pushing against him harder, faster, chasing the high that I knew was coming.

"Baby," he whispered, wrecked, and that one completely unexpected word sent me straight over the edge. My cock pulsed between us, cum shooting onto our stomachs and his cock as I lost myself in a white haze of pleasure.

Ander groaned low in his throat, pumping his hips faster. "Fuck, fuck, fuck," he moaned in between desperate, sloppy kisses, and then he was coming too, his release combining with mine.

His body slumped down onto mine, and I held him as we both came down from our high. That had been...everything. The intimacy of what we'd been doing...there was no penetration involved, and there hadn't needed to be. That was easily the best sexual experience of my life and one I wanted to repeat again, and again, and again.

I loved this man so much.

When my brain recovered enough to allow thinking again, I realised that something was wrong. Ander's face was buried in my shoulder, and small tremors raced through his body. I froze beneath him. "Ander? What's the matter?"

A choked sound came from his throat, and he pushed his head further into the space between my neck and shoulder. I could feel wetness against my skin, and my heart stuttered. Wrapping my arms around him, I held on to him, trying to let him know without words that I was there for him.

It only lasted for a moment before he suddenly tore himself away from me. Completely naked, he threw my door open and ran without a backwards glance. A few seconds later, I heard the sound of his bedroom door opening, rebounding against the wall, and then slamming closed.

I collapsed onto my back, rubbing my hand across my face. What had just happened? I played back through everything that had happened in my mind, desperately trying to swallow around the sudden lump in my throat. There was a tremble in my hand as I pressed my fingers to my shoulder, and then to my neck, to the place his head had been.

My fingers came away wet, and when I touched them to my lips, I tasted the unmistakeable saltiness of tears.

TWENTY-ONE

ANDER

How could this have happened? Somehow, I'd caught feelings for my best friend.

Okay, yeah, I already knew that I had feelings for him. But tonight, I'd discovered something, and it had hit me right around the same time that I'd had the most spectacular fucking orgasm of my life, and it had come purely from rubbing my dick against Elliot's. The free-falling feeling, the roller-coaster ride that my body kept taking, the fucking butterflies that had me calling him "baby" out of the blue, shocking us both—it had all culminated in the realisation that I was falling hard and fast for him. My feelings for him went way deeper than I'd thought, and it had scared the shit out of me.

Because this meant that this couldn't be just sex between friends. We'd admitted we liked each other as more than friends, and we'd also agreed that we wouldn't let sex fuck up our friendship. But this wasn't about my dick.

This was about my heart.

I'd told Elliot not to overthink things, but now here I was, being dragged under by the force of the thoughts crashing down on me. How long had I been falling for him? Had it been even longer than I'd realised?

I took a deep, shuddering breath, burying my face in my hands as I finally faced the truth. I'd been falling for him ever since the first time we'd kissed. That kiss was supposed to be fake, but my feelings were real.

What the fuck did I do with that knowledge? And how the fuck did I approach things with Elliot? I knew that he'd be panicking about the way I'd run out on him, and everything in me wanted to go back to him, to reassure him that things between us were okay. But I didn't trust myself to act normally around him. Could I hide my feelings from him? I didn't want to scare him away by coming on too strong or by making him think that he owed me anything more than sex or, worst of all, actually fuck up our friendship.

A sudden thought struck me out of nowhere, and I bolted upright. *Yes*. If I was lucky, maybe things could work out between us. I wasted no time running into my bathroom, cleaning myself off, and splashing some water on my face before throwing on the closest item of clothing, which happened to be a pair of football shorts. Then I took a second to make sure that all evidence of my mini breakdown was gone, running a hand through my hair to tousle it in a way I knew looked sexy. I glanced down at my body and smiled to myself as I tugged my shorts lower on my hips. If I was going to get Elliot on board with my new plan, I needed to use every weapon I had at my disposal, and I already knew that he thought I was hot based on his actions and words tonight.

After one final glance in the mirror, complete with a wink at myself, I made my way back to Elliot's bedroom. The door was now closed, but he hadn't locked it, and I walked straight in. The room was empty, but I could hear the sound of running water coming from his en-suite bathroom, so I took a seat at his desk chair to wait.

Hang on...was this my most flattering pose? I wanted him to look at me with that hungry look in his eyes, like he couldn't wait to touch me. Standing, I glanced around the room before deciding to lean back against the edge of his desk, my arms on either side of me and my fingers curled around the desk edge. That way, I could flex my pecs and my abs.

Except...the water was still running in the bathroom, and the edge of the desk was digging into my ass uncomfortably. Fuck it. I'd sit in the chair again. I looked hot either way, right? I wasn't going to recline on his bed or anything like that because I didn't want him to feel like I was pressuring him into anything more.

Before I could change my mind yet again, the water shut off, and I collapsed into the chair so hard it went flying backwards across the room. Fucking wheeled chairs. I managed to stop its trajectory just as the bathroom door opened, but there was no time to pose in a sexy way.

"Ander!" Elliot's eyes widened, and his mouth fell open. "W—what are you doing?"

Too busy trying to recover from my unplanned ride across his room, I didn't answer for a minute. His eyebrows lifted as he looked down at me, a small smile appearing on his lips.

"Why is my chair all the way over there?"

"Stupid fucking wheels," I muttered, narrowing my eyes. Scooting the chair back into its proper place, I spun around to face him fully. "This wasn't how it was supposed to happen."

"Huh?" Elliot cocked his head, chewing on his lip as he studied me, and fucking hell, the desire to kiss that lush mouth was almost overwhelming. I had to shove my hands under my thighs to stop myself from reaching for him.

Okay. Time to put my plan into action. I breathed out deeply and then met his gaze, lowering my voice. "Come here."

Heat flared in his eyes, and he immediately moved towards me. I smiled. *Yes.* I could easily become addicted to this new effect I was having on him. It made me want to do so many things to him. If only he wasn't dressed in those thick joggers and a T-shirt... No, that wasn't why I was here.

"Closer." Crooking my finger at him, I held my hand up until he was right in front of me, his legs almost brushing against mine. "Stop."

"Are...are you going to tell me what this is all about now?" Hesitance entered his gaze, and I knew he was remembering the way I'd fled from his room. His lips were slightly parted as he stared down at me. They were glistening from where he'd been chewing them a few moments ago, and I really, really wanted to kiss him.

Fuck it, plans could be modified. Reaching out, I pulled him down onto me. He made a startled sound, his arms flailing for a second, but then he got hold of the back of the chair, and then he was right where I wanted him. Straddling me, his gorgeous face just inches from mine, which meant... Cupping the back of his head, I pulled him into a slow, soft kiss, sliding my tongue gently against his, the press of his lips against mine an addictive touch that I couldn't get enough of.

When I finally managed to disconnect our mouths after several minutes of slow, deep kisses, I rested my forehead against his, closing my eyes. I wrapped my arms lightly around his waist, and he removed his hands from the back of the chair, bringing them down to rest on my shoulders.

"I'm sorry I ran away," I murmured. "It was...I needed a minute. But I need you to know that I don't regret anything we did. The complete opposite, in fact."

Elliot exhaled heavily, his warm breath hitting my lips. "Good. I thought—never mind. It doesn't matter what I thought if you didn't regret it."

I opened my eyes and drew back my head a little so that I could focus on his face. My stomach flipped again as I took him in. Moistening my lips and clearing my throat, I shook my head. "Never. I want to ask you a question. Will you go out with me? On a date?"

His eyes grew wider than I'd ever seen them before. "A *date*?"

"Yeah." A smile spread across my face. Even though my heart was beating abnormally fast and my palms were a little sweaty, I injected as much confidence as I could into my voice, keeping my tone light. "We like each other. I think we've both proved that we're sexually compatible tonight. So why don't we try going on a date? It might be fun."

Lowering his gaze, his lashes sweeping down, he sucked in a breath. "Um. You really think that's a good idea?"

Yes, I really fucking did.

"Yeah. C'mon, what do we have to lose? One date. You can even pick the place."

"Okay," he said eventually. "One date. If you promise that it won't affect anything between us."

"I promise." Angling my head forwards, I pressed a kiss to the tip of his nose. "It'll be fun."

Finally, his lips curved into a small smile. "It better be. You can choose the place."

"Deal. Now, why don't we kiss some more, then we both need to get that coursework finished for our marketing module." Not that I wanted to do the coursework—I'd rather have been kissing Elliot all night, but sadly, our lecturers wouldn't accept kissing as a valid excuse for handing it in late. Bastards.

"Coursework first, then kissing," Elliot countered, his smile widening.

I sighed. "You drive a hard bargain, Mr. Clarke. One kiss, then coursework, then more kissing."

He closed the final couple of centimetres between us, brushing his lips against mine. "Okay."

TWENTY-TWO

ANDER

"I know why you like marking Noah up now."

"What?"

Shit. I turned my head to see Liam regarding me with raised brows. The words had slipped out without thought, and as soon as I'd said them, I knew they were a mistake because now Liam's radar would be pinging. When I'd come downstairs this morning to grab some breakfast, I'd run into Elliot in the kitchen doorway, and my eyes had gone straight to the mark on his neck. I'd had such a sense of satisfaction from the sight, knowing that other people would see it and know that he was spoken for. Not that he was my boyfriend, but he was...no one else was getting near him if I had anything to do with it.

At least I was now next door at number 3, and Elliot was safely back at home in number 1, away from Liam. The last thing I wanted was questions from my nosy friend.

"Yeah. I was reading about how love bites are like a possessive thing. And you, mate, are possessive of Noah."

Liam laughed. "I'm not that bad. I just like people knowing he's mine."

"Yeah. Hey, did you finish off that coursework for Bob's class?" Hopefully, the distraction technique would work.

"Ugh," he groaned. "Submitted it two minutes before the deadline. Who sets coursework that's due the day after KED? Everyone knows we're gonna be getting hammered on KED. It's tradition."

"Hungover, are you?" I grinned at him, noting the green tinge of his skin. I hadn't even had a hangover, thanks to leaving the party early to go after Elliot. And that had turned out better than I could've ever imagined.

He raised his middle finger in reply just as Preston appeared in the doorway, yawning, dark circles under his eyes.

"Morning. Afternoon. Whatever. Why do you Brits drink so much?"

"You drank just as much as I did," Liam told him. "Personally, I blame Travis. He's supposed to be the responsible one, but he was the one handing out shots. Him and Kira, in fact."

"Yeah, let's blame Travis." Preston collapsed down onto the empty sofa. "I bet there won't be many students going to lectures today."

"Noah said—"

"Noah said what?" A voice came from the doorway, and Noah appeared, interrupting whatever Liam was about to say. Catching movement out of the corner of my eye, I turned to see Elliot right behind him.

My heart fucking skipped a beat. I couldn't hold back a smile as Elliot's eyes went straight to mine. *Hi*, he mouthed.

"I thought you said you were going to your lectures today," Liam said, pulling Noah down onto his lap.

"I thought about it, but then I decided to invite Elliot over instead. It's raining, and it's cold, and if everyone else is staying at home, I'm staying too." He curled into Liam. "Can we cuddle under a blanket and watch *Attack on Titan* or something?"

My brows rose as I stared at Liam, watching as he acquiesced to Noah's every demand, promising they'd watch the show and then tucking a blanket around them both. Who even was this person? I'd never expected to see him getting so sickeningly domestic.

"Come and sit here." Glancing back at Elliot, I patted the remaining space next to my leg. He sank down next to me, rubbing his hands together.

"It's so cold today. There was ice on the pavement outside—I nearly went flying."

"I'll warm you up." Holding out my hand towards Liam, without looking away from Elliot, I said, "Mate, pass me that spare blanket." When he threw the heavy bundle of fabric at me, I wasted no time in wrapping it around Elliot. He gave me a soft smile, his cheeks flushed and his blue eyes sparkling. The urge to kiss him again was so strong I found myself leaning towards him before I remembered where I was. I slumped back against the sofa, forcing my gaze away from my best friend.

"I vote for a movie," Preston said, diverting everyone's attention, which was good because I'd just realised that I'd been treating Elliot the same way that Liam was treating Noah. But Elliot was my best friend, and we'd always taken care of each other. It wasn't a boyfriend thing to do, was it? Or maybe it was if you weren't already best friends? I groaned aloud. This overthinking shit was getting seriously annoying.

"Are you okay?" Elliot whispered, leaning closer to me. I inhaled his clean, fresh scent, forgetting that he'd asked me a question until he nudged my arm.

"Yeah, I'm good." Raising my voice, I said, "Yeah, let's watch a film. Something we've seen before because you three look like you might pass out halfway through."

"I think Elliot wants to watch a vampire movie."

Everyone turned to Liam, who was smirking as he stared straight at... My eyes followed his line of sight...for fuck's sake. Straight at the huge, unmissable mark on Elliot's neck. Elliot must've realised at the same time as I did because his cheeks turned red, and he clapped his hand over his neck, burrowing down into the blanket. I turned back to Liam, glaring at him, and he laughed.

"Did a vampire move into your house?"

Noah kicked his shin, shaking his head at him. "That's Elliot's private business. Leave him alone."

The smirk fell from his face. "Alright. Sorry, Elliot. I was only joking." He pulled Noah closer, whispering something in his ear that made Noah's eyes widen, and then suddenly, both of them were staring at me.

Fucking great. Liam had put two and two together and made...well, he'd obviously come to the correct conclusion, that I'd been the one to mark up Elliot, based on what I'd told him earlier. It wasn't like I was averse to telling people, but there was nothing to tell at the moment. What Elliot and I did behind closed doors was our own business. It would be different if we were boyfriends, and when that happened—okay, I was getting waaay ahead of myself. We hadn't even had a date yet. Which reminded me...

"Put on the latest *James Bond*. We've all seen that," I instructed Liam through gritted teeth, still annoyed by his antics. He must've felt bad because he immediately grabbed the remote and navigated to the movies app. While he was occupied, I turned to Noah. "Want to show me where the snacks are? I know Liam has popcorn."

Noah raised a brow, but then he shrugged and followed me out of the room and into the kitchen. I leaned back against the counter, folding my arms across my chest as he began rummaging in one of the cupboards. "I want to do something nice for Elliot. Take him somewhere. Do you have any ideas of what he might want to do? Anything he's mentioned lately?" I was counting on the fact that with Noah's relationship with Elliot being different to mine, he could offer a different perspective, and I could take Elliot somewhere he wouldn't expect me to choose.

The cupboard slammed shut, and he spun around to face me. "Like a date?" he asked sharply.

"Like a...thing that best friends do." When he just stared at me, I sighed in defeat. "Fuck, okay. Yeah, a date. But this is...I don't want to pressure him into anything. I want it to be a fun experience for him. Keep it low-key."

He pursed his lips as he studied me. "Does Elliot know

about this?" When I nodded, he said, "Does he know it's a date?"

"Yes. We..." I paused, thinking. Elliot was close to Noah. Would he have told him about the kiss? Or kisses? There was only one way to find out, and I resigned myself to the fact that Liam was probably going to find out about this afterwards, too. "Did he tell you that we kissed?"

Noah nodded slowly.

"Both times?"

He nodded again, and I took a deep breath.

"Okay. Last night, I, uh, told him I like him. As more than friends. He agreed to go on a date with me. But I don't wanna push him for more than he's ready for."

Noah's mouth opened and closed a few times, clearly at a loss for words. Eventually, he cleared his throat. "You *like* like Elliot?"

"That's what I just said."

He shook his head, mumbling something under his breath that I didn't catch. When his eyes met mine again, his gaze was assessing. "If I help you, I want you to promise me that you won't take this lightly. I don't want you to hurt him."

"Noah, he's my best friend, and he's the most important person in my life. I never, ever want to hurt him."

"Alright. In that case, he mentioned a new restaurant that opened up last month. It's a sushi restaurant with a big floor-to-ceiling aquarium inside. Or...there's—"

"A restaurant where you eat fish while watching fish swimming around in a tank?" I interrupted him. Because what?

"Uh, yeah." He shrugged. "Apparently. I can find out the name—I can't remember it off the top of my head. It might be a bit much if you're trying to keep it low-key, though. I think it's expensive."

"No, I'll do that." I was already decided. It wasn't low-key, but fuck it, if he wanted to go there...I'd just tell him it would be part of my Christmas present to him. "Can you text me the name when you find out? Just don't say anything to him because I want it to be a surprise."

Before he could reply, a voice sounded behind us. "What's taking you so long?"

I sighed. "Hi, Liam. I was getting Noah's advice on something. He can tell you about it later." Giving Noah a nod to let him know that I was okay with him telling Liam, I headed back into the lounge, leaving them to sort out the snacks. Back on the sofa, I gave in to my desire and placed my arm around Elliot, pulling him into me. We'd cuddled together before, so it wasn't new, but the feeling that went through me as I held him close...that was new and different, and I couldn't get enough.

He made a pleased sound, leaning his head against me, and I couldn't hold back my smile.

I didn't know what was happening between us, but I knew that I didn't want it to stop.

TWENTY-THREE

ELLIOT

"Tell me."

Ander shook his head, grinning. "That's the fifth time you've asked me, and I'm still not telling you."

I pouted, and his gaze slid to my lips, his eyes darkening. Heat shot through my body, and I had to forcibly remind myself that we were in public. Very much in public—out on the streets of London, surrounded by people.

Would I ever get used to him looking at me like that? It gave me a heady rush every time. I still couldn't believe that this was my life, that it was *Ander* taking me on a date, and he'd been the one to suggest it.

We were walking side by side, both wrapped up in thick coats, gloves, and scarves. My ears were freezing, but I hadn't wanted to wear a hat—I'd tried to make an effort to style my wavy hair, and from the look on Ander's face when he'd seen me, it had been worth the effort. But was good hair really worth my ears freezing off? Hopefully, we'd arrive at wherever we were going before we got to that point.

It was a nice day, though, despite the cold temperatures. To my right, the sun sparkled on the River Thames, the London Eye right up ahead with its queues of tourists. Across the river was the familiar sight of Big Ben and the Houses of Parliament.

"Here we are. Stop one." Ander came to a halt. I glanced at the building next to us, my brows pulling together. Oh, no.

"The London Dungeon? Uh..."

His smile grew wider. "E, I'd never take you there. I'm still partially deaf from your screams when we watched *The Purge*, and that wasn't even scary."

I punched his arm. "Hey! You jumped more than I did."

"You can't prove it. Anyway, no. We're going there." Gripping my shoulders, he manoeuvred me around so I was facing a different entrance a little farther away from where we were standing.

"Shrek's Adventure? Really?"

He laughed softly, his breath tickling the side of my face. "No. Keep looking. The entrance next to it."

My stomach did a little somersault as I read the words on the sign. "You're taking me to the aquarium?" I glanced over my shoulder at him, a smile tugging at my lips.

"Yeah." His hands slipped from my shoulders. "There was...Noah told me about that sushi place you wanted to go to with the aquarium. But when I googled it, it said that the aquarium bit was for private dining only. I'm only a poor student, so I couldn't afford the fuck-knows-how-many-thousands it would cost to hire out the space. Soooo...I thought this would be the next best thing. We get to see the fish, and then we can go and eat sushi afterwards. Is—do you think that's okay?"

I love you. The words were on the tip of my tongue. The fact that he'd obviously put thought into this, even getting advice from Noah...and now here he was, suddenly unsure about whether I'd like what he'd planned for our date.

Reaching out and gripping his arm, I pulled him towards the building, stopping when I was touching the grey stone wall. Now that we weren't at risk of being jostled by the throngs of tourists, I turned to face him fully. "Ander. It's more than okay. It's amazing. And just so you know, I would've been happy whatever we did."

Relief entered his gaze as he wrapped his arms around me. "Except for going to the London Dungeon."

"Except for that," I agreed, hugging him back and winding my arms around his neck. Butterflies were going crazy inside me.

His lips skimmed over my cheek, and then he angled his head to my ear. "Do— Fucking hell, E! Your ear is like a fucking ice cube."

Great, I really was at risk of my ears freezing off, after all. "Yeah, I know. But I wanted to look nice for you, so I used product in my hair. I couldn't wear a hat."

"Bloody hell, you look hot as fuck without doing anything. It's not worth the risk of frostbite." His hands came up to cover both of my ears, and then he began rubbing them with his gloved fingers. "You really did that for me?"

"It's a date, isn't it? I wanted to make an effort."

He pressed a soft kiss to my lips, and I gasped because it felt so natural and effortless and completely unexpected in the best way. "Believe me when I say that your effort is very much appreciated." His voice lowered, taking on a husky tone. "I'll show you how much I appreciate it later. What's your opinion on sex at the end of a first date?"

I pretended to think about it while desperately trying to stop my cock from hardening at the thought of what we might end up doing later. "Hmm. I'm not sure. Ask me again at the end of the date, and I'll let you know."

He smirked at me. "I won't need to ask. You'll be begging." Before I could reply, he was tugging me inside the aquarium entrance. As we stood in the queue, he leaned into me and whispered too low for anyone else to hear, "Thinking of you begging for my dick gave me a boner."

"Ander!"

Every. Single. Person in the aquarium foyer turned to look at us as my shout echoed around the space. My ears had been frozen, but now they were burning, as was my entire face.

"Hey, it's okay." Ander pulled me into him, wrapping an arm around me, and I turned my face into his neck to hide. His shoulders were shaking as he tried to bite back his laughter, and I pinched his side in warning. "All you did was screech my name. On the list of embarrassing shit that could happen...that doesn't even make it onto the list."

His words calmed me down, and by the time we'd entered the main aquarium, I was relaxed enough to look around and enjoy the fact that I was here with Ander. On a date. Our first date.

"Look at that. It's so cute." I peered into a little tank containing a tiny seahorse, watching it move around in the water.

"*You're* so cute." Ander smiled at me. "Take your gloves off so we can do the whole date thing and hold hands."

"You really want to do that?" I stared at him.

"Yeah, of course I do. I'm committed. This is a date, so we have to do date things. Isn't that how it works?"

"I think we can do what we want. But that, um, yeah. That might be nice." In case he changed his mind, I ripped off my gloves and shoved them in my coat pockets and then reached for his hands, tugging off his gloves while he grinned at me with amusement dancing in his hazel eyes.

When his gloves were safely stowed, I reached for his hand and threaded my fingers through his.

We were holding hands.

And throughout our entire journey through the aquarium, he didn't let go of me, not even once.

The icing on the cake was when we left the aquarium just as dusk was falling and walked across Westminster Bridge to the north side where the restaurant was. Ander made me stop by one of the ornate black lampposts next to the river, the London Eye across from where we were standing. Strings of lights went from one lamppost to the next, and even though it wasn't yet dark, they were lit up, and they looked beautiful.

"Wait there," Ander told me. Leaving me for a moment, he jogged over to a couple who were walking alongside the river, arm in arm. He said something to them before gesturing to me, and they both nodded, smiling.

When he came back to me, I found out that he'd asked the couple to take a photo of us, and he'd told them he'd do the same for them in return. Handing his phone over, he made us do a few different poses before turning to face me. His gaze held mine as everything else faded away and it was just me and him. I wanted to freeze the moment because it was so fucking perfect.

"I'll give you copies of the photos," he murmured, stepping even closer, and before I knew it, I was leaning forwards and pressing a light kiss to his lips. When I drew back, he was smiling widely with a flush to his cheeks, his eyes lit up.

Every time I thought I couldn't possibly fall for him any further, I was proven wrong.

"I'm too full." Ander rubbed his stomach, groaning. "I'm gonna have to go extra hard at the gym to burn all this off."

"Me too." We'd both overindulged way too much, but the food had been so good I couldn't help myself. The restaurant had been a great choice—one with an open kitchen where we could watch the chefs preparing the food, but with an intimate atmosphere, all decorated in blacks and golds. Ander had planned for us to walk outside afterwards, but it had started raining, and it was that freezing winter rain that was like icy needles on your skin. So instead, we'd caught a cab, and we were now back at the house in Ander's bedroom.

Stretching out on his back on his bed, he patted the

space next to him. "Come here. Let's nap, let our food go down a bit. And then afterwards..." He let his words trail off, but we both knew exactly what he was implying.

Climbing onto his bed, I lay down next to him, both of us sharing a pillow. "Afterwards."

TWENTY-FOUR

ANDER

"Ander. Get your lazy ass out of bed. I need your help."

The loud, insistent knocking wouldn't stop. I groaned. "Fuck off."

"You'd better not be telling me to fuck off." The door burst open, and JJ was standing there with his hands on his hips, an indignant look on his face. A look that immediately disappeared when he took in the person currently blinking a haze of sleep away from his face, looking so fucking gorgeous and soft and sleepy that I didn't want to share him with anyone.

Throwing my duvet over Elliot to hide him from JJ's gaze—currently flicking between shock and amusement, complete with an all-too-knowing gleam in his eyes—I cleared my throat. "Joshua James. Why the *fuck* are you interrupting my sleep at this ungodly hour?"

JJ strutted into the middle of the room, folding his arms across his bare chest. It was only then that I took in what he was wearing—sparkly ice-blue short shorts and matching boots that came to mid-calf. I raised a brow as he glared at me. "Check your fucking phone, babe. It's twenty past eleven. You promised you'd help me with my routine, remember?"

Oh, yeah. I had said that. He'd been working on some new moves for his lap dance routines at the club he worked at, and I'd promised to give my opinion because ever since that lap dance competition at Revolve, he'd been telling me I had a natural talent and could probably help him come up with a few new ideas. Which, yeah, I did have natural talent. I came second, after all, and JJ danced for his job, so he'd only won because he had an advantage over me.

"Sorry, mate. I didn't realise the time."

"You don't say," he muttered, but the glare melted from his face. "I guess you had a good excuse, though, didn't you?"

"A very good excuse," I purred. A shocked sound came from the lump under the covers, and I grinned.

"That answers my question, then." JJ gave me a smug smile, which disappeared almost as soon as it had arrived, a frown taking over his face. After blinking a few times, he widened his eyes at me and slowly mouthed, *If you want to talk about it, I'm here.*

I nodded at him, mouthing, *Thanks*, in return, before speaking normally again. "Fine. Give me half an hour, yeah?"

"I've got a dance class at one. Sorry. We can do it another time if you're busy." His mouth twisted as his gaze flicked between me and the lump in my bed.

The covers were suddenly flung back, and there was Elliot, still bleary-eyed, his clothes creased and his hair wild, still looking so fucking gorgeous that it sent me reeling. He gazed up at JJ, a small smile curving over his lips. "Give him ten minutes. He'll be there, and he'll be in a *much* better mood, believe me."

"Elliot Clarke. Well. Why have I never seen this side of you before?" JJ looked at Elliot with new interest, and I narrowed my eyes at him. If he even thought about trying to flirt with my—no, he wasn't mine. Yet.

"Easy, tiger." JJ smirked at me. "I'm not making a move on your man."

"I'm not his man," Elliot blurted out, panic on his face, and both JJ and I stared at him in surprise. What was all that about? And why the fuck did it hurt to hear him say those words?

"Uh, okay. I'll leave you to it. Ten minutes. I'll be in the lounge." JJ backed out of the room, and the second the door closed behind him, I turned on Elliot.

"Not my man?" I tried so hard to hide the hurt in my voice, but I wasn't sure I managed it.

He bit down on his lip, his gaze lowering. "Well...no. We've had a date, but..."

So this meant something more to me than to him, did it? Fuck. This was...I'd complicated everything by catching feelings, hadn't I? And who knew that it would hurt so much to know I was more into him than he was into me?

"Yeah," I said hoarsely. Clearing my throat, I sat up straight, pushing my feelings down. Way, way down. "Right. I'd better get ready. Get out of yesterday's clothes. I can't believe we slept through the whole night and didn't even wake up until now."

"Food coma." Elliot glanced up at me, giving me a tiny smile.

"I don't even think I need breakfast today." Climbing off the bed, I headed to the bathroom. "But I do need to clean my teeth."

Heading straight for the sink and turning on the tap, I heard the sound of my bedroom door opening and closing. I did my best to ignore the feeling of disappointment that Elliot was gone and picked up my toothbrush.

A few minutes later, I was naked other than the towel hooked loosely around my waist, waiting for my shower to get to the perfect temperature. It always took forever to warm up because the plumbing in this Victorian house was old as fuck. Eventually, though, the shower screen began to steam up, and I dropped my towel on the floor and—

A body pressed against my back. A long, lean, very naked body. With a very hard cock.

Arms slid around my waist, and a mouth pressed a kiss to the side of my neck. "Want me to improve your mood?"

I fucking loved this sexily self-assured side of Elliot. Was this what it would be like to have him as a boyfriend?

"Mmm." I pressed back into him. "What did you have in mind?"

"We've got seven—no, six minutes. So there's not time for much, but..." His hand slid down my stomach, and then lower still, until his fingers were curving around my hardening cock.

"I want you to get off too," I rasped, wrenching open the shower door. "Get in the shower with me. Save time."

He released his grip on me, following me into my shower, which suddenly seemed very fucking small with two grown men inside. Thankfully, some previous student with more money than sense had installed a large rainfall showerhead, so at least the water was hitting us both at the same time. I turned to face him, angling my head so that the water didn't fall into my eyes, and slid my hand down his body, my knuckles bumping against my torso as I did so. Because there was no fucking room in this shower stall. When I owned my own place, I was going to make sure I got a much, much bigger shower.

But none of that was important right now. What was important was the person in front of me, whose expressive blue eyes were dark and determined as his hand followed mine and wrapped around both of our cocks.

"Fuck, that feels so good," I groaned, my words echoing around us, bouncing off the tiled walls.

"So good. Put your arms around me," Elliot instructed in a low, throaty tone, and my dick jerked in his grip.

"You being bossy is so fucking hot." Sliding my arms around his back, I leaned forward to tug his lower lip between my teeth. I lowered my hands to his ass, running them across the rounded curves, his soft skin slick with water. He moaned against my mouth, and I pulled him into a kiss, running my hands over every part of him I could reach while he stroked our cocks together. The combined friction of his hand, his cock, and our bodies pressing so close together was so good that I knew once wouldn't be enough. How had I managed to get this addicted to him already when I never had with anyone else before?

All my thoughts disappeared when he twisted his hand over the head of my cock, and then I was coming all over both of our stomachs. I was closely followed by Elliot, who buried his face in my shoulder as his cock pulsed against mine, his cum shooting onto my skin.

So fucking good.

"Okay?" Leaning back against the tiles, I supported his body as he collapsed against me. I felt him nod and I smiled, pressing a kiss to his wet hair. "Good. We've probably got about a minute left before JJ comes looking for me, so we'd better get a move on."

He stepped back, closing his fingers around the shower door handle. "I'll shower in my own bathroom. There's not a lot of room for us both here."

"Okay." He'd already slipped out before I'd even said the word, leaving me even more confused than before. Fuck this overthinking shit. It was not good for me.

I washed as quickly as I could and threw on a pair of shorts, not bothering with a T-shirt. If JJ wanted me to dance, then I needed to show the goods. In fact... Exiting my room, I jogged up the stairs to the top floor of the house, where JJ's and Charlie's bedrooms were. JJ hardly ever bothered locking his door unless he had someone over, and today was no exception. I entered his room, heading straight for his wardrobe.

Jackpot. I pulled out a pair of metallic blue...shorts? Hot pants?...holding them up against me. They should fit. JJ had what I'd call a bubble butt, but my ass was in great shape, thanks to all the workouts I did. Not like Elliot's, of course—that sexy fucking rounded curve that was all natural and— I shook my head. No time to think about that now. I had a performance to prepare for.

Ditching my shorts, I pulled on the very short shorts, turning in front of the mirror to check how they looked. I wasn't disappointed. These things were miracle workers. They somehow made my thighs look more muscular than usual and my package look bigger—not that I needed any extra enhancement. And my ass...fuck, yeah. I couldn't wait for Elliot to see me.

I bounded down the stairs and into the darkened lounge, skidding to a stop in the middle of the room, where JJ was standing, fiddling with something on his phone. He'd pushed back the sofas to create an open space, and he'd placed one of the dining chairs in the centre. The curtains were closed, and I spotted Elliot's lamp cycling through a rainbow of colours from its new place on the TV console.

"Alright, mate?"

My head shot around to see a grinning face, and it was at that point I realised we had an audience comprised of my housemate Levi and his boyfriend, Asher.

"Ash. Levi. Here for the show?" I smirked at them, and Asher laughed, holding up his phone.

"You think I'd pass up a chance to see you make a fool of yourself? I've got my camera ready so I can post this online."

"Levi. Your boyfriend's a dick," I informed him as I gave Asher the middle finger.

Levi nodded, shooting Asher a grin. "He can be a dick, but I love him anyway."

Asher jabbed him in the ribs while planting a kiss on his lips. Those two had a weird way of showing their love sometimes.

Shaking my head, I returned my attention to JJ. "What do you want me to do?"

He glanced up from his phone and shuffled closer to me, lowering his voice. "I meant what I said earlier. I'm here if you ever wanna talk."

"Cheers. I appreciate it." I squeezed his arm in thanks and then squeezed it again. "Fuck me. Your bicep's like a fucking rock."

"That's the product of too many hours in the gym and the dance studio. And the club. I don't know—it all merges into one. Basically, lots of exercise."

"And sexercise. You sleep with more people than I did—*do*."

"Did?" He gave me a scrutinising look. Glancing over at the sofa, where Asher now had his tongue down Levi's throat —seriously, did they not realise there were other people in the room—he lowered his voice again. "Is this thing serious, then?"

I shook my head. "It's...I get the impression that I like him more than he likes me. I think I want more than he wants to give."

"Oh. That could be a problem." JJ's mouth twisted. "At the risk of sounding repetitive, I really did mean what I said earlier. Really. If you need to talk about anything."

"Yeah. Thanks."

In an attempt to lighten the mood, he patted my shoulder. "You know... If you want any advice about gay sex, you can come to me. And if you want me to introduce you to the magic of toys, let me know. There's a great prostate massager I can—"

I cut him off with my hand over his mouth because now both Asher and Levi were staring at us curiously. The last thing I needed was for even more people to find out about my private business.

JJ shoved me away, smirking, and I rolled my eyes. He started tapping at his phone again, but then his head shot up, his gaze scanning my body. "Hey! Did you take those shorts from my room?"

"Did you only just notice I was wearing them? I thought I'd get into character, and they look good on me, right?" I grinned at him, and he shook his head.

"I need to introduce you to my friend Cassius. I think you'd get on well." Swinging into the chair, he patted his thighs. "Anyway, back to the matter at hand. You dance. Ash and Levi are going to film it for me—*not* for social media—so I can break it down later."

"That's it? Are you gonna dance too? I thought I was giving you my opinion on your new moves."

"I'm not happy with it yet. But I'll be asking your opinion when it comes to the time." He tapped on his phone one final time, and "Have Mercy" by Chlöe started playing from the speaker next to the TV. "Okay. Go."

I didn't need any more encouragement. Dropping down, I went for it, moving as I had in the club, and as my hands slid over JJ's hard torso, all I could think of was that I really fucking wished that I had Elliot beneath me.

"Fuck, yeah, Ander!" JJ was all excitable encouragement. "If you ever want a job on the side, I bet I could get you a place at Sanctuary."

"Bloody hell," a voice breathed from the doorway behind me, and I almost lost my momentum. Elliot was here, watching me dance. Did he like what he saw?

I rolled my hips down, and I heard a noise that sounded like a whimper that was immediately cut off. Yeah, he was enjoying this.

"On my lap. Turn around," JJ instructed, and that was when I got my first look at Elliot. He was leaning against the doorframe, dressed in jeans and an oversized hoodie that I was 99 percent sure had belonged to me at one point, staring at me with his lips parted and his eyes huge and dark.

I knew he was remembering, just like I was. And I wanted him to be the one I was dancing on. He was the one I was dancing for.

When the song came to an end, I straightened up and then took a bow to the sound of catcalls from Asher and Levi. JJ headed over to them to check out the video footage, and I made my way towards Elliot.

I braced my arm against the doorframe, leaning into him, watching as his pupils dilated. I couldn't even remember what it was like to not feel an insane attraction towards this boy. How had we ever been just friends? "You liked that, didn't you?"

"I had a hard-on and you weren't even dancing on me

this time," he whispered, and then his face drained of colour. "Shit. Can we pretend I didn't say that?"

Grabbing his wrist, I pushed off the doorframe and into the hallway because I didn't want anyone to overhear our conversation. I pulled him into the empty kitchen, hopping up on the kitchen table, and then tugged him to stand between my legs. "Just so there's no confusion, you got hard when we were at Revolve because I was dancing on you? Or would it have happened no matter what?"

"Um." He bit down on his lip. "It was my first lap dance, so..."

I gripped his chin, lifting his head so he had no choice but to look at me. "E."

"Fine. Yes, it was because it was you." His cheeks flushed, and I smiled.

"Good." Releasing my grip on his chin, I let my hand fall to my side. Although I really, really didn't want to, I changed the subject. "Want to go down to the student union and play pool? See if Noah and Liam are up for it? Or Asher and Levi?"

What I actually wanted to do was to take him back up to my bedroom and suck his dick until he came down my throat, but I kept remembering his earlier words. *I'm not his man.*

I couldn't let him know how hard and fast I was falling for him. I couldn't scare him away.

I wasn't ready for this thing between us to end.

So this was my next best option. Change the subject away from dancing and sneakily suggest a double date that wasn't a double date.

He stepped back, and the expression on his face was unreadable. "Okay. If that's what you want."

Making a mental note to google how long you should wait before asking someone on a second date, I nodded. "Yeah. It'll be fun. We're the dream team, remember? Ace and E-Zee, just like when we were kids and used to pretend we couldn't play pool, then we'd fleece people and use the money to feed your ice addiction."

He growled under his breath, shooting me a warning look, although I noticed that he was trying not to smile. "I told you not to call me that name. Are you asking to have your mouth taped permanently shut?"

I grinned, rubbing my hand over the bulge in my shorts. "Your violent side makes me hard."

His mouth clamped shut, and his cheeks flushed darker. "Stop flirting with me."

"I actually don't think I can. It's hardwired into my personality or something." Flirting was okay, right? He was used to me acting this way. It would seem weird if I didn't flirt. I just had to make sure that he didn't find out how much I wanted him. Not yet, anyway.

He sighed. "Yeah, I know it is. Come on, then, let's go and see who we can fleece money from today. But do not refer to me by that nickname again, please."

"Deal. My vote is for Levi. He's rich as fuck—it'll be like he's doing a charitable deed, donating to us poor students."

Elliot rolled his eyes, huffing out a laugh, and for a minute, it was like it used to be between us.

It was an illusion, though. Things between us could never be the same.

TWENTY-FIVE

ELLIOT

"Why does it have to be him?" Ander groaned dramatically, and I rolled my eyes, grinning.

"Because the universe likes to torture us. Well, you. But I'll be with you to protect you from big, bad Dr. Wilder."

"I should be the one protecting you," Ander protested as we made our way down the corridor towards Dr. Wilder's office.

"Yeah, but I'm not the one that fucked up the assignment," I pointed out, which made him sigh loudly.

"Yeah, yeah. Pray that he's in a better mood than usual."

Laughing, I shot him a sideways glance. "That would take a miracle."

"True. I've said it before, and I'll say it again. Dr. Wilder needs to get laid, badly. It has to be the reason he acts like such a—"

"Mr. Loveridge."

From behind us came a low, smooth purr, stopping both

Ander and me dead in our tracks with what I was sure were identical expressions of panic on our faces. Shit.

"Uh, Dr. Wilder." Ander swallowed hard as he slowly turned to face our international business management lecturer. "I was just, uh, coming to see you about my assignment, like we discussed."

"Yes, I assumed that was why you were loitering around in the staff building. Mr. Clarke, why are you here? Your assignment was perfectly acceptable. Is Mr. Loveridge incapable of going anywhere without you?"

"Um..." I glanced over at Ander. "There's so much history in this building, you know? I'm really intrigued by the, uh, the stonemasonry." Words were spilling out of my mouth, and I had no clue what I was saying.

Dr. Wilder raised one dark brow. "Stonemasonry? Are you considering changing your major to history or architecture? Unless you are, I suggest you wait for Mr. Loveridge outside the building. And don't let me catch you in here again unless you have an appointment."

"Yes, sir." Shooting Ander an apologetic look, I backed away, mouthing, *I'll wait outside*, once I was safely out of Dr. Wilder's eyesight. I would not want to be in Ander's position right now, especially because there was no way that our lecturer hadn't heard his comment about needing to get laid. To be fair, Ander was probably correct. The man was incredibly good-looking—the epitome of tall, dark, and handsome, and the way he wore a suit was...let's just say, if you were into suit porn, you'd appreciate the sight. But his personality was like a human repellent. Unless he acted differently outside of the university...no, that couldn't be possible.

Why was I even wasting time thinking about my lecturer? I needed to be thinking of ways to cheer up Ander because he'd undoubtedly be in a bad mood after Dr. Wilder had finished with him.

Fifteen minutes later, Ander appeared, his mouth turned downwards and a defeated look in his eyes. He came straight over to me, wrapping his arms around me and burying his face in my shoulder. My arms came around him, and I stroked his back soothingly. "That bad, huh?"

"He's a wanker," Ander said, his words muffled by the fabric of my jacket. "I know we were going to get coffee before our next lecture, but he wants me to rewrite this assignment now and bring it back to him by the end of the day."

"Okay. Why don't we go to the library, and I'll get us a coffee, then I'll go through your assignment with you? I did alright on it, so maybe I can give you a couple of ideas?"

His arms tightened around me. "What would I do without you? You're the *best* best friend in the world, E. I'm so fucking lucky to have you."

Best friends. I wanted us to take the next step so badly, to be able to call him my boyfriend, to tell him that I loved him. But now that I'd had a small taste of what it might be like for us to be together, I was so scared of him deciding that it was all too much. He'd said he liked me, and it was obvious that he was attracted to me, but I had to be realistic. Ander didn't do serious relationships, and despite what he said, I still couldn't help feeling like when he'd satisfied his curiosity about being with men, he'd back away from me. And I'd be devastated.

I knew that heartbreak was coming, but it wasn't enough to make me pull back all the way. I'd take what he wanted to give me, and then when it was all over, I'd...I'd cross that bridge when I came to it.

Pasting a smile on my face, because right now, Ander needed cheering up, I said, "As part of my best friend duties, I'm going to make sure that you kick ass on this assignment, and Dr. Wilder will be so impressed he'll actually give you a compliment."

Ander raised his head, huffing out a laugh. "Miracles don't happen when it comes to him." Leaning forwards, he surprised me with a soft brush of his lips over my cheek before releasing me. "Come on. Let's get this assignment over with."

My smile melted into a genuine one as I followed him into the library. Maybe what I wanted wasn't so hopeless after all. Miracles didn't happen when it came to Dr. Wilder, but maybe they'd happen when it came to me.

"I think I caught a hint of a smile." Ander burst out of the faculty building with a grin on his face. "He said, 'Why couldn't you have written it like this in the first place?' which I'm taking to mean that he was impressed with my work."

"I knew you'd do it." I returned his smile, falling into step with him as we took the path through the centre of the grassy quad. "You hadn't even written it that badly last time. I think he was just looking for an excuse to make you do some extra work because he's sadistic like that."

"Yep. Total sadist." Ander nodded. Tugging his phone from his pocket, he glanced down at the screen, his brows pulled together in thought. "E? Do you wanna go to Sanctuary tonight? Where JJ works? He wants to show off his new routine, and he's on the pole tonight too."

"I guess so. As long as we don't drink too much—I've got a 9:00 a.m. lecture tomorrow."

"Yeah, I've got to be at the gym early tomorrow anyway, so I won't be drinking much." He groaned. "We sound so responsible. Fuck. Are we getting boring?"

"Maybe we are." Our eyes met, and the look of horror on his face made me laugh. "Okay, look. We're young. We can deal with workouts and lectures with a hangover. We just have to make sure we line our stomachs before we go out."

Ander threw his arm around me, planting a loud kiss on the side of my head. "I knew there was a reason I loved you."

Warmth spread through me, and even though I knew that he meant he loved me as a friend, at that moment, it didn't matter. To have a best friend like Ander... It was everything.

TWENTY-SIX

ANDER

"Looking sexy, Mr. Clarke." I looked Elliot up and down, appreciating his outfit of tight, midnight-blue jeans and a sheer black sleeveless T-shirt that clung to his torso, similar to the one that he'd worn to Revolve. He'd looked hot as fuck then, and he looked even hotter now. How was that even possible?

After handing my coat over to the attendant, I turned back to Elliot. "Ready?"

He nodded, his eyes sparkling, with that little flush on his cheekbones that I was starting to develop a bit of a fetish for. I loved seeing the physical evidence of what my words did to him.

Placing my hand on his back, I steered him into the cavernous interior of Sanctuary, decorated in shades of black and midnight blue, with burnished gold embellishments. As guests of JJ, we were allowed into the VIP area, which was a mezzanine level accessed by a set of glass stairs. After stating our names and flashing our IDs, the security guy unclipped the rope marking the stairs as out of bounds and waved us through. We ascended the stairs to the mezzanine level, where Elliot suddenly stopped dead, and I had to grab the handrail on the glass balcony to avoid running into his back.

"What's wrong?" I hissed into his ear.

"Are you sure this is the right place? It's all secluded booths. No dancers. Look at those people there—they look like they're having a business meeting." He subtly indicated his head towards the central booth. I followed his gaze to where four people sat in serious conversation. There were three guys, all dressed in business suits, and a woman with blue hair twisted into a bun, an iPad in front of her that she was tapping on. When the guy on the right raised his head and his golden eyes met mine, chills went down my spine, and not in a good way.

I blinked, returning my gaze to Elliot. "Uh, I think so." Pulling my phone from my pocket, I checked JJ's text again. "Yeah, see. He said to come up the glass stairs to the VIP area, and...oh, yeah. We need to go through this bit. There should be a black curtain at the far side, leading to another room."

Elliot visibly relaxed. "Good. Let's go." He made a beeline for the far side of the VIP area, speed walking to get there as quickly as possible, which made me smile. He was so fucking cute. Also, his ass and legs in those jeans...mmm. I liked the view. Very much.

I caught up with Elliot as he reached the curtain, our route blocked by an intimidating-looking bouncer. Turning on my charm, I gave him a wide smile. "We're guests of JJ. He's expecting us."

The bouncer looked me up and down, blank-faced, taking in my attire. JJ had said to dress smart, so I was wearing my nicest pair of black jeans, paired with a navy shirt that I'd unbuttoned the top few buttons of and rolled up the sleeves.

"Ander," the bouncer stated and then turned to Elliot. "Elliot."

"Correct." My smile widened. "It seems that my reputation precedes me."

The bouncer almost cracked a smile at that, I could tell, because his mouth twitched. Stepping aside and pulling back the curtain, he indicated for us to walk through.

Down a short corridor was another room. This one was entirely black with sparkling floors and a mirrored wall, in front of which was a small stage and a pole. There were booths similar to those in the VIP area, but these had heavy curtains that could be pulled across the opening for privacy. Dancers performed for patrons in some of the open booths, and I assumed that there were more private dances happening behind the closed curtains. There was another door leading out of the room, and I wondered if it led to even more private places. A stunning woman in a silver G-string was writhing on the pole, her long blonde hair cascading down her back. *Honey Rose.* Once, it was my life's ambition to get a lap dance from her. Standing here now with Elliot, though, I found that I wasn't interested. Not even a bit. It was fucking weird, to tell the truth, because she was hot like lava. Or the sun. More evidence that I was getting in way too deep with my best friend because right now, he was all that I saw.

"Wow. I didn't picture JJ's workplace looking like this," Elliot murmured, pulling me out of my thoughts.

"No?" I placed my hand on the small of his back again because I wanted to touch him. Steering him in the direction of the bar, I leaned closer, inhaling his fresh, delicious scent. "What did you think it was going to be like?"

He shrugged. "I don't know. For some reason, I thought it would be all red velvet. But I don't see any velvet. Not even those curtains."

I laughed, amused. "E, are you actually disappointed that there's no velvet?"

"No."

"I'll buy you some velvet curtains for your bedroom for Christmas," I promised as we reached the bar, and he elbowed me in the side.

"Don't you dare. But you can buy me a drink if you want. I'll get the next round."

After scanning the drink menu, I ordered a gin and tonic for Elliot with extra ice to feed his addiction and a Japanese beer for myself. My eyes watered at the price—no exaggeration—and I quickly realised that we wouldn't have to worry about drinking too much tonight. Instead, we'd have to worry about draining our bank accounts.

"Did he charge you extra for the ice or something?" Elliot asked me as we slid into an unoccupied booth facing the stage.

"No, that was just the price of the drinks. We're not

going to have to worry about getting drunk tonight at this rate."

"Babes, I've got you covered."

Elliot jumped at the sudden voice, and I grinned at him before turning to JJ. He stood in front of us, brandishing an ice bucket with a bottle of champagne and two glasses.

"This is on the house. I had to sweet-talk Austin—he's the owner of the club—into letting me have it. I told him that it was in his best interests to keep you onside because when you've both finished your degrees, you'll become rich and powerful businessmen, and he'll want you as contacts."

"Did you hear that, E? We're gonna become rich, powerful businessmen. JJ said so." I nudged him in the side.

He laughed, picking up one of the glasses that JJ had placed on the small table in our booth. "Speak it into existence, JJ."

"Whoa, hands off the glasses. I'm here in a professional capacity tonight, so don't make me look bad." Effortlessly opening the bottle of champagne, JJ filled the flutes. "They're letting me dance on the pole when Honey's finished. It's my first time, so I'm glad I have you two for moral support."

"What do you mean, letting you?" Elliot arranged his flute next to his glass of gin and then fished out an ice cube.

"Normally it's just Honey Rose and a few of the other female dancers on the pole, but I'm all about equal opportunities, so I've been working on Austin to let me dance too. I'm hot, and I'm a good dancer, so why shouldn't I get to go up there and show off my moves? It's a show, and I'm here to perform."

"Fuck, yeah. The more variety, the better, in my opinion." I lifted my glass to him. "E and I will be here, cheering you on."

He grinned widely. "I'm hoping I'll catch someone's eye. A sexy, rich businessman, preferably. I want a sugar daddy."

"Yesss, mate. Aim high." I high-fived him while Elliot looked on, shaking his head.

"I can't believe you two sometimes. You're really on the hunt for a sugar daddy?"

JJ tapped his fingers on the table, his lips curving into a smirk. "Nah, not really. I have other ambitions for myself. I'm not going to be someone's sugar baby. I'd just like a hot fling with an older guy. And if he's here in this part of the club, he's going to be either rich or connected or both, and you won't hear me complaining." He glanced over at the stage. "Gotta go. I need to finish getting ready for my performance. Enjoy. There's more champagne if you finish that one."

When he'd strutted off, I picked up my glass of beer, taking a small sip. Mmm. This was good. As it should be because I'd had three-course meals that cost less than one of these. Next to me, Elliot crunched on his ice cube, and it made me smile. Shifting closer to him in the booth, I placed my hand lightly on his thigh, just resting it there. A soft gasp escaped from his mouth. Yeah, this was what I wanted. I'd suggested coming here partly for JJ, but the reason I'd asked Elliot to come along was that I wanted to take him out again, but I didn't want to scare him away. So by doing this,

I got to have a sneaky date with him without being obvious about it.

"Having a good time?" I murmured close to his ear, blowing out a little so that he'd feel my breath on his skin. He shivered, slowly turning his head. His eyes met mine, and a look came into them that I'd never seen before. It was confident, even a little bit arrogant, and it was so fucking hot.

He glanced at my mouth, and then his tongue swiped across his lips. His gaze returned to mine, hot and heavy-lidded. "Two can play that game."

My cock was hardening rapidly, and I was grateful for the darkness of the club and the fact that the booths were so secluded. I held my breath, waiting to see what he'd do next. Confident Elliot was my very favourite Elliot.

A finger lightly traced across the veins on the back of my hand, which was still resting on his thigh, and the noise that fell from my throat was almost a whimper. No one had *ever* done that to me in my life, and fuck me, when did the back of my hand turn into an erogenous zone?

The game was on, and I was here to win.

Sliding my hand higher up his thigh, scraping my nails against his jeans for extra sensation, I leaned in, bypassing his enticingly plush lips and skimming my nose across his cheek. Freshly showered and shaved, his skin was soft against mine. He released an unsteady breath, his head falling back against the padded backrest of the booth. I took that as my cue to move my head lower, my nose skimming down his throat. I didn't kiss him, not yet, just enjoying getting to play with him like this.

"Ander."

"Yeah, baby?"

He straight up moaned, immediately clamping his hand over his mouth, although I doubted anyone would hear him with the thrumming bass of the music around us and the fact that we were so secluded.

"Don't hide from me." I gave in, kissing a line back up his throat, tasting the salt on his skin as my hand moved higher up his thigh. His eyelids fluttered closed, his finger still tracing patterns on my hand. After a moment, he began to move his finger higher, sliding it up my forearm to the place at my elbow where my sleeves were rolled up. Then he traced a line back down to my hand, still using a light, teasing movement. It was driving me fucking insane, and this was only one finger on my *arm*, of all places.

I mouthed at his throat, moving my hand off his thigh and onto the growing bulge between his legs. When I rubbed my hand over his dick, his moan vibrated against my lips. So fucking hot. My cock was painfully hard, trapped in my jeans, and I knew that he had to be feeling the same restriction. My fingers went to the button of his jeans, but he stopped me with a hand over mine.

"Not yet."

Raising my head, I met his heavy-lidded gaze, his eyes dark with arousal. This time, I couldn't resist leaning in and capturing his lips with mine. The kiss went from zero to a hundred in just a couple of seconds, Elliot's hands cupping the back of my head as he pulled me closer. "Can't get enough of kissing you," I panted against his mouth before attacking his lips again. Somehow, I ended up straddling him, grinding my bulge down against his as his hands moved all over my body, driving me completely fucking insane.

"That's one of the hottest things I've ever seen, and I'm friends with several porn stars, so believe me, I've seen a lot. But there's a privacy curtain for a reason."

We sprang apart instantly like we were magnets repelling each other. Collapsing back into the booth, I pressed a hand to my chest, attempting to slow my racing heart rate before meeting JJ's amused gaze.

"Sorry for interrupting," he said. He wasn't sorry. "I was coming over to tell you that my performance is about to start, but then I saw you two tongue fucking each other. I got sidetracked watching you."

"You stood there watching us?" Elliot's unconvincing attempt at an outraged hiss made me smile.

"Yep. I'm a gay man with twenty-twentyish vision, and you two are fucking hot together. Who wouldn't wanna see that?"

"He has a point," I said. "We are hot together. Very fucking hot."

Elliot's cheeks were flushing again, and I wanted to kiss him so badly. Bloody hell, I never lost control like this. I'd completely forgotten that we were technically in public because all I saw was him.

"Even though we can all agree it was hot, this is my workplace, and there are things you might be able to get away with doing in other places that you can't do here where my boss is entertaining business clients. Dry humping is one of them. So just use the curtain, okay?

You're my guests, so I'm responsible for you." JJ stepped closer, smirking. "Plenty of things happen behind the curtain. You want condoms. Lube. Wipes. A change of clothes. I've got you covered."

Elliot's mouth fell open as he stared at JJ. JJ just winked at him, his eyes glittering with whatever black-and-gold sparkly shit he'd just lined them with.

"We'll use the curtain." I went to slide out of the booth, but JJ shook his head.

"Wait until I've finished my dance."

One hot-as-fuck kiss from my best friend and my brain was so scrambled that I'd forgotten we were here to support JJ. "Yeah, of course. I wouldn't miss it," I said truthfully. "You gonna show us your lap dance moves after?"

"Yeah. I'll find one of the other dancers to do my demonstration on, unless either of you want a dance from me?" He shot me a knowing look.

"No," I said immediately. Yeah, Elliot had enjoyed watching me dance on JJ, but I didn't want anyone else to have the privilege of dancing on Elliot. Hello, double standards.

"I thought not. I'll find someone. For now, sit back and watch the master at work." Blowing us a kiss, he backed away from our booth and then bounded over to the stage.

"Bloody *hell*. I had no idea JJ had so much talent," Elliot whispered, his gaze fixed on the stage where JJ was hanging upside down on the pole, barefoot and wearing another of his endless supply of tiny shorts—this time in gold. His entire body was shimmering gold, in fact, even his hair, and I made a mental note to ask him how he'd done it. Not that I was planning to paint myself golden or anything, but you never knew when information like that would come in handy.

JJ twisted and spun in a graceful, athletic routine, all rippling muscles and shimmery skin, and honestly? I was insanely jealous of his moves. "He's amazing." I sighed heavily. "There's no way on earth I can compete with him."

Elliot dropped the ice cube he'd been fishing out of his glass, sending a small tsunami of gin cascading over the edge. His wide eyes met mine. "Why would you want to?"

Good question. "To impress you?"

"Ander." He shook his head, incredulous. "Why on earth would you think that you had to be better at dancing than JJ to impress me? Don't you remember how—" He paused, biting down on his lip and lowering his gaze.

"Remember how..." I prompted.

"How much I liked you dancing on me. And watching you dance on JJ. You *know* I did. And yes, JJ is amazing, but he impresses me in a whole different way than you."

My lips curved into a smile. "Yeah? Different how?"

"You know how." He huffed. "Don't play dumb." Fishing the ice cube back out of his glass, he crunched it viciously.

Dropping the teasing, I leaned into him, placing my hand over his in what I hoped was a reassuring gesture. It was so fucking weird how easily I kept slipping between hot-for-him mode and best-friend mode. Weird, but at the same time, it was so easy. Effortless, in fact. "I know. I'm sorry, E. I like knowing that I have an effect on you, and I like hearing you say it."

"Of course you do," he muttered, climbing to his feet. "Watch JJ. I'm going to find the toilets."

Then he was gone, and although I returned my attention to JJ, all my thoughts were to do with wondering what was going on inside my best friend's head.

TWENTY-SEVEN

ELLIOT

E xiting the toilets, I wasn't looking where I was going and almost stumbled into a group of guys. Apologising, I darted around them and then did a double take because one of them closely resembled Dr. Wilder. But no, I was mistaken. As if he'd be here, of all places.

"I thought I saw your favourite lecturer just now," I said to Ander as I slid back into the booth. "Imagine if he was actually here."

"If you're talking about Dr. Wanker, then I can't think of anything worse. I swear, he haunts me in my nightmares." Ander gave an exaggerated shudder. "Hey, you missed JJ doing this thing on the pole with his legs where he stretched them straight out, and then he was walking them up through the air...I can't describe it. But it was so fucking impressive. His core strength is insane."

He began talking about core exercises, and I smiled at his enthusiasm. Tonight had been so unexpected, and instead of worrying about it like I normally would, I was doing my best to go with the flow and enjoy whatever happened. The time for overthinking would come later, I was sure, but for now, I wanted to be in the moment and have fun with the man I loved.

"JJ's bringing Honey Rose over to demonstrate his dance," he said after a pause, shooting me an unreadable look.

Oh. Honey Rose. The beautiful woman who was supposedly the most popular, in-demand dancer in the club.

I swallowed hard, fighting to keep my voice even as I said through gritted teeth, "Sounds good." Jealousy was an emotion that I was used to experiencing when it came to Ander, but it had always been tempered by the fact that I knew nothing would ever happen between us. Now, though, after everything we'd been through recently...I wanted to fucking claim him. Mark him up, as he'd done to me.

The thought shocked me into silence. Where had that come from?

"Elliot."

The firm, uncompromising tone in Ander's voice had my eyes flying to his, temporarily diverting my mind from my sudden revelation.

He held my gaze steadily. "I'm only interested in seeing which moves JJ has picked up from me. We'll go downstairs to the main club and dance after that."

"Oh. Okay." I was a little taken aback by his words and his demeanour, but...he said he was only interested in seeing whatever moves JJ had picked up from him.

If he really meant that...

Stop daydreaming, Elliot, and get your head out of the clouds.

Go with the flow. That was what I'd been doing so far tonight and what I'd continue to do.

My glass of gin was now empty, so I picked up one of the champagne flutes JJ had left for us. "Toast? To tonight? To you inspiring JJ?"

Ander's lips kicked up at the corners as he reached for his champagne flute, having also emptied his glass of beer.

"To me inspiring JJ. And to us, for being fucking amazing. Not just tonight but every night."

Laughing, I clinked my glass against his. "Cheers."

Almost as soon as I lowered my glass to the table, JJ appeared in my field of vision, clasping Honey Rose's hand. She had a sultry smile on her pouty lips, and it pained me to admit it, but I suddenly felt so insecure.

A warm palm slid onto my thigh, and then Ander's breath was hitting my ear. "Did I tell you how gorgeous you look tonight?"

I couldn't help turning to face him. He was...blushing? That was unusual, but the reason became clearer when he spoke again.

"It feels...weird sometimes, I guess...saying things like that to you. But I want you to know."

Fuck. He was my everything. "Ander. I know...I know it's—it's weird." I was tripping over my words. Inhaling deeply, I squared my shoulders. "I feel the same."

He smiled, happy and bright, and I relaxed back into the booth as JJ came to a stop in front of us.

"Ander, Elliot, meet Honey Rose, our best dancer and a

goddess among mortals. Honey, meet two of my house-mates, Ander and Elliot." He twirled Honey Rose around, her body shimmering under the club lights like JJ's, her glossy blonde hair floating around her like she was in a shampoo advert. She was exactly Ander's type—not that he was particularly discriminating when it came to choosing partners, but they always had one thing in common, and that was that they were very, very pretty. This woman was beyond pretty. She was—

Ander squeezed my thigh, his thumb stroking up and down. "You're even more beautiful in person than the pictures JJ showed me. Not that I have eyes for anyone other than Elliot here." He leaned in, pressing a soft kiss to my cheek that took me completely by surprise.

"You two are together? I thought so—I can tell how at ease you are with each other. You make a gorgeous couple." Honey Rose gave us a bright, genuine smile, and suddenly, my insecurities melted away because Ander wasn't showing any interest in her—he'd practically claimed me as his in front of her, and she was being nothing but friendly to us both.

"They do, don't they? That's what I said." The smug smile on JJ's face didn't even bother me because if even a stranger thought that we made a good couple, then maybe...

I couldn't let myself get carried away, but I was going to hold on to this feeling for as long as I could.

"I want you," Ander rasped in my ear, grinding his hard cock against my ass, his hands an iron grip on my hips as we moved to the music on the main floor of the club. "Do you want me?"

The way he spoke those words, low and throaty, just for me, as he rubbed his cock against my ass had all my blood rushing to my dick. How could he expect me to form sentences? I threw my head back against his shoulder, reaching back to pull him even closer. "Yes."

"Good," he murmured in between mouthing at my neck. "I haven't been able to think of anything else since you dragged me on this dance floor and started grinding your hot body all over me."

"*Please*." One-word answers were all that I was capable of.

He didn't make me wait. "Let's go."

The taxi ride home was an exercise in self-restraint. I was practically vibrating out of my seat with the need to touch him, and Ander held himself tense against the cab door, clearly thinking along the same lines as I was. As soon as we pulled up and paid, he was wrenching the door open and then tugging me down the short pathway to our house. He crowded me up against the black front door while I fumbled with my key, attempting to jam it into the lock. Why wouldn't it go in? And why were my hands shaking so much?

"Let me." His fingers closed around mine, and together, we fitted the key into the lock and turned it. Finally, the door was open, and we stumbled through into the hallway, Ander at my back, one hand still grasping mine, the other banded around my waist. He was so hot and hard, and the only thing I wanted was for him to pin me down on the bed and let me find out exactly how it felt to have him inside me.

"Your room," I said breathlessly, arching back into him, and he groaned in reply. We somehow made it up the stairs and into his bedroom, and then he was kicking the door shut and pressing me up against it. The bright streetlight right outside his window offered enough illumination in the room for me to be able to read the lustful expression written all over his face, and it made my dick throb. *We were really doing this.*

Tugging off my top, leaving my torso bared to him, he ran his hands greedily down my body. Kissing down my throat again, he rolled his hips, his voice a hoarse vibration against my skin. "I'm so fucking desperate for you."

I was just as desperate for him, and I'd never known just how fucking much it was possible to want to be consumed by someone. And this wasn't just anyone. It was *Ander*.

My fingers were clumsy on the buttons of his shirt, and we were both feeling the same sense of impatience because I hadn't even unbuttoned it all the way before he was yanking it off over his head. Now it was my turn for my hands to roam the hard lines of his body while we kissed each other with increasing desperation, rutting against each other up against his door.

"Jeans. Off," he growled. Somehow, we managed to pull apart long enough to remove the rest of our clothes, and then we were crashing onto the bed with me on top of him. I mouthed at his jaw, unable to get enough of the feel of his body plastered against mine, with the undeniable proof of his arousal pressing into my belly.

I swallowed hard. "I'm gonna come too fast, and I really want you inside me."

"Fuck, E. Me too. Or you inside me. Fuck, I want it all. I want to fill you with my cock, but I want you to fill me too." He sucked a mark into my neck, his hips jerking upwards, and I nearly lost my mind. This was...he was everything I'd ever wanted, and it was so much better than I could've ever imagined...

"Need you. Fingers." I gasped the words into his hair.

He was completely self-assured, slicking his fingers with lube from his bedside drawer, and then he was dipping them between my ass cheeks. I didn't even think about the experience he must've had to know what to do because he was circling his finger around my hole and pressing on my perineum, and it felt so fucking good. I was going to come way too quickly if he kept this up.

When he pushed one finger inside, I gasped. I needed more. Maybe people had exaggerated how painful it was, or maybe it was the fact that I'd not only fingered myself...a lot, but I'd fucked myself on a dildo—all I knew was that one finger wasn't enough to satisfy me. I needed more. I needed his cock.

"More," I begged. "Give me more."

"Fuck, you're so hot," he groaned, easing another finger inside me. I pulled him down into a kiss, unable to hold back any longer, so overwhelmed again in the best way because it wasn't an exaggeration to say that all my dreams were coming true.

"More." I scraped my fingers down the smooth skin of his back, feeling his muscles flexing underneath my touch. "I want your cock."

Pulling back a little, he looked down at me, and although his gaze was dark with arousal, there was concern in his eyes. "I don't want to hurt you, E. I never want to hurt you."

"You won't. I promise I'll tell you if it's too much."

My words must've reassured him because he added another finger, taking care to stretch me out. "Does that feel good? There's meant to be..." He trailed off, his brows pulling together as he moved his fingers and brushed over my prostate.

"Ander. Yesss. *There*. Oh, fuck." I arched into him, willing him to keep touching me in the place that lit my body up from the inside. Except, no, I needed his cock. Now.

"You're making me jealous. You're doing this to me next. No. Now? Please?"

He was killing me. I wanted his cock, so fucking badly, but I wanted him to have everything he wanted. I wanted to make him feel as good as I was feeling. The way his cock was like an iron bar against my leg, dripping precum, made it clear that he was enjoying what we were already doing, but if I could make him enjoy it even more... Forget my inexperience—this was me and him, and I was suddenly certain that I could blow his mind.

"Yeah, okay. Do you want to go on your front or your back?"

He slowly withdrew his fingers from me, and I instantly

felt the loss, but at the same time, I couldn't wait to have him fall apart beneath me. "On my back. I want to see you."

"Okay." Rolling to the side, I grabbed the lube and a strip of condoms, then slicked up my fingers. When I turned back around, Ander was lying on his back, a pillow propped under his ass and his hand wrapped around his cock. I just stared, unable to believe that I had him here in bed with me. I was in love with him for so many reasons, and I knew that I would always love him, no matter how he looked, but fucking hell, he was like a god with those carved muscles and beautiful face that I loved so much. I got a million butterflies in my stomach just looking at him, and to be able to see all of him like this? It was a gift that I'd treasure always, even if it never happened again.

Crooking a finger at me, he stared right back, his gaze sweeping over my body, hot and heavy, making my dick jerk. "Come here."

When I crawled back across the bed to him, he widened his legs, and I slotted into place effortlessly, like we'd done this a hundred times before. I didn't even feel nervous, not when he was looking at me like this, like I was the only thing he saw.

When I pressed the tip of my finger inside him, his eyes fell closed, and he exhaled a deep, shuddering breath. "You're the first person to ever touch me this way." His eyes opened, and his gaze connected with mine. "I'm glad it's you."

"Ander," I whispered. Slowly pushing my finger all the way in, I kept my gaze fixed on his. It suddenly felt imperative that he knew how important this was to me. "Thank you for trusting me to do this with you. I've never...you know this is the first time I've done any of this, and I'm so glad it's you too."

I couldn't hold his gaze after that because I was afraid that he'd recognise the truth in my eyes, that I was completely head over fucking heels in love with him. Instead, I lowered myself down and placed kisses over his warm skin while I slowly worked him open. When I had two fingers inside of him, I crooked them, feeling around for that magic place that would make him see stars. He swore loudly, bucking against me, his cock jerking against my skin.

"Fucking *hell*. Do that again."

A smile spread across my face as I obliged. He began palming his cock, pushing down on my fingers, biting down on his lower lip. When I added a third finger, he tensed up for a moment but then relaxed, breathing out as he thumbed the head of his cock.

"You're so gorgeous. I can't believe I get to do this to you," I murmured, placing a kiss on his chest, right over his pounding heart.

His gaze turned soft as he returned my smile. "Me too. I've been missing out all this time. Is it like this for everyone?"

"I don't know. I don't think it's the same for everyone. Different sensitivities or whatever." Kissing a line up his chest and onto his throat, I began to slowly circle my fingers, stretching him out. "Guess you're one of the lucky ones."

"Yeah, I fucking am. Come up here and kiss me." He ran his free hand up my back and then brought it around to cup my jaw as I closed the final bit of space between us. His lips slid against mine, hot and hungry.

I needed more. I wanted to take this final step with him, to know what it was like to feel him inside me. "Ander, I need you inside me. Or me inside you, if you want."

He groaned against my mouth. "Fuck. Yes. Whichever way you want, E. I want it to be good for you."

"It will be. It is." With one last kiss, I eased my fingers out of him and then sat up, reaching for the strip of condoms I'd thrown on the bed. "I really want to feel you inside me."

"Let me." Ander reached for the packet. "Get the lube. I want to make sure I don't hurt you."

When he was sheathed and ready, I straddled him on my knees. Fuck, I'd dreamed about this moment so many times. Had so many fantasies about it, alone in my bedroom, coming into my hand, never imagining for one second that it would really happen.

He ran his hands up my thighs, looking up at me with a question in his eyes. "I'm ready," I assured him, gripping his cock to hold it in place as I carefully lowered myself down. When the head of his cock was lined up with my hole, I exhaled shakily, trying to remember everything I'd read about anal sex, and then carefully pushed down.

"Fucking *fuck*," Ander groaned as I slowly sank onto his cock, the muscles of my thighs taking all the strain as I lowered my body in the tiniest increments. It burned a little, but I didn't even care because it meant that Ander's dick was inside me. My erection hadn't even flagged—the expression of lust and hunger written all over my best friend's face made my cock throb, and when he reached up to wrap his hand around my cock, I moaned.

"Fuck. So full." No dildo could have ever prepared me for this. Ander's hot, thick length filling me up, his strong thighs beneath me, his chest rising and falling with unsteady breaths as he avidly watched his dick enter my body. When I was all the way down, I stopped for a moment, savouring the fact that this was happening, and then I began to move.

"You feel so fucking good around my cock," Ander ground out as I raised myself up and then down again, still slow, getting used to the feeling of him being inside me. Releasing my cock, he pushed his knees up, his hands coming around to cup my ass as I braced my hand against his chest. "Is it good for you?"

"So good." I moved again, and this time, he moved too, raising his hips. I didn't know if we were more attuned to each other because we knew each other so well or if it was just luck, but we were so in sync right from the beginning, and as I'd just said, it felt so good. So, so good. We moved against each other, and then I angled myself slightly and...

It was another fucking level. A cry tore from my throat as Ander's cock hit right where I wanted it to, sending pleasure fizzing through my entire body. I gripped my dick and began to stroke, hard and fast, losing myself in the whole-body sensations that were overtaking all my senses.

"Fuck, E, yeah." Ander's hips moved faster, and I was right there with him. His eyes met mine, pupils completely blown, his lips slick and reddened from our kisses. "You're the hottest fucking thing I've ever seen. I wanna see you come all over me."

I was lost. His words sent me over the edge into a blinding orgasm, my cum shooting all up his chest, and I was only vaguely aware of his hips stuttering and his fingers tightening their grip on my ass as he rode out his own climax.

When I came to, I realised that I was slumped over him, letting him take my entire weight, our chests pressed together, hot and slick with sweat, both of us struggling to catch our breaths.

"I don't think first times are supposed to be that good. That was amazing," I mumbled into his shoulder. Amazing was an understatement. Having sex with someone you loved so fucking deeply...okay, I couldn't compare it to anything else, but that *had* to be why it had been so mind-blowingly good. Ander remained silent, and I raised my head to look at him. "Hey, are you okay?"

He nodded, just once, staring blankly into the distance, and I realised that his body was beginning to tense up beneath me. My stomach churned. Was he regretting it? It had seemed like he'd been really into it, but now I wasn't so sure.

What should I do? I eased myself up, letting his soft-ening cock slip out of me, leaving me feeling empty and a little sore. I'd definitely be feeling it tomorrow. I fumbled around for the box of tissues that he kept beside his bed and placed it next to him before I began cleaning myself up, unsure if he would welcome me touching him.

The bed shifted, and then Ander was climbing off,

disposing of the condom in his wastepaper basket, keeping his back to me. He walked across to his desk and braced his forearms against the edge, staring out of the window, his shoulders tense.

"Elliot." His voice was low and hoarse. "I want you to know that what we just did was..." He paused, gripping the edge of his desk so hard that his knuckles turned white.

"Was?" I whispered shakily.

"Was fucking perfect. I think...fuck." Breaking off, he brought one of his hands up, rubbing it across his face. "I don't want you to take this the wrong way, but I need a bit of time on my own now."

Oh, *no*. I swallowed hard around the sudden lump that had come into my throat. Scrambling off the bed, I hunted around for my clothes, gathering them into a pile as quickly as I could, only stopping to yank on my boxer briefs. My hands were shaking, and I knew that I was going to do something stupid like cry any second.

When I made it to the door, Ander spoke again, still not looking at me. "I don't regret it, E. Not at all. I just...I need some space right now."

I nodded jerkily, hoping he could see me out of the corner of my eye because I didn't trust myself to speak.

When I was back in the safety and privacy of my bedroom, I curled up into a ball under my duvet, squeezing my eyes shut and gritting my teeth in a useless attempt to stop myself from crying, desperately hoping that what we'd done tonight hadn't been the biggest mistake of my life.

TWENTY-EIGHT

ANDER

I couldn't breathe.

I was fucking drowning.

I'd never been so shaken in my life. What the fuck did I do? I was so fucking unprepared for this. Sometime during what had been, hands down, the best sexual experience of my life, because it was with Elliot, I'd realised something.

I wasn't falling for my best friend any longer. I'd fallen all the way. I, Ander Loveridge, serial player with no intentions to start a relationship with anyone, had completely and utterly fallen in love with Elliot Clarke, and to make things worse, I wanted everything with him. Every-fucking-thing. Maybe it was because he was already the other half of me that I'd fallen so hard and fast, but now that I'd been hit with this bomb of a revelation, I was so unequipped to handle these feelings.

I'd told Elliot to leave because what else could I do? How could I untangle this mess of feelings and pretend like my entire world hadn't just been shattered? How could I act like I was okay to carry on as we had been, taking it slow so I didn't scare him away, when all I wanted was for him to be mine in every way? To be my boyfriend for real, not just as an act for an asshole in a bar? To tell everyone that he belonged to me?

My palms were digging into the edge of my desk, the wood biting into my skin, and my head was pounding. Fuck, I really needed to talk to someone. Liam, maybe. Surely, he'd have some advice—not that he'd been through quite the same situation, but I knew how in love with Noah he was.

Except it was two in the morning. Everyone would be asleep.

A wave of panicky, sick feelings crashed over me, and I forced myself to inhale and exhale deeply, counting in my head until it resided a little. When I felt like I was no longer at risk of drowning, I stiffly uncurled my fingers from my desk and made my way to my drawers on shaky legs, grabbing a pair of grey joggers and pulling them on. Then I picked up my phone and made my way up to the top floor to JJ's bedroom. He was the only person I knew who'd still be awake because he'd been working tonight, and there was no way I could sleep after everything. I had to talk to someone.

Collapsing back onto JJ's bed, I pulled up Google on my phone and typed, "What do I do if I've fallen in love with my best friend?"

After less than a minute of scanning the results, I threw my phone down, defeated. I really fucking needed to talk to someone about this. Where was JJ?

Jumping up from JJ's bed, I began pacing his room but stopped dead when I reached his bookshelves. On one of the shelves, a space had been cleared where there were usually books, and instead, there was an aquarium tank with the biggest snail I'd ever seen in my life inside. I wasn't even kidding—that thing was *huge*.

It stared at me with its stalk eyes, and I stared right back. Would it be weird if I started talking to a snail? I guessed not—people had therapy pets that they talked to, didn't they? Why not snails? Maybe I should get one myself...actually, no. Elliot wasn't a fan of snails.

"Do you know when JJ's gonna be back?" I asked the snail. It didn't reply.

"Have you ever been in love with your best friend?"

The snail moved sloooowly along the floor of the tank, stopping in front of what looked like a piece of lettuce.

"What am I saying? You're all alone in there." Moving closer, I reached out to trace my finger over the glass. My vision was getting blurry as tears gathered in my eyes. "That's so fucking *sad*."

I threw myself face down on JJ's bed.

That was the last thing I remembered.

"Not that I'm complaining about finding a hot boy waiting for me in my bed, but what the actual fuck are you doing here?"

I blinked my eyes open, groaning at the brightness. When my surroundings came into focus, everything came rushing back. I was in JJ's room, and last night, I'd...well, I was still feeling exactly the same way as I had been then. A lot in love and a lot freaking the fuck out.

"The snail's all alone," was the first thing that came out of my mouth, and JJ's brows shot up. He propped his hands on his hips, eyeing me incredulously.

"You're telling me that you slept in my bedroom to keep a snail company, who, by the way, isn't even mine?"

"Whose is it?"

JJ waved his hand in the air dismissively. "I'm looking after it for a friend for a couple of weeks while he has the time of his life in Thailand. He's out there by the pool, living his best gay life drinking cocktails and dicking down hot boys while I'm stuck here in cold, rainy London with— No, don't sidetrack me. Why are you here really? It's not the snail, is it?"

"I came up here last night to talk to you, but you weren't back. I must've fallen asleep." Sitting up, I rubbed my eyes, yawning. "Did you only just get home?"

He smirked at me. "Wouldn't you like to know? Sorry, babe, I don't kiss and tell."

"You bloody well do, you liar."

"Okay, okay, I do. Sometimes. But not this time. Let's just say that maybe I had a good time at the club after you'd gone." His smirk faded, and he huffed, folding his arms across his chest. "Again, stop sidetracking me. What's the matter?"

Drawing up my knees, I buried my head in my arms so that I didn't have to see his face. I gritted my teeth, forcing the words from my lips. "Nothing much. Just that I realised that I'm completely head over fucking heels in love with Elliot."

A shocked gasp came from JJ, and then the next minute, I felt the mattress sink under his weight, and he placed his hand on my shoulder, rubbing gently. "Are you sure?"

"Yeah. I'm more sure about this than I ever have been about anything, probably. I don't know what to do. I feel like I'm drowning."

"Can I ask you a question, just so I have it straight in my head? Are you panicking because you've fallen in love with a guy or because it's Elliot?"

"The second," I said instantly. "The fact that he's a guy is irrelevant to me. It's because he's my best friend and the most important person in the world to me. I know he likes me as more than a friend, but we're on totally different pages here. Different stratospheres. I'm in too fucking deep, and I don't—what do I do?"

JJ shifted closer, slipping his arm around my shoulders, and sighed. "Oh, Ander...I—I really don't know."

That made two of us.

TWENTY-NINE

ELLIOT

Everything was so messed up. Ander was avoiding me again, and with every hour that passed without him, it felt like my heart was breaking, piece by piece. He'd texted me the following morning to say that he needed some space, and I couldn't help but feel like the longer we left it to talk, the wider the cracks would become in our friendship. If he wanted to go back to just being friends again, I'd jump at the chance. I'd do everything in my power to hide the love I felt for him because losing him as my best friend couldn't be an option.

Even so, things would never be the same again. Not now that I knew him so intimately, had experienced pleasure with him that I hadn't even known existed, and had fallen even more deeply in love after getting the privilege to share this new part of him.

Everything had changed, and this was why you shouldn't sleep with your best friend. Unless you were prepared to lose them, and I wasn't ready to lose mine. But the longer the time and distance stretched between us, the more hope I lost.

"Have you seen him yet?" Noah asked me as we took our seats at a table in the student union.

Picking up my burger, I shook my head. "Not at all. Even in the lectures we share, he's been arriving late and leaving early, like he wants to make it obvious that he doesn't want to speak to me." I bit into my burger, and it tasted like ash in my mouth, just as everything I'd eaten had since Ander told me he needed space.

Swallowing a mouthful of fries, Noah shot me a sympathetic look. "I wish I knew what to say, but I guess if he's asked for space, you have to respect that. Do you want me to speak to Liam? See if Ander's said anything to him?"

"No, it's okay. Thanks for the offer, but I'd rather not involve anyone else in my issues, especially not when Liam's so close to Ander. I feel like I'm putting you in the middle a bit, now Liam's your boyfriend, but I don't have anyone else to talk to about it. No one else knows how I feel about Ander." Uncapping my bottle of Coke, I tipped it to my lips, hoping that the fizzing liquid would do something to ease the churning in my stomach.

"Hey, don't even worry about that. You're my friend—of course I'm gonna be there for you. And Liam respects that—he's not going to ask me to tell him anything private that you've spoken to me about." He gave me a reassuring smile. "Remember that Ander's your best friend. You're going to work this out."

"I've tried to be objective." Lowering my voice, I glanced around the busy student union to check if anyone was listening in. "He was definitely into it when we, you know. It was just afterwards—he completely froze up and shut me out and hasn't spoken to me since, other than sending a text to say he needed space. It's been three days now. I haven't even seen him at home, and do you know how hard it is to avoid someone you're living with?"

Noah chuckled humourlessly. "Yeah, I have an idea of that. Liam did that to me for a bit." He played with his bottle of water, flipping the sports cap on and off. "Maybe you should send him a text. Just say that you're respecting his space, but you're ready to talk whenever he wants to?"

"Yeah, maybe I will." Tapping my fingers on the table, I thought about it. Was it a bad idea? Fuck it. I pulled out my phone and tapped out a quick message.

ME:

> Take as much time as you need, but I wanted to let you know I'm here to talk whenever you're ready

Message sent, I returned my attention to Noah. "It's hard, you know? I don't know what to do. It probably sounds dramatic, because it's been three days, which isn't a long time, but I really, really miss him."

"It's not dramatic. It's—" Noah cut himself off as Adam and Nick, two of the guys from our running club, approached our table.

"Are these seats free? It's so busy in here today we can't see anywhere else to sit," Adam said.

I attempted and almost successfully achieved a small smile. What could I say? I was experienced at compartmentalising everything Ander-related. I'd been doing it for most of my life, after all. "Yeah, take a seat. Everyone's in here escaping the rain, I think."

"Cheers, mate." Nick pulled out the chair next to mine. "I think you're right. It's pissing it down outside."

Adam groaned. "Yeah. Tell me about it. I stood in a puddle that was more like a pond on the way in and got fucking soaked. My socks are wet, and it's fucking disgusting having them squelching in my trainers. It's meant to rain for the next few days. Anyone up for holding our next running club meetup inside? With a film and popcorn?"

"Isn't that what the film club does?" Noah raised a brow, grinning, and I found myself returning his smile. Here, just for now, I could pretend that everything was normal.

"Why don't we crash the film club's next meetup instead?" I suggested, making an attempt to contribute to the conversation.

In the middle of stuffing fries into his mouth, Noah nodded and gave me a thumbs up, which I took to mean that he was up for it, and Adam followed suit.

Nick turned to me. "Do we even know what kind of films they watch? Isn't it all arty foreign ones with subtitles?"

I shrugged. "No clue. They have a page with the list-ings, though...let me find it." Tugging my phone from my pocket, I unlocked the screen. The first thing I saw was a new message alert, and my stomach flipped. My hands were trembling as I navigated to the messages, and I bit down hard on my lip to stop myself from reacting to the words that were written there.

ANDER:

I need more time. Sorry E. DON'T STRESS.
We're still best friends *smiley face emoji*

Still best friends.

"Did you find it?"

"Huh?" My voice cracked, so I cleared my throat and tried again. "What?"

"Did you find the page?" Nick was eyeing me expectantly.

Clearing my throat for a second time, I once again pushed everything Ander-related down, and it took all my effort because all I wanted to do was overanalyse the message he'd sent me. "Sorry. Um...just give me a minute." Quickly logging into the LSU network, I scrolled to the clubs and societies section, then scrolled through the alphabetical list until I found the film club.

"Here." I placed my phone down between us so Nick could see it as I thumbed through the dates. "It says the next film is *The VelociPastor*. What the fuck? With a title like that, there's no way it can be an arty foreign film."

Nick's brows flew up. "What? That can't be a real film, surely? Check IMDb."

Pulling up my web browser, I opened IMDb and typed in the movie title. "It actually exists. Look."

As we read the film's description, which involved a man who could turn into a dinosaur, and ninjas, apparently, Nick began chuckling, and I unexpectedly found myself laughing along with him. When Nick read the synopsis aloud to Adam and Noah, they were in instant agreement that we 100 percent would be crashing the film club's next meetup.

It felt good to laugh with my friends, but at the same time, it was hollow. I knew that as soon as I was alone again, I'd be back to feeling low and hopeless, missing my best friend, and wondering if things between us would ever be the same again.

———

Stepping outside the student union, I grimaced as the freezing rain hit my face. I burrowed deeper into my coat, tucking my hands in my pockets and hunching my shoulders to protect as much of myself as I could from the elements. Thanks to the weather, there was hardly anyone around, other than a few students dashing between buildings. Keeping my eyes on the ground, I made a run for the library, dodging the puddles as I went. It was on my route home and would give me a minute to shelter from the rain before I had to face the full force of the elements.

Because my eyes were on the ground, I narrowly avoided colliding with a girl, changing my trajectory at the last second and skidding on the wet ground as I twisted around her.

"Sorry!" I called out automatically, the wind whipping away my words.

Then I looked at her. And then looked again.

It was Daisy, the girl I'd met at the student union with Ander.

And she wasn't alone.

Ander was right there next to her, his arm across her shoulders, the two of them looking very cosy together sheltering under his coat, her body curling into his and her arm around his waist.

A sharp pain stabbed at my chest, and I gasped for breath. I'd known that we weren't on the same page with our feelings, knew that eventually, he'd move on once the novelty of being with me had worn off, but seeing him like this, even if it happened to be something innocent, hurt way more than I thought it ever would.

His wide eyes flew to mine, guilt written all over his gorgeous face. Even though all my instincts were telling me to leave, I couldn't stop myself from drinking him in. I'd missed him so, so much.

But when he opened his mouth, I knew that I wasn't ready to hear him break my heart.

I ran, and I didn't stop.

THIRTY

ANDER

It was day three since my life had been turned upside down, and things weren't improving. After my talk with JJ, I'd made the decision to pull back from Elliot, to create some purposeful distance between us so that I could attempt to let my feelings fade to a more manageable level. I knew that I was hurting Elliot by staying away, and I was also hurting myself, but it was the only thing I could think of doing. Being in love with your best friend and knowing they didn't feel the same way was so fucking hard. If I was lucky, the time apart would mean that I didn't just blurt out that I loved him the second I saw him again, like I knew I would've done if I'd gone back to him that night. And then we could move on, and I could come up with a plan to get him to love me back.

Meanwhile, I was miserable as fuck and annoyed with myself for making my life harder by sneaking around like a ninja, trying to avoid him. Right now, I was in the student union bar, playing doubles pool with Preston, Travis, and his girlfriend, Kira, when what I really wanted was to be back at home in my nice warm bed with Elliot while we watched something scary that would make him cuddle into me and bury his face in my shoulder.

Fuck. Was that why I liked watching movies with him that I knew would make him jump?

"Ander!"

I came to, realising I'd zoned out in the middle of my turn. The others were all staring at me, unsurprisingly. There was a clear question in Preston's eyes, but I shook my head at him.

"Sorry." Lining up my pool cue, I tapped it against the white ball, and it rolled a little way, nudging the orange-striped ball into the pocket.

"Great job." Preston lifted his hand, and I slapped my palm against his before he moved into position to take our next shot. As he passed me, he leaned into me, speaking low in my ear. "Hey, man, is everything okay?"

"Yeah," I said, hoping he'd take the hint and drop it. He did, stepping back and clapping me on the shoulder. Thank fuck for that. I slumped back against the wall, propping my pool cue up next to me.

My phone buzzed with a text alert, and when I unlocked the screen, I found a message waiting for me from the person I was trying to stop thinking about.

ELLIOT:

Take as much time as you need, but I wanted to let you know I'm here to talk whenever you're ready

Shit, how did I reply to that? He had to be worrying about the fact that I'd been avoiding him. I didn't want to upset him, but I did want to stick to my plan of avoiding him until my feelings were less overwhelming.

I wrote, *I need more time. Sorry E. DON'T STRESS*, just so we were clear. Then I thought about it for a second and added, *We're still best friends*, followed by a smiley emoji so that he would know I wasn't upset with him and his friendship was important to me. Even as I hit Send, I wasn't sure if I was doing the right thing, but I didn't know what else to do.

Fuck, I needed air. "Be back in a minute," I muttered to Preston, then strode out of the bar as quickly as I could. Fucking brilliant—it was pouring with rain outside, and my coat was back in the bar with the others. Turning on my heel, I made a detour towards the cafeteria. Maybe a snack would boost my mood. Something sweet that my football coach wouldn't recommend.

I stopped dead just inside the entrance as my gaze caught a familiar sight. It felt like all the breath was punched from my lungs as I watched my best friend, aka the fucking love of my life, sitting with another guy who I recognised as a member of his running club, their heads close together as they looked at something on a phone screen. A few seconds later, both Elliot and the guy started laughing, and *wow*, that really fucking hurt. It was clear that he wasn't suffering like I was. He was fine without me. He was *happy*.

I also realised something else. Something important.

My feelings—the ones that I was trying to suppress or

reduce or whatever? They were even stronger than before. The realisation hit me like a sledgehammer. How fucking stupid had I been to think that avoiding Elliot would make a difference? I was in love with him, and time and distance didn't mean anything. My feelings weren't going anywhere.

What was I supposed to do now?

I couldn't watch them anymore. My brain somehow remembered how to work my feet, and I got out of there as quickly as I could, feeling lonely and hurt and so fucking miserable.

Being in love fucking sucked.

When I got back, my three friends did a good job of pretending that everything was okay, and I appreciated it. While I'd been gone, Travis and Kira had managed to pot the same number of balls that Preston and I had, and now we were down to our last two each. I didn't even know how I made it through the rest of the game, but somehow I did, although Preston and I lost. As soon as it was over, I grabbed my coat and muttered a quick goodbye to my friends before getting out of there.

Sheets of rain were hammering down outside, and I was so fucking glad I had my big coat and boots on because this weather was no joke. I readied myself for a run back home, but I was stopped in my tracks by an inside-out umbrella blowing straight into my leg, followed by a cry of despair.

"No! Ah! Oh my gosh, I'm so sorry!"

I turned to see a girl, soaking wet—like drowned rat drenched, her hair plastered to her head and her eyes wide and filled with tears as her gaze darted from me to the umbrella.

Wait, I recognised her. Fuck, had I slept with her?

It took a second for me to register that she was Daisy, the girl I'd met in the student union not so long ago. As soon as it clicked into place, my brain caught up with the fact that she was obviously distressed and in need of help.

They didn't call me a knight in shining armour for nothing. Okay, no one called me that, but I wasn't someone who'd just walk past when a person needed my help. Thinking fast, I shrugged off my coat and pulled it over my head, then moved to where she was standing, dripping with water, and threw it over her as well. I was going to get soaked myself, but at least the coat would protect the upper parts of our bodies.

"Daisy, right?" I leaned into her, resting my arm across her shoulders because she was shivering and more or less crying at this point.

"Y—yes," she sniffed. "My umbrella...the wind blew it inside out, and it broke, and I don't have a hood on my coat. I'm so stupid. I checked the forecast before I left, but I thought I'd be okay with the umbrella."

"Where were you going?"

She pointed in the direction of the library. "I have a study room booked, and I'm supposed to be meeting up with some people for a group project in half an hour."

I nodded. "I'll take you there. Maybe by the time you finish, the rain will have stopped."

Her eyes welled up with even more tears, and another shiver racked her body. "Really? It—it's okay if the rain hasn't stopped by then. I can get my housemate to bring my other coat when she comes." Glancing down at herself, she huffed out a laugh. "And a change of clothes."

"Yeah, good idea. You don't wanna catch pneumonia or bronchitis or whatever it is." Lifting my head, I set the library entrance in my sights. "Ready to make a run for it? Hold on to me. I'll make sure we get there in one piece."

We ran for the library—or she ran, and I jogged. We'd almost made it when a figure came out of nowhere, almost knocking Daisy over. She squealed, falling into me, and I braced my legs to steady us both, trying not to lose my own balance on the wet ground.

"Sorry!" a very familiar voice called, and my head shot around, meeting wide clear blue eyes brimming with so much pain I couldn't fucking breathe.

"Elliot," I whispered, but he was already gone, racing away from me as fast as he could.

"Was that your friend?"

I became aware of Daisy, who was still holding on to me, and then I suddenly realised how this whole completely innocent thing might have looked to Elliot.

"Fuck!" I swore loudly, herding her towards the library doors as fast as I could. "I need to go. You sure you'll be okay?"

"I'll be fine. Thank you," she called, but I was already gone, tearing after my best friend, attempting to wrestle my coat on properly as I ran. Elliot was fast as fuck, but I was fit from all my hours of football and the gym, so I just had to hope I could catch him.

I ran as hard as I could, jumping over puddles and skidding around the other unfortunate people who happened to be out in this weather. The whole time, I was focused on the distant blur in front of me. Was I getting closer?

Pumping my legs as hard as I could, I sprinted down the street, realising that he was heading in the direction of our house.

It seemed like he slowed down a little, so I increased my pace, gradually closing the distance between us. We were on our road now, thank fuck, because my lungs were burning. I was fit, but I wasn't a sprinter by any means.

Up ahead, Elliot darted between two parked cars, flying across the road. I saw the minute he realised that he was going to land in the massive puddle on the other side. He swerved, but he tripped, splashing straight through the middle, water soaking through his already drenched jeans, right up to his calves.

I heard his broken sob before the wind tore it away, and it was like an arrow to my heart. I *never* wanted to hear that sound from him again. He stumbled up the path to our house, fumbling to put the key in the lock with shaking hands, the rain pouring down on him as his shoulders shook with his cries.

Seeing someone I loved in so much pain fucking killed me.

I caught up with him at last, gasping for breath as I came to a stop right behind him. Reaching out, I placed my hand on his shoulder. "Elliot."

He spun around, his mouth falling open and the colour draining from his face as he took me in. Tears dripped from his lashes, joined by the rain, and his bottom lip trembled. "Go away," he croaked.

Stepping closer to him, I tightened my grip on his shoulder. I shook my head. "No."

"P—please." His voice broke. "*Please.*"

"I can't do that, E." Holding his gaze, I moved even closer, pushing him back against the door to give him some shelter from the rain. "I'm not leaving you again. I made that mistake already."

Shaking his head violently, he lifted a shaking hand to press it against my chest, trying to push me away. "No. I can't do this with you."

My own eyes filled with helpless tears, hot against the chill of the rain on my skin. "You...you don't want to be around me?"

"It's not—" Taking a deep, shuddering breath, his gaze swept downwards, hiding his eyes from me. "I...I love you."

A sudden warmth spread through me at his words. "Elliot. I love you too."

He shook his head again, slumping back against the door. His breaths came faster, his body trembling. "It's not the same," he sobbed. "I know you love me as a friend. But I —I'm in love with you. I'm sorry. I tried not to be. I tried so fucking hard. But I can't do this anymore, and—and I've ruined everything between us."

He *loved* loved me? Not just as a friend? The same way I loved him?

The rain was pouring, but it felt like the sun was coming out.

Releasing my grip on his shoulder, I brought my hand up so that I could cup his face, my fingers sliding across the wet skin of his jaw. "Elliot Clarke. Look at me." I waited until his distraught gaze met mine, and then I leaned closer so that his beautiful face was the only thing I saw. "I'm in love with you. So fucking in love with you, you wouldn't even believe."

"What?" His stunned whisper was snatched away by the wind, but I was close enough to hear.

"Yeah, you heard me. I love you. I'm in love with you. I want everything with you. You're my best friend in the whole world, and you're *my person*."

"*Ander*," he choked out, and then he kissed me, or maybe I kissed him, hot and salty from his tears or mine, and it didn't even matter that we were standing outside our student house with the rain pouring down on us. All that mattered was the fact that I had the person I loved in my arms, where he belonged.

THIRTY-ONE

ELLIOT

I couldn't stop shaking. This had to be a dream. Was Ander really here? Was *I* really here? Was my hand pressed against his chest, the other curved into a fist where I was clutching my keys so hard that the metal was digging into my skin? Were my lips moving against his?

Had my best friend really just told me he was in love with me?

"You're shivering. Let's get you inside," Ander murmured against my lips, and then he pried my keys from my death grip and unlocked the door of number 1.

By the time we were in his en-suite bathroom and he was carefully stripping my wet clothes from my body while steam from the shower filled the room, I was beginning to believe that maybe this wasn't a dream, after all.

"Is this real?" I whispered.

Ander paused in unbuttoning my soaked jeans, his gorgeous hazel eyes meeting mine. His gaze went so soft, and I could see the truth written all over his face as he cupped the back of my neck, pressing his forehead to mine. "Yeah, it's real. I love you."

My breath hitched, and I swallowed hard. "H—how? I thought...I thought this was just something fun for you. That when you'd decided you'd had enough, you'd move on. I never even dreamed..."

I shivered again, and he released me, going back to unbuttoning my jeans again. "Need to get you out of these wet clothes," he muttered, peeling the denim from my legs, then my drenched socks, and finally my boxer briefs. He then tugged off his clothes in what felt like three seconds and led me into the shower.

The warm water rained down on us, chasing away the chill from my skin, and I sighed with relief.

"Better?" he asked, applying a liberal amount of shower gel to a washcloth. The clean, lightly spiced fragrance filled the cubicle.

I nodded, and he smiled, pressing the cloth to my shoulder. He began to move it across my torso in slow, circling movements, and I relaxed, my muscles letting go of the strain I hadn't even realised I'd been under.

"What you asked me. How could I love you?" His free arm curved around my back as he held my gaze steadily. "Loving you is easy. So easy. Everything we did felt so natural and so right, and when I started falling for you, it was effortless. Then that night when we...when you let me inside you, when we both completely let go, I realised that I'd fallen all the way. It was so fucking much—I didn't know what to do with it because I knew you liked me, but I didn't think your feelings were as strong as mine, and I was so fucking afraid that I'd scare you away."

"Ander." I wrapped my arms around his neck, pressing my body into his. The washcloth dropped to the floor as he wound his arms around my waist, his wet skin sliding against mine. I cleared my throat. "Is that why you said you needed space?"

The corners of his lips curved up into a rueful smile. "Uh, no. Yeah. Partly. I thought that if I stayed away, I could get my feelings under control. Make them fade a bit so that we could carry on as we were and then you might love me back someday."

"Your ideas are really fucking stupid sometimes," I said affectionately, and he laughed.

"Yeah, I know that now. I saw you in the student union earlier, and I realised that my feelings weren't going anywhere. You were with that guy from your running club. You were laughing, and you looked really happy, and I thought...I dunno, I thought you weren't bothered about the fact that I'd been avoiding you."

I slid my hand up the side of his face and then tapped the side of his head. "Use this brain. What you saw was me compartmentalising. Attempting to feel normal. It was the complete opposite of how I was feeling inside."

"Yeah? Why don't you use yours?" He smacked my ass lightly, making me jump and shoot him a half-hearted effort at a glare, although we were both smiling too widely. His smile faded as he continued. "I saw your face when I was with Daisy. I know what you were thinking."

I shook my head. "No. I know. I didn't really think there

was anything going on between you...it was the fact that I was already upset about everything between us, and I was unprepared to see you. So when I saw you with her, it reminded me that you would move on from me, and I'd be left to pick up the pieces. I panicked, and I ran."

"Let's agree that we were both idiots, and we can make sweet, sweet love to make up for it later when you're all warm and dry. Yes?"

Giving him an eye roll, which only made him laugh, I released my hold on him, stepping back. "If you want to get to the lovemaking part, you'd better get on with washing me."

"Bossy," he murmured with a smile, but he picked up the washcloth anyway. As he resumed his ministrations, keeping everything gentle and not even trying to make it sexual, he angled his head to my ear. His voice was so soft and hesitant as he asked, "When did you know?"

I knew exactly what he was asking me. Letting my head fall forwards, I buried my face in his shoulder as I admitted the truth. "I've been in love with you for a long time, Ander. It...it's only ever been you."

He made a choked noise, and I felt his Adam's apple bobbing as he swallowed hard. "I had no idea," he said hoarsely. "None."

"Yeah..." I sighed against his throat and then pressed a soft kiss to his damp skin. "I was good at hiding it. At keeping that part of me locked away because our friendship was too important to me. I never wanted to do anything to jeopardise it."

"You don't have to hide it anymore. We're going to be

together. Do all that boyfriend shit and be nauseatingly in love like half of our friends seem to be."

Boyfriend shit. Raising my head, I met his gaze. "Is this your way of asking me to be your boyfriend?"

He smirked, back to being his usual confident self, and I loved him so much. "I thought that was a given, E. You're mine now. And I'm yours."

"I guess I can deal with that." Brushing my lips across his, I smiled. "I love you."

His eyes shone brightly, happiness radiating from him. "I love you too. I missed you so fucking much these past few days. Let's never do that again."

"Deal. And in case it wasn't obvious, I really missed you too. Now, let's hurry up with this shower because my skin's starting to prune, and I want to get out of here."

"I know what you want." His hand slipped between us, and he stroked it just once over my half-hard cock. "The same thing I want. And I'm going to give it to you."

Ander had towelled me dry, slowly and carefully, not even letting me lift a finger, and now I was bundled up in his duvet while he disappeared to get "supplies."

When he returned, his towel slung low on his hips and his gorgeous body on display for me, my mouth went dry. I was so busy drinking him in that I didn't even register what he was carrying— "Is that a *baking tray*?"

He grinned at me, all pleased with himself. "Yeah. I

271

didn't want to have to make two trips, and I couldn't find another tray, so I improvised."

My smile was wide and helpless as I watched him place the tray down on his desk. "What did you get?"

Dramatically clearing his throat, he gestured to the tray with a flourish. "We have...two bottles of water for when we're thirsty for something other than each other. A glass full of ice cubes to feed your addiction. Snacks for when we get hungry. Baby wipes, courtesy of JJ, for a quick clean-up so we don't have to leave the bed. The lamp I stole from your room, so it feels more romantic and I don't accidentally set fire to anything, like I did that time you wanted to burn those scented candles in your bedroom." He shuddered. "That could've been so much worse. Candles are great, but—"

"As long as you don't light them right underneath my poster of Zac Efron. Poor Zac." We both took a minute's silence to remember the way he'd gone up in flames. Thankfully, I'd had a full pint glass of water sitting on my desk, and after Ander had launched it at the wall and then frantically started smacking at the smoking paper with a towel, it was all over. Except for the fact that I had to explain to my parents why we needed to repaint the wall.

"Yeah. That." A smile curved over his lips. "Anyway, no chance of setting anything on fire now. I think we have everything except for the condoms and lube—can you get them out of the drawer? Oh, by the way, JJ and Sid say hi and they're glad that we've worked things out."

"Sid? Who's that? JJ's latest conquest?"

For some reason, Ander cracked up laughing, falling

onto the bed next to me. "No. *No.* Sid's a snail. Actually, JJ doesn't even know its name—can you believe that?—so I named it temporarily. JJ's looking after it for a friend, and I told him that he has to buy it a companion before his friend gets back because Sid's all alone in the tank. Don't you think that's sad? JJ's gonna look into it."

I raised my brows. "A *snail*? What the fuck are you talking about?"

He rolled onto his side, reaching out to cup my cheek. The humour faded from his gaze as he drank me in. His eyes flared with heat, and suddenly the atmosphere changed. Leaning down, he pressed soft kisses to my cheeks, my eyelids, my forehead, my nose, and then finally, my lips. "Never mind. It's not important."

"Mmm." I cupped the back of his head, sliding my fingers into his hair, still a little damp from the shower. "You're right. Less talking, more kissing."

"Yes." His lips met mine again. "Let me show you how much I love you."

THIRTY-TWO

ANDER

Everything was set up and ready to go. Elliot's lamp was setting the mood, along with music playing softly from my phone. Fuck if I knew how to do romance, but I was going to do my best to romance the shit out of my best friend.

If I didn't lose control too quickly, that was. Because right now, seeing him lying there all spread out on my bed, naked and so fucking delicious, I just wanted to get inside him. Or have him inside me.

I looked down at him. Where to start...

"Touch your cock. Keep your grip loose," I instructed him, the hoarseness of my voice a dead giveaway for just how fucking turned on I was for him. He moaned softly, his hand coming down to wrap around his erection, and my dick jumped. Fuck. I needed a distraction if I was going to have any hope of lasting.

My gaze went to my desk where his glass of ice cubes sat, condensation beading on the sides.

Yes.

I wasted no time in moving the glass from the desk to my bedside table and then fished out one of the cubes. Bloody hell, it was *cold*. I mean, yeah, it was obviously cold since it was ice, but it was sticking to my skin, and I didn't want to give Elliot ice burns or anything. Slipping the cube into my mouth, I sucked on it a bit, just to take the edge off the chill, and the whole time, Elliot tracked me with his heated gaze. Who knew it would be so fucking hot to do something as simple as putting an ice cube in my mouth?

My mind flashed back through a series of images of Elliot taking an ice cube between his plush lips and swirling his tongue around...fuuuuck. I was so hard. I was never going to be able to watch him eat another ice cube again without getting a boner.

I crawled across the bed to him, and when I was on my hands and knees over his body, I thought for a minute about the best place to start and then lowered my head to his chest. His breathing came in rapid movements, and as the ice cube slid over his nipple, he gasped, arching up.

"*Ander.* It's..." He trailed off, and I took that to mean that he wanted me to continue. I moved to his other nipple, repeating the same process, and his reaction was so fucking satisfying that I had to repeat it all over again.

When he was whining in his throat, writhing underneath me and pushing my head down, his nipples all reddened, I took the hint and moved lower. The cube was a lot smaller by now, so I bypassed his stomach and headed straight for his cock. I'd just have to make sure I gave his abs plenty of attention next time.

I drew the ice cube out of my mouth, holding it in my hand, and then dragged it over the head of his cock.

He shouted so fucking loudly that I hoped our house-mates had earplugs. Immediately, I sucked him into my mouth, licking over his head with one long, slow drag of my tongue, and he moaned, his hands tugging at my hair in a way that I never knew I was into until that moment.

"Ace," he gasped. "*Fuck.* It was too much and then your mouth and then it was so—fuck."

"Want more?" I kissed the tip of his cock, wet with precum and my saliva. My mouth was fucking watering.

"Mmm, *yes.*"

I didn't need any more encouragement. I swirled the remains of the ice cube around his cock, the ice dripping and melting between my fingers, and then I took him into my mouth again, sucking him down as far as I could without triggering my gag reflex, tonguing the underside of his shaft and rolling his balls in my hand. The way he pulsed around my mouth was like nothing else I'd ever experienced. It was so. Fucking. Good.

"D—don't. I don't want to come yet," he moaned. "Want you to... Can we try it the other way around this time? Me in you?"

My cock was throbbing and leaking precum. The thought of Elliot's dick inside me...it suddenly felt like I couldn't live for another second without knowing what it was like.

"Yeah. Yeah, we can do that," I rasped, kissing all up his body until I reached his mouth. We kissed like we were starving, desperate for each other, our bodies grinding together, hot and hard and fast.

When he fumbled for the lube, his fingers brushing across my ass, my cock jerked against his hip, and I groaned. "E, fuck. I need you in me."

"Yes. Yes." His hands were shaky as he drizzled the lube onto his fingers, and then he was rolling us so I was beneath him and shoving a pillow underneath my hips. "Love you so much," he breathed, circling a finger around my hole before carefully pressing it inside.

"Love—*fuck*—you," I ground out, impatient to feel his cock inside me. "More. Give me more."

He pressed another finger inside me, circling and scissoring and opening me up until I was the one writhing on the bed, my cock hard enough to cut glass, needing him inside me with a desperation I'd never experienced before.

"Fuck me, E. *Now*."

Our eyes met, and they said everything. Everything we couldn't put into words. Quickly rolling on a condom, he paused at my entrance, the tip of his dick a too-light, teasing touch. He held my gaze as he pushed into me, glacially slow, his body trembling with the effort of holding himself back.

It burned like fire, it stretched me, and it made me feel a thousand things. It was the love of my fucking life entering me with so much fucking love written all over his face I couldn't breathe. The burn faded into insignificance as I took Elliot in. Felt the heat of his body against mine, his hot breath against my skin, his chest rising and falling rapidly as he struggled to stay in control.

But I didn't want him to stay in control. I wanted him to fall apart.

I pulled his head down to mine. "Fuck me, baby."

He moaned again, loudly, and I couldn't get enough. I wanted to spend the rest of my life drawing those noises out of him. I wrapped my legs around him, and he gasped out a sexy-as-fuck noise that I couldn't even explain, his mouth going to my throat as, finally, he began to move.

"Not...going...to...last..." he panted, thrusting in and out of me, and oh my fucking days, the way he was falling apart on top of me was the hottest thing I'd ever experienced in my life.

I felt it the second he came, pulsing inside me, his moans muffled by my neck, his body shuddering as he lost himself to the pleasure. Fuck me, it was enough to tip me over the edge, but somehow, with every bit of focus I possessed, I managed to hold off, applying pressure to my cock with my fingers until the urge to come had subsided somewhat.

Only because I wanted to draw it out. This was our first time as boyfriends, the first time with us both knowing that we loved each other. I wanted it to last.

"E. You're so fucking sexy," I groaned, my cock fucking dripping between us. "I want to fuck you. Make it last."

"Do it," he panted, withdrawing from me. I immediately felt the loss, but at the same time, I needed to be inside him more than anything. He pressed a condom into my hand, and I wasted no time in rolling it on, hissing as my overly sensitive dick throbbed at the sensation. The bed was moving, and I suddenly realised that he was fingering himself open, and fuck. Me. That was so, so hot.

"Fucking hell, E. You'd better be ready in the next couple of minutes because I'm in serious danger of coming the second I get inside you."

He adjusted his position, lying back on the bed and pulling me on top of him. His cock was already hard again, sticking straight up between us, and I had to make him come again. I needed him to come on my cock.

"I'm ready," he gritted out, and I slid my hand up his calf muscles, lifting his leg and hooking his ankle over my shoulder so I could go even deeper when I got my dick inside him. I lined myself up, pushing inside that tight, slicked-up heat. My eyes rolled back in my head, shivers of pleasure racing up and down my body, Elliot's arms tightly clasped around me, his body so fucking hot against mine.

I rolled my hips down. "Do you think you can come again?"

"Y—yes." His words were muffled, his face buried in my neck again, his mouth hot and wet against my skin as he sucked and licked and bit me. Digging the pads of my fingers into his fucking gorgeous ass, I yanked him even closer, bringing his other leg up so that we hit a different angle, an angle that had my climax barrelling towards me like a runaway train or something.

I was so fucking deep inside him, and he was so hot and tight, I couldn't hold off any longer. I came, hard, my whole body shuddering, holding on to him as tightly as I could.

The second I stopped and managed to catch my breath, I lowered his legs and wrapped my hand around his cock.

"Come for me, baby." I stared down at his gorgeous face, stroking him hard and fast, knowing he was right on the edge. His hips jerked up, and his eyes rolled back. He gasped out my name, his cock pulsing in my grip, and warmth shot between us as he went boneless beneath me.

He wrapped his arms around me, and I placed soft kisses to the side of his head, letting myself sink down onto him, slowly sliding my softening cock out of him. Neither of us were ready to move, and we lay there, wrapped up in each other for what felt like forever. Eventually, though, I dealt with the condom and used the wipes to clean us up. We were both exhausted, and I collapsed onto my back, pulling Elliot half on top of me, my arm around his waist.

"Sleep well, E. I love you."

I felt him smile against my collarbone. "Sweet dreams. I love you too."

THIRTY-THREE

ELLIOT

Ander had a football match today. Ander...my best friend, my boyfriend, and the person who was in love with me. How the fuck had this happened?

I couldn't stop smiling as I piled into Noah's car along with Kira and two of her friends, Emily and Maura. It was cramped, but they all managed to squeeze in somehow. Scooting my seat as far forwards as I could to give them more room, I folded my legs into the small footwell. Noah glanced at me, brows raised, and I shook my head, grinning. *Tell you later*, I mouthed, and he returned my grin.

When the radio was on and the girls were occupied in a discussion amongst themselves, I spoke, keeping my voice low. There wasn't necessarily a need to hide my news because Ander hadn't indicated that he wanted to keep it quiet, but since most people thought he was straight, I wanted to make sure that he was the one to make the decision about who he told and when.

"I've worked things out with Ander. We're on much better terms now."

Noah laughed as he flipped the indicator, moving into the left turn lane. "By the size of the smile on your face, I'd say those terms are even better than they were before."

I didn't confirm or deny, but I knew he could tell.

When we arrived at the grounds where the LSU football team were playing Crawley's university team, I was hit with a jolt of excitement. The last match that Ander had invited me to, when I'd been in the studio with Curtis and then Ander had been injured, felt like a lifetime ago. This time, for the first time ever, I was here to support my boyfriend.

The five of us made our way down to the pitch, wrapped up in scarves and gloves and hats. Kira had brought a thermos of hot chocolate with her, and I kind of wished I'd done the same because it was cold enough that I could see my breath, and the railings of the tiered seating were frosty. But I forgot all about the cold when the teams came onto the pitch, and I got to see Ander for the first time that day.

He grinned widely when he caught my eye, and I waved, butterflies going fucking crazy in my belly. It was such a heady, exhilarating feeling. After loving him in secret for so long, knowing that I'd never be able to have him, he was now mine. He'd chosen me, just like I'd chosen him.

The match got underway, with Noah leaning into me every now and then to ask me for clarification on various rules of the game. It seemed like he was starting to enjoy the matches now, or at least the ones Liam played in.

Just before half-time, Preston scored, and I jumped to my feet with the rest of the LSU supporters, shouting and cheering. A little farther down my row of seats, the pride and happiness on Kian's face as he watched his boyfriend blow him a kiss had me smiling even wider.

The second half kicked off, and Crawley equalised seventy-four minutes into the game. After that, it was a tense sixteen minutes where both sets of supporters willed their team to score. Ninety minutes approached, and the linesman held up a board indicating that there would be three minutes of added time.

Ander passed the ball to Travis, who made a split-second decision and passed to Levi. It was a long shot, but somehow, he managed to kick it just right, and the ball went soaring over the heads of the Crawley defenders, curving to the right, and went straight into the top corner of the goal, with the tips of the goalie's fingers brushing it as it flew into the net. A minute later, the whistle blew, and it was all over.

"That was great!" Noah bounced on the balls of his feet. "I think I'm starting to see the appeal of football now. Don't tell Liam, though—he'll probably make me watch all the matches on TV with him, and I'm not sure I'll ever be that much of a fan."

I laughed as I wound my scarf more tightly around my neck in preparation for leaving the pitch. "He probably won't be that bad. Ander only asks me to watch some of the matches on TV with him, and we always do a swap so we get to watch something of mine afterwards."

"Hmm. Good idea. I did get Liam hooked on *Attack on Titan*, so maybe I can get him to watch another anime with me in return for me sitting through a match." He weaved through the groups of people heading towards the car park, instead heading for the changing rooms, and I followed behind him.

"It's all about give and take." I grinned at him as we joined the other families and friends of the players who were gathered around the exit to the changing rooms. There was a palpable sense of celebration in the air, like there always was when we'd won a match, and I couldn't wait to see Ander, to share his happiness.

The doors opened and the players piled out, freshly showered and most in their LSU football team hoodies. As soon as I saw Ander, he gave me a wide, bright smile and held out his arms.

I didn't need any more prompting. I launched myself at him, throwing my arms around his neck while he gripped me around the waist. His lips were on mine before I'd even had a chance to take a breath.

A loud wolf whistle broke through the private little bubble we'd created, and I remembered that this wasn't so private after all. The opposite, in fact. I could feel my cheeks flushing as Ander ended the kiss, smiling against my lips.

"Hi," he said softly. "I love you."

"Hi. I love you back." Had I ever been this happy before?

We both turned to the source of the wolf whistle—a smirking Kian—and Ander lifted a hand from my back to give him the middle finger. He then tugged me into his side, turning to face the assorted players and supporters who were staring at us with unconcealed curiosity—which I was betting had something to do with the fact that everyone knew me as his best friend and him as a player. Of women, as well as football.

"I can see you're all nosy buggers, wanting to know my business," Ander spoke loudly. "So I'll satisfy your curiosity here and now. I, Ander Loveridge, am officially off the market, thanks to this one." He pointed a thumb at me, following it up with a smacking kiss to my cheek, and I couldn't help laughing.

I caught Noah's eye, and he mouthed, *So happy for you*, before giving me a thumbs up. Meanwhile, Liam was making a rude gesture at Ander involving his tongue in his cheek, and Ander was responding by flipping him off.

"Why are our friends such bellends?" Ander wondered aloud.

"They probably say the same about us."

He shook his head. "Me, definitely, but not you. You're the nicest, kindest, fucking sweetest person I know. Did I tell you how cute you look in that woolly hat and scarf?"

"I'm not cute," I protested as he dropped a kiss on the tip of my nose.

"You are. Cute. Sexy. Fucking beautiful." He punctuated his words with kisses. "And you're all mine."

A hand suddenly came down on Ander's shoulder, and we both jumped, finding his football coach shaking his head at us. "Okay, Loveridge, enough of the lovey-dovey crap. Get out of here; they're waiting to lock up." His face was stern, but there was a twinkle in his eyes, and when Ander saluted him, his hard exterior melted away.

"Good job today. Go and celebrate, both of you. You've earned it."

He was right. We had earned it.

A large portion of the team and their significant others had gathered at number 3, sprawled across the sofas and the floor. Beer cans littered the coffee table, and pizza boxes were strewn around the room, the signs of our celebrations. I was squeezed on one of the sofas, the arm of the chair on one side, and Ander on my other side. His arm was around me, and I was playing with his fingers while we argued with Travis and Liam about whether to watch a film or play on the PS5. In the end, Travis decided that he had the final say as the head of the house, and because neither Ander nor I lived there, our votes didn't count.

"We're watching a film. Half the guys here won't pay any attention anyway, and we won't have people arguing about whose turn it is to play," he said.

"Okay, but I'm choosing what we watch." Ander swiped the remote from the coffee table. "Unless anyone has anything they really wanna watch?"

No one objected, and with a grin, he navigated through the various streaming apps until he found what he was looking for.

"*Scouts Guide to the Zombie Apocalypse*," I read aloud and then groaned. "Is this going to be another one that scares me so much I can't sleep?"

Ander laughed. "Look what it says. It's a comedy."

"It also says horror."

Hitting Play, he tugged me closer, placing his mouth to my ear. "Exactly. I want you to cuddle me when you get scared, and then I want to cuddle you in your bed all night long to protect you from any zombies that want to eat your brains."

"There's something wrong with you. Why would you purposely want me to get scared?" My complaint was half-hearted at best, and Ander knew it because he grinned widely and then kissed me.

"It's romantic. Look, everyone else is doing it."

I looked around the room at the few people who were actually paying attention to the TV screen. He was right—they were all looking quite cosy with each other. Although a lot of that probably had to do with the fact that we were all crammed in, so we couldn't help being practically on top of each other.

With a sigh, I angled my body towards him, releasing his hand and throwing my arm across his waist. "You'd better cuddle me all night. And if I get nightmares and need therapy, you're paying."

"You are definitely the dramatic one in this relation-ship," my liar of a boyfriend said, so I shut him up with a kiss. Because now I could.

THIRTY-FOUR

ANDER

As we drove through the outskirts of Bournemouth, back in our hometown for the Christmas break, Elliot made a little noise in the back of his throat.

"What's up?" I glanced over at him before returning my eyes to the road. He was staring out of the passenger window.

"The golf club. Do you remember our leavers' prom? Seeing the golf club reminded me."

"Yeah. That was a good night..." I trailed off, thinking hard. I'd had a good time, but had Elliot? Guilt suddenly hit me like a brick to the head. Fuck. I'd been so occupied having fun I'd lost track of Elliot after a while. I hesitated before asking the question. "Was it a good night for you?"

Elliot sighed. "It was and it wasn't. Parts of it were good, but it was just..."

Letting go of the gearstick, I curled my fingers around his thigh. "Tell me, baby."

He shivered beneath my grip like he did every time I

used that word, which was why I mostly kept it for special occasions. When I glanced over at him again, he was chewing on his lip, clearly debating with himself.

Eventually, he spoke, low and quiet. "When you turned up at my house and I saw you, you made me feel—you looked so good. So untouchable. Something I knew I wasn't allowed to want. And you were with Zoe, and everyone thought you looked so good together. I...it was okay for me most of the time. Pushing away what I felt for you, pretending to myself that I only loved you as a friend. But sometimes it would just really hit me hard."

"Fuck, E. I—"

He cut me off with a shake of his head. "You shouldn't feel bad about it. You didn't know. You couldn't have known. I was so careful. Anyway, that night, I thought—I thought I was doing okay, until—" His voice cracked, and I needed to pull over because I had to hold him in my arms. There was a petrol station just ahead of us, so I pulled into it, turned off the engine, and then leaned over to him, cupping his face in my hand.

"Until what?" I asked softly.

There was a faraway look in his eyes. "Until I was standing at the side of the dance floor and the DJ started playing that cover of "Dancing on My Own" by Calum Scott. The lyrics killed me. It felt like there were suddenly couples everywhere I looked, and I was there on my own, but the hardest thing was when I saw you dancing with Zoe. You s-smiled down at her, and then you kissed her, and I hated it." His lip trembled, and a tear fell from his lashes. "I hated it so fucking much. And then—and then they were taking the photo booth down, and I never got to take a photo with you."

There was a huge lump in my throat. Fucking hell, how had I been so wrapped up in my own world that I hadn't even noticed how much he'd been hurting? I knew he'd just said that I shouldn't feel bad, but I did. *So* bad. I loved him so much, and the thought of him being so upset that night... it killed me.

I had to make it right somehow.

"Come here, baby." Pulling him into me as best I could with us both being restrained by our seat belts and trapped in a small car, I kissed away the tear from his cheek. "I know I can't change the past, but I'm going to do everything I can to make sure your future is as happy as possible."

He gave me a wobbly smile. "I don't know why I'm getting so upset. I thought I was over it, and we're together now. It was just...I don't know, passing the golf club triggered the memory or something."

"You never have to worry about seeing me with anyone else again. You're it for me, Elliot."

A proper smile curved over his lips at my words, and my heart swelled with everything I felt for him. I loved him so fucking much.

He exhaled deeply and then cleared his throat. "Same. Speaking of our relationship...are you ready to break the news to our families?"

I grinned back at him. "Fuck yeah. Let's do this."

Both of our families were gathered together at Elliot's parents' house, as they often did around this time of year. When we arrived, we were immediately pulled into the mayhem, being hugged and kissed and exclaimed over by a million different relatives. You'd think we'd been away for years with the welcome they gave us.

By unspoken agreement, Elliot and I drifted towards the huge fireplace in the centre of the lounge, which was traditional "announcement" territory in the Clarke house. We looked at each other, and he smiled, sliding his arm around my waist. I did the same to him, pressing soft kisses to the side of his head while I counted under my breath to see how long it would take everyone to notice.

It took 3.5 seconds. Jean, Elliot's mum, screeched at the top of her lungs, pointing a shaking finger at us, clasping her other hand to her heart and her eyes filling with tears as she beamed at us. Seriously. Elliot thought I was the dramatic one, but dramatics ran in his family.

By now, everyone was staring at us, and Elliot's cheeks had gone red, and bloody hell, mine felt hot too. It was weird having our combined families all staring at us like this. Elliot's aunt Sadie elbowed Jean, and she broke out of her frozen state to turn to her, both of them whispering excitedly.

"Well, boys, I had a feeling this would happen." Sadie swept over to us, pulling first Elliot and then me into a bone-crushing hug. "I can't say I'm surprised."

That broke the dam, and then there was an unstoppable wave of people congratulating us and asking way too many prying questions about our relationship. Elliot's parents came over to us, Jean wiping tears from her eyes.

"I hoped. Ever since Dee's party, I hoped. You make my son so happy," she said, hugging me. "I'm so glad it's you."

She drew back and moved to Elliot, whispering something in his ear that made him smile and blink rapidly, discreetly swiping his hand over his eyes, and I was left with Elliot's dad, Brian.

"You're already a part of this family, so it feels a little redundant to say this, but welcome to the family, Ander." He held out his hand, and I shook it.

It felt suddenly formal, and I found myself saying out of nowhere, "I promise to take care of your son."

"I know you will." Shooting me a wink, he added, "He'll take care of you too."

Then it was the turn of my parents. They approached us together, my dad handing us glass mugs of spiced apple cider, steam curling from the tops. "Time for a toast. We're proud of you two." He squeezed my shoulder, lowering his voice. "I'm so proud of you, Ander. I had faith that you'd work everything out."

We all clinked glasses, and then my mum hugged us both and made us pose for several photos in front of the fireplace, fussing with Elliot's hair and telling me to stop slouching. I rolled my eyes but smiled at her because it was her way of showing she cared.

Finally, after five million years, Elliot and I were free, escaping to the freezing cold garden where we could steal a minute together alone. He pulled me into him as soon as the sliding door closed behind us, pressing a kiss to my lips, soft and slow and so fucking sweet, it made my stomach do that roller coaster thing again.

An idea began to form in my head, and I broke away from the kiss. "Do you have any family things to do tomorrow? Can you get away?"

He eyed me suspiciously. "Any reason?"

"Maybe. Are you free or not?"

"I think we're going to see my godparents in the morning, but I'll be free later on."

I kissed him lightly. "Good. I'll pick you up at...not sure what time yet. I'll text you."

Time to cross my fingers and hope I could pull this off.

THIRTY-FIVE

ELLIOT

I had no idea what was happening tonight. All I had to go on was a single text from Ander.

ANDER:
Pick you up at 9

About two minutes after I received the text, my mum knocked on my bedroom door and then waltzed in, a familiar sky-blue suit draped over her arm.

"Is that the suit I wore to Craig's wedding?" I asked, even though I knew the answer.

She laid it out on my bed and smiled. "It is. I thought you might like to wear it tonight."

"Really?" I raised my brows, eyeing her with suspicion. In reply, she mimed a key locking her mouth shut. There was no point in pushing her for answers, I knew from experience. So when she'd left, I showered and obediently put on the suit, eyeing myself critically in the mirror. I guessed if I was going to be wearing this, I should style my hair to match.

When I made my way downstairs, my mum ushered me into the lounge and made me stand in front of the fireplace.

"Wait there. Don't move," she instructed me before disappearing out of the room. My heart was pounding as I wondered what exactly was going on—all I knew for sure was that my mum was in cahoots with my boyfriend. Why else would she be forcing me to wear this suit and stand in front of the fireplace for no reason whatsoever?

The mantlepiece clock began its annoying chime, letting me know that it was 9:00 p.m., and at exactly the same time, like it had been purposely planned, the doorbell sounded.

"Stay there!" my mum shouted from somewhere in the hallway, her footsteps sounding on the tiled floor. The next minute, I heard the front door opening, and I held my breath.

It felt like I'd been waiting forever, but then Ander appeared in the lounge doorway, and my jaw dropped as the air left my lungs in a rush. His body was wrapped in a fitted navy suit; his hair was also styled, and there was a light dusting of stubble on his jaw. He looked fucking incredible. The most beautiful man I'd ever seen, inside and out.

It took me a moment to realise that he was looking at me the same way I was looking at him, devouring me with his gaze, and then I felt like I'd been set alight. My cock stirred, hardening more rapidly as he crossed the room to me and slanted his mouth over mine.

"You look so fucking sexy," he rasped against my mouth, sliding his arms around me. I could feel his length hardening against mine as he palmed my ass. "Mmm. You feel even sexier."

There was a delicate cough from somewhere across the room, and it was an *immediate* boner killer. We sprung apart, Ander turning to face the fireplace, taking deep, calming breaths, while I forced myself to slowly raise my head and give my mum my most innocent look while my face was burning hotter than the sun.

Thankfully for Ander and me, my dad was also with her and had taken the time to distract her by showing her something on the back of the SLR camera he must've pulled out of the loft. I prayed for my hammering heart rate to slow, while Ander, now fully recovered, took his place next to me and slipped his arm around my waist.

"Photo time!" my mum said brightly, looking up from the camera. She patted my dad's arm, shooting him an expectant look, and he rolled his eyes good-naturedly in return. Lifting the camera, he snapped several photos of us, my mum pausing to inspect each one on the camera screen, and then they left us alone.

"Ready to go?" Ander began steering me towards the door.

"Where are we going?" It was pointless to ask him, really—it was obvious he was enjoying the mystery way too much if the huge, excited grin on his face was anything to go by.

"You'll see," was all he said. We ended up in his car, and I couldn't work out where we were going until the sign for the golf club appeared and Ander turned into the entrance.

The car park was busy, and along with the usual December festive decorations, it appeared like it was decorated for a wedding or some extravagant party.

Ander parked a little way away from the other cars in a corner shadowed by a large oak tree. "Ready?" he asked, and before I could reply, he climbed out of the car, slamming his door behind him. I'd only just unbuckled my seat belt when my door was thrown open, and Ander was there, holding out his hand to me.

I placed my hand in his warm, solid grip, and he pulled me up to him, closing the door behind me. The automatic locking beep sounded as we began walking in the direction of the golf club, our hands still clasped.

When we made it onto the terrace that led into the golf club's function room, Ander placed his mouth to my ear. "Act like you belong here," he murmured. "Like you know the people inside."

My head shot around to his, my eyes widening. "Ander! Tell me we're not crashing someone's party."

"Uhhh. No, we're definitely not crashing someone's party." He wouldn't meet my gaze.

"*Ander.*"

"We're, uh...we're crashing a wedding. It's okay, though. It's a big one—I checked. Half the people here should be well on their way to being drunk by now, so they won't know or care, and the others will just assume we're guests because of the way we're dressed."

I groaned. This had the potential to go horribly wrong.

"If this ends up being like the time we tried to sneak into Bobby's eighteenth and we not only got caught by his parents, but I spent the whole night throwing up blue sick from that bloody vodka drink, then I *will* kill you."

"That one was your idea." He met my gaze, a smirk on his lips, and I wanted to simultaneously kiss him and strangle him. Okay, it was like 90 percent kiss and 10 percent strangle, but you know how it is when your loved one acts like a bit of a bellend.

"It was *not* my idea," I hissed. "Anyway, please tell me why we're crashing someone's wedding."

His next words had my admittedly minor irritation-slash-anxiety melting away in an instant, replaced by a wave of love so fierce, I could've happily drowned in it.

"Because you deserve another go at the prom. I know it's not a replacement for everything you missed out on, but I don't want you to be sad anymore when we drive past. We're going in there, and you and me are going to dance together and be all in love, and then we'll take some selfies before we go."

The sudden lump in my throat was too big for me to speak, but Ander seemed to get it; he gave me a soft smile and squeezed my hand before leading me inside.

Thankfully, he was right about it being a big wedding. As I looked around at the groups of guests—a large number already inebriated, lit by colourful sweeping lights—I relaxed. We headed straight over to the dance floor, where we spent at least forty minutes just dancing and making fools of ourselves, interspersed with a quick bar break to quench our thirst.

After Ander had quite an impressive go at the Cha Cha Slide along with the drunken bride and groom while I recorded the entire thing on my phone, we headed outside for a minute to get some air. Standing next to one of the patio heaters that dotted the terrace, we wrapped our arms around each other. I lowered my head to his shoulder, pressing my cold nose into the side of his throat.

"Thank you for this. This was exactly what I needed, but I didn't know it."

He rubbed his hands up and down my back. "Good memories from now on."

"The best," I agreed softly.

"There's just one more thing before we take our selfies. Actually, no, let's take a selfie here first." Tugging his phone from his pocket, he held it in front of us. Our faces were lit by the glow of the fairy lights that were strung around the terrace, and the patio heater flames sent flickering shadows dancing across us. We'd already taken several selfies this evening, but Ander was fixated on taking some right before we left, which made me fucking melt inside. The things I'd told him about our leavers' prom...I hadn't even planned to tell him, but it had all spilled out in the car. I'd never meant to make him feel guilty or feel like he needed to make it up to me because he'd done nothing wrong, but he'd taken my words to heart.

We wore matching wide smiles as I pressed the side of my face against his, our faces appearing on his phone screen. He snapped a photo, and then gasped, making me jump.

"Wait. I almost forgot." Rummaging in his pocket with

his brows pulled together, he muttered, "Where is it?" When he lifted his hand, his fist was closed, and I raised my brows, eyeing him with suspicion.

"What are you doing?"

He grinned at me. "Adding the finishing touches. Remember how our prom had all those green decorations for our school colour?" I didn't have a chance to reply before he opened his fist, tiny green star-shaped confetti raining down on us.

This man. He'd thought of everything. "You're amazing, you know? I love you." I didn't think I'd ever get tired of finally being able to say those words to him. The words I never thought I'd get to say outside the context of friendship.

"Same. I love you back." Brushing a kiss across my lips, he took one more photo, then pocketed his phone. "Let's go back inside for this final part of the plan. Then we can go and kiss in my car and maybe wank each other off because I don't think there's room for us to do anything else in there."

"Romantic," I said drily, but I couldn't help my smile. Or my cock from taking an interest in the thought of Ander gripping me in his palm—whoa. Time to stop that thought in its tracks if we really were going back inside.

When we were back in the function room, Ander asked me to wait for him at the side of the dance floor. He disappeared into the crowd of dancing bodies and then reappeared next to the DJ booth. I watched, my heart pounding, as he spoke to the DJ. And then he was back in front of me, tugging me right into the centre of the dance floor.

"This one is dedicated to all you lovers out there. May

you never have to dance on your own again," the DJ crooned into his microphone, and if I hadn't been here with Ander, I would've cringed so hard and probably cried a bit.

The music began, and from the first note, I knew what the song was. Ander's arms came around me, and he looked into my eyes as we began to sway to the music. "This is going to sound cheesy as fuck, but I wanted them to play this...because I want you to know that you'll never have to dance on your own again."

It was cheesy, and it was perfect, and right there, holding the man I loved under a glitter ball at a stranger's wedding, I knew that it was a moment I'd hold on to forever.

ELLIOT

EPILOGUE

FIVE YEARS LATER

"Looking at the photos from our private prom again? You're getting as bad as Noah with all the collecting pictures." Ander swatted my ass as he passed me where I was leaning over the iPad that rested on our kitchen island, swiping through an album from our university days.

"It's the anniversary of our do-over prom date," I informed him, leaving the iPad and following him into our small but cosy lounge. Baxter, our Shih Tzu cross, came running across the room, his tongue hanging out, happily sniffing at Ander's bare feet with his cold, wet nose.

"Ugh!" Ander leapt up onto the sofa and gave Baxter a stern look. "Don't even think about coming up here."

Baxter wagged his tail, pleased with Ander's attention, but obediently stayed where he was. Ander sighed, pulling a dog chew from what might have been the sofa cushions or his back pocket. He threw it to our dog, who caught it in his mouth, quite impressively, in fact, and then ran off to his basket to feast on it.

I switched on the lamps and turned off the ceiling light, then joined Ander on the sofa. "How was work?"

He slid his arms around my shoulders, pressing his body weight into me so that I had no choice but to sink lower into the sofa until I was more or less lying down with him sprawled on top of me. "Hi. Work was good. You were there, remember? How exactly did you manage to leave an hour earlier than I did?"

I wound my arms around him. "Because I managed to avoid the big boss man by telling him I had a time-sensitive task, and you were too late to come up with an excuse?"

"It's your fault," he murmured against my lips, rolling his hips down and making us both moan. "You were too distracting, standing there at the photocopier in those tight trousers. You know what they do to me."

"Yeah...blame me," I said breathlessly, arching into him, forgetting about the fact that we had an audience of one small dog, although he was successfully distracted, thanks to Ander.

"Wait. Before we get naked, come outside with me for a minute." Ander's weight suddenly left mine, and he tugged me up off the sofa. "I'll be back in a second."

When he returned, he was holding my coat and a scarf and was wrapped up in his own jacket, which looked a little odd given that he was currently barefoot. I smiled at the sight. Fuck, I loved this man so much.

After shrugging my coat on and letting him drape my

scarf around my neck, I made a detour to the hallway to grab my shoes, and then I followed him back through the kitchen. He stopped only to shove his bare feet into his trainers, and then he unlocked the door that led to our tiny walled back garden—our little patch of greenery here in central London. His hand came up to my face, obscuring my vision. "Close your eyes."

I closed them, and he led me a little way across the garden before telling me to sit down. Taking a seat on what I knew was the wooden bench that was placed against the wall, underneath the trailing honeysuckle that grew across this section of our compact space, I kept my eyes squeezed shut.

He left me, and I breathed in and out slowly, the chill of the night air tempered, probably by the small gas firepit we'd installed in this space. It was difficult to tell with my eyes closed. I felt a little disorientated.

"Open," Ander said softly.

My eyes opened, and a gasp fell from my throat, my hand flying to my mouth.

Our little space had been transformed. The small firepit was alight, as I'd presumed, but the hundreds of candles placed all around the garden were new. They glowed and flickered, tiny, hypnotising flames dancing and throwing shadows all around us. It was like we were surrounded by hundreds of fireflies, and it was so beautiful.

And then, as my gaze lowered, I saw the most important thing of all, right in front of me.

Him. The person I loved the most in the world, down

on one knee, looking a little bit nervous and a lot in love, a small velvet box cradled in his palm.

He opened his mouth, and before he even said a word, I already knew what my answer would be.

Yes.

THE END

THANK YOU

Thank you so much for reading Ander and Elliot's story! If you want to know what's coming next, sign up to my news-letter for updates or come and find me on Facebook or Instagram.

Check out all my links at https://linktr.ee/authorbeccas teele Feel free to send me your thoughts, and reviews are always very appreciated 🖤

Are you interested in reading more from some of the other characters? Check out the following:

Blindsided (Liam & Noah)

Cross the Line (Kian & Preston)

Savage Rivals (Asher & Levi)

Becca xoxo

ACKNOWLEDGMENTS

They say it takes a village, and it's true. It was thanks to the support of some amazing bookish friends that I was able to write Ander and Elliot's story. And when I wrote it, I fell in love with watching them fall in love, both so unsure, taking that step from best friends to lovers.

So I want to say thank you as always to Claudia and Jenny for everything, and to Megan & Corina for your beta skills. Thank you to my amazing blogger and ARC teams, to Sandra, Rumi, Wordsmith and GRR, and to the bloggers & bookstagrammers - I love and appreciate all the reads, reviews, promo, edits etc. Ivy—our sprinting sessions were a lifesaver! And to the other authors and readers who have supported me along the way, I appreciate you so much! To my awesome narrators of the LSU series, James Joseph and Will Watt, thank you for bringing my words to life. And to James, thank you for providing the most perfect illustration for Ander & Elliot's special edition cover—you're awesome!

Finally, thank you so much for taking the time to pick up this book and read Ander and Elliot's story. LSU will be back!

Весса хохо

ALSO BY BECCA STEELE

M/M Standalones

Cross the Line

Savage Rivals

Blindsided

Sidelined

Cirque des Masques

LSU Series

Blindsided (M/M)

Sidelined (M/M)

The Four Series

The Lies We Tell

The Secrets We Hide

The Havoc We Wreak

A Cavendish Christmas (free short story)*

The Fight In Us

The Bonds We Break

The Darkness In You

Alstone High Standalones

Trick Me Twice

Cross the Line (M/M)

*In a Week (free short story)**

Savage Rivals (M/M)

London Players Series

The Offer

London Suits Series

The Deal

The Truce

*The Wish (a festive short story)**

Other Standalones

Cirque des Masques (M/M)

*Mayhem (a Four series spinoff)**

*Heatwave (a summer short story)**

Boneyard Kings Series (with C. Lymari)

Merciless Kings (RH)

Vicious Queen (RH)

Ruthless Kingdom (RH)

Box Sets

Caiden & Winter trilogy

(The Four series books 1-3)

**Key - M/M = Male/Male (gay) romance

RH = Reverse Harem/why-choose (one woman & 3+ men) romance

ABOUT THE AUTHOR

Becca Steele is a USA Today and Wall Street Journal bestselling romance author. She currently lives in the south of England with a whole horde of characters that reside inside her head.

When she's not writing, you can find her reading or watching Netflix, usually with a glass of wine in hand. Failing that, she'll be online hunting for memes or making her 500th Spotify playlist.

Join Becca's Facebook reader group Becca's Book Bar, sign up to her mailing list, or find her via the following links:

facebook.com/authorbeccasteele

instagram.com/authorbeccasteele

bookbub.com/profile/becca-steele

goodreads.com/authorbeccasteele

Made in the USA
Coppell, TX
19 June 2023

18272582R10192